Next Week's Graduate

Terry Gavin

NEXT WEEK'S GRADUATE

iUniverse books may be ordered through booksellers or by contacting:

iUniverse
1663 Liberty Drive
Bloomington, IN 47403
www.iuniverse.com
1-800-Authors (1-800-288-4677)

ISBN: 978-1-4917-5829-8 (sc)
ISBN: 978-1-4917-5828-1 (e)

Library of Congress Control Number: 2015900639

Printed in the United States of America.

iUniverse rev. date: 02/02/2015

For Mom

If we do meet again/
we'll smile indeed.

Shakespeare

Prologue

A thick layer of dust sits atop an old fashioned scrapbook housed in an empty bedroom closet, once used by a mother who left an eleven-year-old boy, his older brother, and their father.

If one were to look through the brittle, yellowed pages, faded color snapshots arranged with flaring, handwritten descriptions under each would be seen.

First Christmas.
First birthday.
First day of school
Rice Lake, 4th grade.
Jonathan Peters, Esq., and me, First Communion.
Mother and son, Halloween. Fifth grade?

But the feminine scrawl under each captured memory stops with a beaming youth and a sad eyed woman named Emma, masking her emotions so the little boy won't detect the torment that his mother endures on a daily basis.

And there the photographs end.

Chapter 1

Mike Warner was graduating from high school, Class of '88, without the foggiest notion of what he wanted to be. Sure there was college, but that was on a three-month horizon. And that is an eternity to a seventeen year old. Not only that, he viewed higher education as a four year distraction: a speed bump designed to put off life's hard choices. Who wants to consider fixed rate loans, health insurance plans, retirement options, and sunblock at the precipice of turning eighteen? Not him. His parents expected the graduate to join the family business and bring new life to a dry cleaning store that had been with the family for thirty-five years, covering two generations and as many mortgages. But Mike didn't see it that way.

"No way. You and dad? That's your domain. Me? I think not."

"That's a fine way to talk," Ethyl barked. "A fine way. Tell him, Bert. A fine way. And just what are you going to do instead? There's only one of you and two of us, and, God forbid, what's to become of us when we retire, and you're on welfare because you snubbed your nose at a fine business? A fine business built by your grandfather, rest his soul, and my mother. Your grandmother. I tell you to plan, and what do you do? A concert, that's what you do. And another thing. Grandpa never wanted anything more than to have my first male born son take over when I, God forbid, could no longer watch over things. So, tell me, Michael. What do you plan to do? Tell me. Our family business isn't good enough for you, so what's left?"

"Porn?"

"Oh, Good Lord. A stroke. A stroke will surely come. I can feel the left side of my body turn numb." Reaching out to Bert, her faithful spouse of twenty years, she seized his free hand and beat it into her drooping breasts, each pounding more pronounced than its predecessor, a mixture of exasperation and melodrama spread across her face as if she were reenacting a scene from *Carmen* with the skill of a high school sophomore.

"Please, get a room," Mike groaned, shielding his face with hands as mighty as a Greek god yet as smooth as a Paris runway model whose cuticles were outlined with residual traces of coke.

"Michael, manners please," Bert instructed his son.

The youth lowered his hands and examined the resigned man who lay plopped in a ripped La-Z-Boy recliner. Bert's crow's feet had become deep ravines in his beet red face, yet as Mike looked closer he could not remember his father ever looking differently. The man's sizable gut dropped well past his abdomen; a pair of black polyester pants struggled to grasp the slick padding that insulated the 230 pound man. Eyeing his father's creased forehead with the intensity of a seasoned pathologist, Mike let temptation guide the moment and ask something that had plagued the youth for most of his adolescent years. "Dad, did you ever want to take off? I mean, was there ever a point in your life when you looked at us and thought, I don't think so. I'm outta here?"

"Oh, for heaven's sake. The Lord look down on you with grace and forgive us for allowing such thoughts to be spoken within these walls. What does a parent do to deserve such treatment? Did you hear your son? Oh, disgrace. Disgrace. Shame. The disrespect. Why, Michael, why? Haven't we raised you a proper Christian? Haven't we closed our doors on Sunday for the past eighteen years to spend more time with you? Haven't we? Make him answer, Bert. He's not answering me."

Selecting each word as if it might be his last, Mr. Warner shifted his weight a few times and began. "Listen to your mother, Michael. She, she's—oh, how can I put it? She's right. Yes, she is right. Quite right indeed. Yes, yes."

"And in the presence of your mother. Why, Michael, why? Have you no concern for those who brought you into the world and led you through life? Is this how we're to be repaid? Oh, good Lord. Where are my Tylenols? Bert, where are my Tylenols? Do you have them?"

Without missing a beat, Mike left behind his riled parents and walked into their small kitchen that looked as if it had been designed right after Nagasaki and Hiroshima received their wake up call. Securing a quart of whole milk, the youth placed it in the crook of his left arm and rocked it as if it were a newborn child. Gliding back into the living room with exaggerated waltz steps, the boy's parents looked at what he held and how he was holding it. "Know what Coach once told me, dad?"

"Football, basketball, or baseball?"

"Coach, dad. Coach. The man. The force."

"Michael, now is not the time for your …"

"You, know. Coach. Singular. Like Madonna."

"Oh, good Lord. May the Blessed Virgin not weep."

"He pulled me aside after one of our victories, placed his arm around my waist, which I thought was a little too friendly, if you know what I mean. No judgment. Not this guy. Live and let live. That's what I say. Absolutely. Just as long as my tighty whities stay snug and secure until I say otherwise, we are fine."

"In the name of the Father, the Son, the …"

"And he says, 'Impressive game, Mark. Impressive.' Kind of tard. Called me Mark. Could never remember Mike. Whatever. So, I thanked him, but then he pulled me closer. I mean, come on. Boundaries, dude. Boundaries. But I play along 'cause I'm a team player. And then he tells me something that I'll never forget. He says, 'A win is only a win if the heart knows it's a win and not a win/win.' Like I say, tard."

"Our Lady of Memorial, pray for us."

"And I say, 'Exactly,' having no idea what he's talking about, and know what I did next?"

Ethyl stopped her incantations as Bert leaned forward, his eyes caught between the milk carton still being rocked in his son's arms and a teenager who held his parents spellbound.

"And?" Bert asked.

"I said, and you can appreciate this, dad. I said, 'Winning isn't everything. The win is.' Get it? The essence of insight. Your tax dollars at work. Pretty *Star Trek* of me, don't you think? *Wrath of Khan* quality, baby."

The man repositioned himself in the chair and shook his head, casting a disapproving look at next week's graduate.

Chapter 2

Dear Mom and Dad,

I'm taking off for a week and will be back in time for Sunday's graduation, at which time I expect to have discovered the real America.

Your best looking son,

Tom Cruise

Chapter 3

Spotting the Nike Warehouse near the Wisconsin/Illinois border, Mike decided that he needed a new pair of shoes to accompany him on his excursion. Although he didn't pack many clothes, he was certain that a decent pair of running shoes would add a certain flair to his temporary exodus from the roost. Didn't matter what the brand was either, for he was not a label maven. Nike, Adidas, and Avia were nothing more than décor that adorned one of many paths that he was determined to explore as life's journey propelled him to adventures yet to be experienced. Navigating his '72 Ford Pinto through the warehouse parking lot, he had little difficulty securing a prime spot near the front of the store, for early evening had given way to sunset, and the store's pulse was soon to expire for another day, only to be revived the next working day.

A yellow Corvette pulled up alongside his Ford Pinto and revved up its engine to reinforce the already apparent automotive superiority. A forty-year-old man and a peroxided woman glanced at the youth's rusted, faded relic plastered with bumper stickers from Mt. Rushmore, Graceland, and NASA. Tasting the pair's condescension, Mike tried to incite his car to mimic the competition. Instead, the only sounds the couple were treated to was a cacophony of coughs, spurts, and eventual death.

With a sunglass arm planted in his mouth and a trail of fingers caressing his cropped black hair, the man stepped out of his car and used one of its windows as a mirror. Smoothing his pink Polo shirt and then centering his belt, he walked over to the passenger door, avoiding any contact with Mike's vehicle. Opening the door, the man held out his left hand, and five manicured fingers made their way into his palm. The high school senior watched long, slender legs extend from inside the car and plant themselves onto planet Earth. Looking up, he watched her stand erect and cast a seductive gaze his way.

Brushing away stray hair strands from her porcelain face, she made direct eye contact with the teenager and placed an index finger in her now parted lips. "Hello," she offered in a sly, Southern drawl.

"Hi," the youth replied, all the while noticing the increased tension in her escort's extended hand.

"Nice car," she replied.

"This ol' thing? I just take this one out when my Bentley's in the shop. Truth be told, I bought this from my Uncle Al. He's a car aficionado."

"I bet," Corvette man scoffed as he released the woman's hand.

"I don't think they make this car anymore, now do they?" she asked, her finger tips gliding across the Pinto's lowered window.

"Yeah, they stopped making 'em years ago. Something about blowing up."

"Yes. I remember that. There were quite a few blowups. Bangs. Big bangs. Certainly wouldn't want you to fall victim to a rough bang."

Resting his head on his forearm, Mike smiled at the woman and wondered how long the sportster couple had been together. He envisioned them meeting at a race track and later dancing at a loud nightclub with flashing magenta lights, jasmine's lingering scent coloring the air.

"If you know what I mean," she added.

Feeling ill at ease, the man shifted his weight from one foot to the other, as if he were a grade schooler waiting to pee, all the while rubbing an index finger under his nose like a poor man's imitation of a drug cartel kingpin wiping away trails of coke.

Intrigued by the couple, Mike commented, "That's an awesome car. Is that a five liter?"

With a sudden rush of impotence, the man responded, "Ah, guess so. How should I know? This is America, son. The USA. We don't recognize the metric system here."

Stunned by the assertion, Mike asked, "Is it really? Damn. I must've taken a wrong turn in Iceland. Dude, what'm I gonna do?"

"I'm not your dude."

"But you could be. Bet you're a real playa when you wanna be—if you catch my drift."

The sportster became more frozen than a museum piece. It's as if he became an object in a diorama exhibit that centered on late 20th century superfluous life, littered with extravagant clothes, cars, and personal stylings designed to produce euphoric moments in ordinary lives.

"Nah, just messin' with you, dude. Total hetero, here. Very hetero. Open minded, though. No judgment here. So, no need for you to worry. It's cool."

The man just stared and continued his master class in impotence.

"Just help me finger—sorry, figure this out. You spend all that money on this car, and you don't know something as basic as your engine's liter? Look at the beast I'm sitting in. I can tell you anything you wanna know about it. Go ahead. Ask me anything. Transmission, engine. C'mon, shoot. Hit it, Sparky. Don't be bashful."

The woman leaned forward and probed, "How fast can you go in there? Bet you're one of those boys that's all speed. Passing 'round curves, droppin' down dark, wet slopes like a seasoned pro, using every ounce of energy that's available to that fine young body of yours. I can see it. Yes, I can see it. I can see it, and I can feel it."

Brushing her tongue against a polished nail, the woman leaned back on the Corvette and rested the small of her back on the upper portion of the passenger door, her bright yellow pants caressing every inch they covered.

"Man, your pants are so tight they probably never wrinkle," Mike reasoned.

"Oh, sure they do, especially after sitting in this canary cockpit for hours upon hours with what's his name." Without ever looking at the man, she waived her hand in his direction and let it go limp after acknowledging his less-than-impressive presence.

Sparky came out of his self-induced coma and responded, "I think it's time we went in."

"But you never asked me about my car," the youth complained. "I know. Ask me how much tire pressure I need, or—let's see. Ask me what size my carburetor is."

"Go on, Philip. Ask him what size he is. I need to know."

"Don't stop there, Prince Philip. Ask about the brake lining. Ask me what it takes to bleed the lines. I can tell you anything about this baby." Mike's hair blew gently in the wind and outlined a face that any modeling agent would love. His hazel eyes refracted the day's diminishing light in a cool, hypnotic manner.

"Oh, come on. Ask him. I'm just dying to find out."

"Forget it. Let's go inside."

"Oh, Philip, Philip, Philip. You're not playing fair. Won't you ask him for me? You know important this is to me."

"Why should you care about anything this kid has to say? Is a rust bucket that intriguing?"

"Philip, please? Please ask him about his torque and his …"

"I graduate next week," the youth interrupted.

"Oh, how nice," the woman marveled. "Isn't that wonderful, Philip? What school do you go to?"

"St. Malachy's."

"Well, that is simply precious. Isn't it Philip?"

"Sounds like an all guy's school to me."

"No way," Mike protested. "We have girls just like when you went." The youth paused and then added, "You did go to school, didn't you?"

"Of course I went to school," the man whined.

"What did you major in, Philly?"

"You don't major in anything when you're in high school, you droll."

Puzzled, Mike inquired, "Droll? Sounds like Mr. Thesaurus is needed. Droll is an adjective, not a noun. I can't be a modifier, can I? Nope. Not in a million years, if you'll pardon the hyperbole."

"Oh, don't you mind him at all," the woman insisted. "He's just a being a baby. A big, fat baby."

"Miss, did you major in anything when you were in school?"

"Why, no. We just went and in four years, well, I guess we were done. I don't even remember what we had to take. Well, you're in school. You tell me what's required."

"English. You had to take that."

"Oh, yes. That was one of my better subjects, even though I had to take sophomore English twice. Teacher hated me. Jealous. Some ol' hag. Used to call her Snaggletooth. Think she had more interest in the ladies than the boys, if you follow, which I'm sure you do 'cause you strike me as a man of the world. A young man and his pet planet."

"Please, I read *The Odyssey.* I know all about the island of Lesbo. In fact, I love lesbians 'cause they love the same thing I do."

The woman fanned herself with both hands and threw her head back. "Oh, stop, kind sir. You're making me blush."

"Well, the Lord save us," Mike added.

Struggling to calm her racing heart, the woman stood up, brushed her pants from the crotch outward, and said, "Bet you're really good with words. Always writing notes to those thirsty little girls."

"Nah, I was never one for passing notes."

"Just little kisses, I bet."

"Are you ready yet?" the nearly forgotten man asked.

"Oh, hush up, Philip. Can't you see that this fine young man and I are involved in a deep discussion? Now you march into that store and buy your Hush Puppy basketball shoes or whatever they are and leave us to our own devices."

"Chuck Taylor. Red High Tops. You're really close."

Bathing Mike with a warm smile, she added, "I can't keep those silly brands straight. Why, you need a pair for walking, driving, running, eating. Now, isn't that the strangest thing you've ever heard?"

Philip remained stationary and examined every feature of Michael that could be seen: his Nordic nose; his tanned face that flashed a perfect, desirous smile; his fiery red, nondescript T-shirt.

"Why, I bet you're one of those boys that just sneezes and ends up with a date. I can see it. Yes, I can. Rows and rows of the prettiest things you ever saw, and you're there as the ring master, whip in hand, directing them to do anything that you command. That's how it is. I know it because I know it. I can see it. And that telephone probably rings its fool head off with all those incoming calls. Your poor mother, bless her heart, being a regular switchboard operator trying to keep track of those girls. Why, I bet they jam up half the state trying to get a hold of you. Yes, yes, yes. All of them and you. Say, how old are you?"

"Seventeen. Turn eighteen next week. Check it out: two days after I graduate."

"Eighteen and a Spring boy. My, my, my. How they're making them these days. And what a fine example of maleness you are. Well, what are you doing at a warehouse in the middle of nowhere when you should be out with your female friends, raising royal heck and celebrating your graduation? You tell me why."

"'Cause I'm on a road trip. Major road trip. Perhaps even epic."

"Los Angeles?"

"Could be. You see, for the next seven days, I'm going to be searching for the real America."

"Well, what a footloose and fancy-free idea. Why don't we ever do that, Philip? Oh, never mind. You're just a stick in the mud. Mud? More like quicksand. All you ever talk about is this silly car, and you don't even know how much oil it takes to run this plastic thing. Why, I've never heard of anything more ridiculous in all my life."

Philip was turning various shades of red while pulling a thin gold chain that dangled from his neck, resting on billows of black chest hair. And as his anger built, his foot provided a staccato bass beat as it softly yet steadily kicked the Pinto's corroded side panel.

"Not the car," an alarmed Mike chastised. "Not the car. Get your feet off my car."

"Philip, really. What's the matter with you? Here we are having a perfectly fine time, and you go ruining it by kicking this young man's car. You should be ashamed of yourself. Why, if someone looks cross eyed at your car, you're ready to call the police. I am ashamed of your behavior. You embarrass me sometimes, you really do. A reckless deed, you just did. You have ruined my day."

"I don't slam my door into your car, and I don't expect you to do it to mine. I don't have your kind of cash, and I intend to keep this car in one piece for as long as I can," the youth commanded. Leaning out the door, Mike strained to see the area that Philip had touched.

"It's not fair. No, it definitely is not fair. Philip, take me home. I'm distraught; I'll never ride in this car again."

"Oh, give me a break. I didn't even …"

"I'll break you, all right. What a fine example you're setting for this impressionable young man. That's what starts juvenile delinquency, you know, and it's all your fault. How can you live with yourself knowing what you have done? Answer me. How can you look at yourself in the mirror knowing that you are a damager of property? Well, I am appalled. I'm, I'm upset. Damned upset. That's what I am."

Mike observed the exchange with a passive resignation. Listening to the fight with his left ear while detecting the on-going traffic with his right, he stared ahead, his eyes fixated on the Nike logo, and pondered a simple fact: in ten short days he would be eighteen, passing the threshold of adolescence into adulthood. The teenager wasn't a fighter because he never had to be. He was one of those rare individuals who could disarm even the most threatening adversary with his carefree demeanor and boyish charm, for he saw life in simple terms and found it unnecessary to become involved in the cerebral preoccupations that so many teens do. He lived his life his way and saw nothing wrong with how others lived theirs. This was important to him because it was the only way he had to make sense of life, and this in return enabled him to experience anything he wanted. According to Mike, every minute had to be filled with adventure; otherwise, he considered it a wasted moment of opportunity.

While the couple's bantering became a long, monotonous moan that harmonized with the traffic sounds, he started to plan his next move. He had earlier grabbed $600 from his sock drawer, a safe haven that he considered more accessible than a bank, so cash was no problem. If he needed any additional clothes, he could pick up another pair of jeans and a couple additional T-shirts at any big box monopoly that permeates the American landscape. Toothpaste? Just as easy. Dental floss? A necessity. Listerine? More important than the $600.

"And another thing. My brother told me that his boss' cousin had this type of car, and it rusted."

"That's impossible. It's fiberglass."

"Well, calling me a liar will get you nowhere but hell."

"How can fiberglass rust? Answer me that."

"It's an imperfect world, Philip. These things happen."

"Oh, for God's sake."

"And I will thank you to leave the Lord's name out of this."

"Excuse me," Mike interrupted, "but do you guys think they sell Listerine here?"

"Listerine? Listerine? Does this look like a pharmacy? Does this look like a grocery store?"

"Oh, hush up, Philip. The boy wouldn't have asked if he didn't think it was possible that they sold it, now would he? These stores sell shoe laces, don't they? They sell running clothes, don't they? So, what is so wrong about asking if they sell Listerine? You are so critical. So critical. And to this fine young man. You've probably scarred him forever, and he won't ask anyone anything again because you are so darn positive about what products stores choose to sell and what can rust and what cannot. You're becoming terrible. Just terrible, and I am very, very tired of it. Do you hear me? Tired as all get out. T-I-R-E-D. Tired. You do know how to spell, don't you?

"Now you listen to me, young man. The only way you're going to find the answers in life is by asking questions. Ask them until the cows come home and then, and only then, will the answers be made ready for the pickin'. Do you understand me?"

"Yes, miss."

"Hey, what do you say we leave ol' Philip with his rust bucket and hightail it to wherever you're going? You wouldn't mind, would you, Philip? Would you, pouty puppy?"

"I don't give a damn what you do."

"Don't you curse."

"I don't give a good goddamn what you or the football captain do because I am walking through those doors, into that store, locating my Chuck Taylors, picking up new socks, checking out, exiting those same doors, getting into this $37,000 rust free …"

"For now."

"Why are you shopping here?" Mike interrupted.

"What?"

"Your car. It's expensive, right? You've got nice clothes, so why are you shopping at a discount outlet? Why don't you just buy your shoes at one of the malls closer to town? You'd be saving time and gas."

"And you wouldn't be driving me halfway across the state either, you lug head."

"Don't call me that."

"And your car wouldn't have a chance to rust either."

"Monica, get in the car."

"Says who?"

"I says."

"You says?"

"Yeah, I says."

"Grammar please," Mike added.

"Well, so what if you says anything?"

"You can ride with me and help me find some Listerine," Mike interrupted.

"See that, puppy? Now, there's a gentleman. A fine, young gentleman who is more concerned with plaque and a woman's safety that you could ever hope to be."

"I am not asking you: I am telling you. Get into this car. Now."

"Oh, blow it out your nose. You don't know the first thing about how to treat a lady."

"Yes, I do."

"No, you do not. You could care less about the difficulties we face every day. Count them. Every single day. One day we're all going to rise up and make you do your own shirts. Do you understand? No more ironing, plastic hangers, or safety colored bleach. And you can forget about your daily *Afternoon Delight.* It bores me. Same moves, same performance. Talk about predictable. I have it down to the second. Replays in my head like some boring movie that never ends." She turned back to Mike and added, "Actually, it doesn't end soon enough—and that's just after the first few seconds. Talk about finished before starting. Can you imagine?" Directing her attention back to Philip, her eyes possessing a zeal normally reserved for a Pentecostal minister, she instructed, "So, listen up, mister: from now on I'll be the one up to bat, and I'll be the one keeping score, so don't get snippy with me, puppy boy, or I'll box your ears."

This is better than Consumer Ed, Mike thought. He found himself in a real life drama, the likes he had never seen. In fact, the closest he had ever come to this type of intensity was when he worked as a busboy and dropped a butter bowl in the mayor's lap. Other than that, drama and the youth were nothing more than casual acquaintances. No major fuck ups, no domestic temper tantrums. Just a peaceful coexistence with one and all.

Indeed, Mike's parents never once laid a hand on him because there was no reason to: he was a model son, one whom every parent dreams of having. An easy delivery, slept through the night, superb grades, never got in the way. Little League, Cub Scouts, 4-H, football star, Spring Play, Prom, clear complexion—he had it all.

"I don't need a ride from you. I could walk all the way back home on my knees. They do it at the Mexican shrines all the time."

"Then may your knees fall off and get run over by a Mack truck," Philip pronounced.

"Wow, talk about melodrama," Mike scoffed.

The yearly parent teacher conferences became rudimentary as his parents were treated to a repetitive litany of, "He could be a bit more serious at times, but other than that he is doing extraordinarily well and is a pleasure to have in class."

Football games helped pass the cool fall nights while pride's warmth satisfied the proud couple. In fact, what it boils down to is this: Mike had a cherished childhood free of any momentous traumas or injuries. And this was, to him, the problem.

"And another thing, Philip. You either watch what you're saying, or this young athlete will beat the tar paper out of you."

"Paper?"

"Whatever. Don't question me."

Opening his car door, Mike stepped out of the car, never once taking his eyes off Philip. Standing next to him, the seventeen-year-old dwarfed the man by a good five inches; a soft moan filled the air as Monica's eyes traveled down Mike's frame, only to rest on a patch of denim that struggled to stay connected to a zipper.

"My Lord, Philip. Will you look at this? The Second Coming comes equipped with second helpings."

Philip withered as a muscular right arm pressed down on his shoulder while a clenched fist arched his head towards the sky. The minor's emotionless face humbled the trembling, perspiring body that had turned limp.

"Do you know what Coach used to tell us, Philip?"

Each time the man shook his head, he felt knuckles pressed against his Adam's apple.

"He always told us, 'Now, boys. The first thing you've got to remember is the last thing you've got to remember.' And then he'd ask if we understood what that meant, and we'd shake our heads like you're doing now. So, he'd stare us down for a couple seconds, kind of psyching us out I always thought, and then he'd say, 'I didn't think so.' And we'd sit there and shake just like you're doing now because we didn't know what he was going to do. Maybe he was gonna yank our heads off and go midnight bowling with 'em. Maybe not. We didn't know. And it didn't matter because he loved us. He loved us like his own, and we loved him. I loved him. I loved that man like a father—just not a father of mine. And when he told us that our team was only as good as the last man sitting on the bench, we listened. Oh, how we listened and obeyed his every command. Nothing was too much to do for that man. He was our lifeline to success. Our blood. Our adrenal gland. Any of this making sense to you?"

Philip's shirt was saturated with an unleashed transfusion of underarm sweat; his knees would have knocked against each other had he not been supported by a boy who looked like a poster child for the American Dental Association. Trying in vain not to sound retarded, Philip attempted a simple yes that sounded more like "Yee."

"Oh, for heaven's sake, Philip, speak up. He asked you a simple question, and you give him baby talk."

Savoring the moment, Mike bore down on his already firm brace and pulled Philip closer. He could now smell the story teller's stale breath and prayed for courage to pull away, but the strength never materialized, and Philip knew that he was as vulnerable to this youth as a newborn is to the elements.

"So, Coach would get this pissed off look, roll his eyes around a couple times, and say, 'Sons, do you know that we have the opportunity for greatness? We have it, we won't give it up, and you aren't going to lose it. We can charge into that void, encircle the enemy, and force ourselves onto the world, or we can retreat and walk away with nothing. Which do you prefer?' Hey, I'm talking to you, soldier. Which do you prefer?"

"Wha?"

"Which do you prefer?"

"Ah, ah."

"Which do you prefer?"

"I'm not sure."

"You're not sure? You're not sure?"

"Yes."

"Yes?"

"No."

"No? No what?"

"No, sir?"

"No, sir?"

"Yes, sir?"

"Yes, sir? No, you've got it all wrong. You take the high road. You go in low and climb your way to the top. You don't stop until you're lookin' down their throats. You don't move until you've knocked 'em out of your way. You don't leave until you've driven in three at the bottom of the ninth. You don't leave until you leave. This make any sense to you, Private? Does it? Does it?"

Philip's arms swung in the air as he broke free and ran to the driver's door in an epileptic state. Yanking it open, he dove in, leaned over, pushed the passenger door open which knocked Monica in to the Pinto, leaned even further and latched onto the seat of her pants, pulled her backwards into the car with his right hand while starting the car with his left, punched the gas pedal with the force of Hercules, threw the car in reverse and accelerated backward like a bad Driver's Ed movie, switched gears, and drove away in a symphony of screeches and burning rubber, as opened doors danced in the wind.

Mike shielded his face with his left arm and then lowered it guardedly, making sure that no more sprayed gravel was forthcoming. Brushing himself off, he walked to the entrance doors and said, "Now, that is one strange monkey."

Chapter 4

Tommy Alvin was not having a good day. He only had three more payments on his Toyota and had just lost his job.

"I don't believe it," he said while walking out the factory, the metallic smell of spray paint still circling through his nostrils.

Now, one might have a vivid picture of disgruntled workers filing out a factory gate, each shaking his head and fanning himself with a pink slip, but it wasn't like that. Tommy was the only one of 1,357 employees who got the ax. When questioning his supervisor, all that was offered was a simple, "Bad break, kid."

"Bad break my ass. I'm always being singled out. None of this is fair," he muttered as he shuffled out the factory, never to return.

It probably would have helped had he had any co-workers with whom he was friendly to vent his endless complaints, but he didn't. The only people who said anything to him were the Hispanic women who worked in the packaging department, and they didn't speak English, for the only person more hated than a college graduate at LD Manufacturing was a college dropout. Young/old men with premature wrinkles looked at Tommy with utter contempt for committing this most heinous crime. Men stopped talking when he entered the checkered tile men's room, the area by the Coke machine, the payphone, the punch clock, the receiving desk. It didn't matter where he was. People ignored him.

Climbing into his source of debt, Tommy sat and watched his wasted, tattered former colleagues exit the parking lot and inch their way to a duplex nightmare with screaming children, chain-smoking wives, and noisy upstairs tenants whose rent covered the monthly mortgage payment.

"Shit."

His fist was still lodged against the dashboard when he first felt a slow, inflamed sensation that preceded a cry of pain as blood dripped down his forearm onto his greased trousers. "Motherfucker," he choked while examining the damaged hand.

Although Tommy was distressed about his latest run of misfortune, he was not that surprised because his entire life was an endless succession of failures. He knew that he was smart. Almost borderline brilliant. Almost. And then there were the times that he was anything but. Once he and a neighbor went to a construction site and demolished a stack of drywall. Two third graders had the time of their lives jumping on individual pieces and laughed as the white dust turned each into grade school ghosts. The house's frame was all that stood, and the two did laps around it before running through the doorless entrance and outlined space where patio doors would be installed. And then a construction worker arrived. It didn't take long for him to realize what the two were doing and without moving an inch yelled a chilling, "Stop." The kids had a clear path to the neighboring woods, and Tommy's partner took advantage of this. But not Tommy; instead, he froze and watched as the worker left his vehicle, walked into the construction site, and grabbed him by the scruff of his neck, ordering him to take him to where he lived. Tommy became the city's first non-prosecuted eight-year-old felon.

Then there was the time that he mixed Sulphur, ground charcoal, and Saltpeter at the annual school science fair and blew up a lab cart after igniting the mixture with a Bunsen burner, all the while trying to demonstrate the principle of combustion. As parents ran towards the exit, he stood stationary and fanned his arms, hoping to clear the billowing smoke while spitting on the white flames that burned through the metal counter as an odorous scent of rotting eggs and carrion permeated the room. His father grabbed the sixth grader by the waist and ran out the room with the boy turned perpendicular. Feeling resistance when sprinting through the door, Tommy's father looked down, only to find his son's head and legs jammed in the doorframe, the unconscious child limp in his father's arms, blood flowing in thick, red bursts. After being revived with mouth-to-mouth, the failed pyrotechnician heard the earsplitting screams emanating from faint mothers.

Mistakenly relieved that adolescence was the second-to-last stage of paternal care, the Alvins were more shocked than ever when driving home on a Friday evening, only to find their spare car pushed halfway through their garage door. Tommy had planned on getting in some lay-up practice while his parents went to a Rotary fish fry but found the family's beater parked directly under the hoop. Sprinting into their two bedroom house, he located the keys that were always placed in the Porky Pig soap dish above the kitchen sink. Tossing the keys in the air and catching them like a television private eye, Tommy walked outside and contemplated the magnitude of this event. He was only two months away from being a freshman, and this was going to be his first experience behind the wheel. The pride that he felt filled him with a masculine rush that engulfed his soul and shook every fiber of his being while reinforcing a long-held belief: he was hot.

Climbing into the car, he positioned himself behind the wheel and turned it a couple times, always careful never to waver from his 10 o'clock and 2 o'clock grip; his left foot pushed on the floor to boost him up a couple inches. Bouncing up and down a few times, he visualized himself on a large urban expressway, guiding a Porsche through a maze of traffic that surrounded him. Turn off signs whizzed by as he passed a slow driver with a petrified look on his elderly face. Two Atlas moving trucks, long as the Mississippi, pulled along each side of the youth's car and boxed him into a submissive position. With little room to maneuver, Tommy accelerated and did a quick forty-five degree between the trucks. The one on the right slammed on its brakes as the driver saw the Porsche's passenger door directly in front of the diesel creature's massive grill, the Teamster sheltering his forehead with his left arm while praying that no one would die. Flooring the Porsche and turning the wheel left, the speed king fishtailed the pride of Germany and slipped out of the trucks' paths. Swinging the car into the service lane, he dominated the machine and darted past a line of motorists who honked their horns in a joyous chorus and waved hands, each flashing the victory sign.

Topping 110 mph, Tommy weaved through three lanes of traffic and observed each passed car become a shrinking memory. A majestic, dark red sunset painted a gallery of striking brilliance on a land that Tommy considered his. Automotive prowess and finesse only added to this earthy, macho perception that he imagined and advertised at bargain basement prices. The landscape, the car, and himself. To Tommy, this was living.

Turning the ignition key, his family's Plymouth fired up. Tension filled the air as he felt the energy generated by the machine. Placing his right arm behind the front seat, he looked over his right shoulder and was pleased with how well he was prepared for this safety-filled adventure. Removing his right foot from the brake, he touched the gas pedal and pressed down. He heard the engine climb.

Batting his eyes, he dreamed of closing them just to celebrate the feeling one gets when he's in control. Fighting off the temptation, he remained turned, concentrated on his view out the rear window, and waited for the car to creep backwards and inch its way from under the basketball hoop.

Nothing happened. He turned back, only to note that the car was still in park. Correcting this silly oversight, he put the car in drive and turned back around. There it was. The feeling he had waited for this entire life. The sensation of movement. The power of control. The destiny of going through the garage door.

"Oh, no," he cried.

Without hesitation, he slammed his right foot down, only to miss the brake and bear down on the gas. The rear wheels screamed with delight and propelled the vehicle through the closed door. Tommy saw wooden panels crashing towards him as he turned back around, only to be saved by an embarrassed windshield that felt sorry for the youth. He heard the metal tracks pulled off the wall as the center portion of the door collapsed and pinned the vehicle with a move that would have made a wrestling coach proud. Blocked by any further movement, Tommy sat and listened to the engine purr as if everything were fine. He tried to think of every possible excuse that could be given to his parents, but nothing worked. Everything was a blur because his only reality was the sound of the engine and an occasional piece of wood bouncing off the Plymouth's hood.

Spotting an entering hand, Tommy watched as his neighbor, Mr. Scanlon, turned the ignition key off. Their eyes met, and he could see his neighbor barely able to stifle a laugh. "Are you all right?"

"I was," Tommy replied,

The man helped the boy out of the car. Looking at him, Tommy became increasingly embarrassed about the occurrence and tried to reassure himself that it was all a bad dream.

"Boy, Tommy. You just spent this year's Christmas gifts."

Walking over piles of splintered wood panels, 2x4s, and twisted track, they stopped at the garage entrance and surveyed the carnage.

"Your birthday, your wedding ..."

Tommy wanted to cry, but he didn't want to do it in front of this guy, for fear of even greater embarrassment.

"Your anniversary ..."

Searching for the perfect alibi was no longer a viable solution because he was way too old to lie. He no longer considered himself a child and decided that he would have to face up to his failure like a man.

"Your son's first birthday."

Tommy's parents were driving down the street when, halfway between Mr. Scanlon's house and theirs, his father spotted the battered door and slammed on the car's brakes, his wife's head bouncing off the sun visor like a ping pong ball.

The boy stood and pondered what his punishment would be, for he knew there was little that he could do to mask the mutilation and make it appear less severe than it was.

Brought back to the factory, Tommy watched the last of his former colleagues file out the door. Blunders filled his life. He knew it and wrestled with them on a daily basis, for he could not shake a feeling of social inadequacy and inferiority. No matter what he did, no matter how hard he tried, he felt that Lady Luck never made an appearance.

All those dreams. All those exciting visions of grandeur and power all seemed meaningless to the nineteen year old who still traveled with his college backpack that was once filled with engineering books. Now loaded with grease-covered shirts, it became a perverse metaphor that reminded him of what he had become.

No one planned his life with such stark conviction and determination as Tommy, but then again no one surrendered those ideals more quickly than he. It wasn't weakness—it was more like fright. The very thought of failure crippled him and prevented any real effort for advancement, much less the all-important follow-through.

"What am I going to do?"

Crippled by feelings of dread, he started his car and refused to consider finding another job. It was so much easier for him to dream about phenomenal success and persecuted failure than it was to be pragmatic and examine his situation and the options available. Why did he behave this way? Because he found it exciting to see himself tormented by a rabid crowd chanting his name, raising their fists in condemnation, and demanding that justice be honored. "He must pay," the swelling masses would scream when a civic leader passed judgment on a man who felt that he was merely taking up space. He could see himself walking through crowds, wiping his spit-streaked face, while Roman bouncers pushed him forward with menacing clubs carved from cypress wood. "Faster," one would command as a whip lashed his lacerated back. Old women, normally a source of solace, would run to him, only to throw salt on his open wounds. He could see himself stop, gaze into a cloudless powder blue sky, and offer the words, "Forgive them, Father. They're assholes."

A car horn jarred him back to the parking lot. Looking in his rearview mirror, he saw Marty Koantchek, otherwise known as Fat Freddy, motioning for Tommy to vacate the spot that he wanted. Discerning muted sounds while watching the driver's blubbery lips bounce off each other, Tommy made out, "Move, move. This is my spot, you punk ass kid. Move it, or I'll throw your rice eater into the nearest compactor." Laying on his horn for added effect, the man bounced in his seat, building up to a frenzied crescendo. Tommy watched this while visualizing a string of siren-screaming squad cars, each racing into the parking lot, encircling Fat Freddy, and dragging him out the car. After kicking him around for five minutes, four of the officers would hold him down while the others performed a stomach stapling operation. Freddy would be kicking, only to be stopped by a firm warning.

"Freddy, put that leg down, or we'll amputate." Crying and rattling off every saint's name he could remember, Marty would be reduced to a slobbering sack of celluloid.

"Sorry for the excitement, Mr. Alvin. Are you all right?" Tommy's imagination provided.

"Yes, officer. Thank you for your concern."

"Will you be requiring an escort tonight?"

"No, thank you, officer. I'd prefer to make an appearance at the club alone."

"Very well, sir. Do have a good evening."

"Thank you, officer. I shall."

Putting the car in reverse, Tommy turned and began to back out of his spot. Seeing this, Freddy smiled and inched his way towards the Toyota, hoping to scare Tommy into thinking that he was about to be hit. Just as the unemployed man slipped the car in drive and moved forward, Freddy slammed on his brakes and created a sharp, screeching sound designed to jar the youth. It didn't work. The teen continued down the parking lot and turned on to the highway, never once looking back to what he was leaving.

Now what? he thought as he pushed the radio buttons repetitively, barreling through five preset stations. He didn't enjoy what any offered but didn't want to settle on one station, trusting that a decent song might soon appear. This only added to Tommy's displeasure. So, he threw caution to the wind and stayed with one, and it responded in an expected pattern, remaining faithful to its grating, predictable playlist and its interchangeable disc jockey who sounded like his predecessor and each who followed.

"Here is somethin' so fine, so hot that you're gonna need some heavy duty mitts to touch this one on your hot, rockin', flame throwin', Z105 hands. Crank it, baby. Yeah! Yank me, crank me 'til those awesome sounds come and get me."

"Whore."

The late Friday afternoon traffic was congested and at a virtual standstill. Rows and rows of cars sat in stalled lanes, spewing forth all the poisons that drivers could inhale. Wedged between a Vega and an Audio 5000, Tommy examined the city skyline and imagined a towering building that bore his name. If only the rock band he had walked away from during high school had become as big as the Beatles. He would have had enough money to invest in high-yield bonds that would have doubled his capital—or so he believed.

The unemployed man could not fathom his bad luck, how utterly cruel chance was. Fortunately, his imagination also helped smooth out anything unpleasant. Each day he punched in at his former place of employment, he pretended that he was starring in a film launched after his first platinum album. The director was a perfectionist, so it was not surprising that a scene be re-shot daily. No matter what Tommy did, he always fantasized that he was walking through the motions specified by one of Hollywood's finest screenwriters. That's why the shoddy treatment he received from his former co-workers never mattered much. Everything was arranged and crafted for an individual scene; he found himself enthralled with the beratements, the belittlements. An obnoxious receptionist was styled to add a subtle irony to the film's sardonic tone. A contemptible, vile slug became a marvelous character actor.

The factory's token wise ass was the finest method actor with whom Tommy had ever worked. Everything was a labor of love because it was just another step in his ascent to superstardom. To Rolls-Royce. To stretch limousines. To awestruck, five-year high school reunions. To snowless Christmases. To A-List parties. To magazine covers. To recognition.

Following the car in front of him, he felt that he was just paying his dues, and greatness was just around the corner. Patience. Tommy didn't have a lot of it, but he knew that if he worked hard, God would oblige and shower the aspirant with the riches of the earth because he was special. He knew it, and the Creator knew it, too.

Yet hoping that something exists and having it exist are two different animals.

"What a painful thought," he murmured, "to think that life doesn't offer anything more than a boring, traditional existence. Nothing special, nothing sacred. Just an empty string of events that ends when you die a nobody."

Tommy was both crippled by this possibility and pleased with his syntax. He could not go through life unacknowledged. He had to be important. He had to feel important. He had to sense the pulse of a crowd electrified by his presence. He wanted to be coy while toying with his fans' adulation. He wanted nothing less than everything and was willing to dream the impossible just to rid himself of his daily existence. No childhood dream was ever too big, and no adult want or desire was ever to be dismissed.

Being a voracious reader, he surrounded himself with biographies of the famous and the How-To pulp scriptures that mass market the promise of success through serial rights and foreign market distribution. Highlighter in hand, Tommy painted the pages with long strokes of yellow that marked ideas that he deemed important. Once completed, he transferred the information to an elaborate catalogue system, centralizing the major concepts of these books—early childhood, investments, motivation, management, efficiency, marriage, parenthood—and drafted a reference chart that enabled him to compare how the successful made it and how he might mirror their efforts and one day rival their accomplishments. Stretching out his mammoth chart on the basement floor, he marked each heading with a person's name. It was not uncommon to see the likes of

Armand Hammer and Joan Crawford side by side because it didn't matter who they were as long as they were successful, and Tommy could learn something from their feat. Any attempt to consider the possibility of never attaining his desired status would be dismissed because the alternative to fame was unthinkable: he could not live life as an unknown.

And that is exactly what he was.

Stalled along a stretch of fast food restaurants, Tommy recalled when he used to ask his sixth grade classmates if they wanted his autograph. "Look at it this way. You can either get it free now or pay for it later," he would tell them. Brazen? Yes. Successful? No. Leaving behind this aggressive posturing, he opted for a more covert method of recognition that bordered on invisibility, a trait that made him one of the most forgettable members of his high school class. His fellow students only remembered him vaguely as the guy who used to play in a rock band that never played out. He was, for all intents and purposes, an imperceptible member of his graduating class. He never got in trouble, never dated, never contributed in class yet always had his homework done on time, wasn't involved in extracurricular activities, didn't work in town, did occupy a space in a yearbook, but outside of that he was on his own. Even his bandmates never knew him. He never drank or got high with them. He'd just walk in with his bass guitar, plug in, play, and leave. Simply referred to as our bass player by the group members, he managed to survive the high school years by refraining from any communication that he considered ancillary and kept all his ambitions to himself, never once wavering from his held belief that surprise was the greatest aphrodisiac.

Imagining his impending stardom nightly, he thought, I still can't believe it, but it's true: I'm going to be one of those few people who makes it—and I mean makes it big. Everyone will want to be me, and that's the best part.

Feeling the right side of his face being bathed by the setting sun, he was buoyant, confident that the day's event would not have happened without a reason; he was glad. This was one more indication that big plans lie ahead, and that he was on his way to the top.

Now, it might appear that Tommy was not all that stable. True, he was somewhat inclined to shape his world around questionable perceptions, but so what if his social skills fell on the short side of traditional? The guy had dreams.

Spotting a video arcade on the other side of the next stop light, Tommy decided to celebrate his newfound optimism and check things out. Traffic was beginning to move, and this only reaffirmed his conviction that better, much better, times were ahead. Barely able to contain himself, he turned up the car radio and grooved to the announcer.

"The hot rockin', flame throwin' Z105 is here today and burn those lovely little ears off that gorgeous bod. Baby, baby, baby—touch me now cuz I'm gonna be too hot to hold any second now. Yeow!"

Tommy raised his bloodied fist and cried a hearty "Yeah!" He felt that life had worked itself out, and that the only obstacle preventing success was any lingering self-doubt. With each progressive movement towards the arcade, fanciful notions danced in his head. The acclaim. The interviews. The press junkets. It was all his for the taking. And take he would.

Spotting several youths leaning against a '67 Galaxy 500 in the arcade's parking lot, Tommy pulled next to them, all the while bobbing his head to the non-stop eloquence of the disc jockey. Although it was a no parking space, consequence meant little to him. "When you roll, you roll," he shouted to the car radio as a feeling of invincibility captivated the man who ten minutes earlier had been a quivering mass of confusion. It was this type of mood swing that should have alarmed him; however, the only sensation that Tommy measured was the feeling of power that accompanied his weighty thoughts of fame. When in this state, nothing could touch him. Nothing and no one. Opening his car door, he nodded to his teenage brethren who passed a joint to each other, all sporting Judas Priest T-shirts.

Soak it in, guys. Remember the now, so you can remember when, he determined as he walked past the youths, approached the mottled front door, and sauntered in.

The arcade was a wonderment of eighties' technology that no teen could do without. A repetitive symphony of polytechnic computer chips slam dancing with various circuits provided the creative outlet that attracted the unemployed man and his quarter-pumping comrades. Dazzling strobe lights flashed through a psychedelic time warp and held captive a pack of thrill seeking youths, each trying to outdo a maverick's highest score. Waists pressed against metal frames that possessed unbridled sources of desire, pounding each to maximize euphoric bursts of pleasure. Tommy loved this place. These were his people. His machines. Anytime he needed a surge of energy or a simple nod of acceptance, he would come here.

"How's she treating you?" Tommy asked a badly complected youth.

Without taking his eyes off a screen filled with racing cars, weaving roads, misshapen trees, and menacing obstacles, the sixteen-year-old junior asked, "Where have you been? Haven't seen you here for two days."

Enjoying this mild form of celebrity recognition, Tommy replied, "Work. Plans. Lotta plans. Projects, you know. Time consuming."

"Sounds like a royal—aw fuck, missed the bastard—royal headache."

"Occasionally."

"I hear ya."

And there the conversation stopped for the two had run out of topics to discuss. So, Tommy stood and watched as the youth set a new score for someone else to break.

There was something about the arcade that Tommy found comforting. Although there wasn't that much of an age difference between himself and the others, he did feel superior because he was older, and that made him one notch above them, for he needed to feel accomplished, regardless of how trivial it might appear. And indeed many of the patrons looked up to him because he dropped out of college, and to them that was mark of independent distinction.

"Well, I'm taking off. Congrats on your new score."

Still staring ahead at the screen, the student responded, "Thanks."

With that Tommy left the machine and traveled to an original Pac Man relic that sported a handwritten Out of Order sign, secured by a Band-Aid. He found this symbolic and found himself getting misty eyed. Here was the premiere video game, one that helped launch a cultural revolution, and it was sick. Caressing one of its red buttons, he thought about all the hours he spent learning how to communicate with the machine. How to pamper and love it.

Grabbing a nearby stool normally occupied by a rent-a-cop, Tommy sat down and gazed into the screen. Seeing his reflection made him think about what it would be like when he came back here a star. He envisioned himself dedicating a new machine graced with a plaque bearing his name. Perhaps even the stool he sat upon would be roped off, and teenage girls would reach over, touch the torn red vinyl, and faint.

"One day," he whispered. "No doubt about it, one day."

Tommy never did drugs. He didn't have to. Thinking about these types of fantasies threw him into any number of mind-altered states. He didn't drink either. He had no idea what beer or wine tasted like because he was completely drug free. Living this type of life, he determined, only primed him for his inevitable rise to the top. "I'm not going to waste myself, only to look like a burnout when I finally make it. No way," he maintained to his reflection. Following a detailed regiment of proper nutrition and rest, Tommy made sure that he was going to be in peak condition when the public learned about him and his meteoric rise; no one would be able to make crass comments about what a wild life he must have led because he determined that his face would be radiant, supple, and smooth. "*Preventive Cosmetics.* That's what I'll call my first fitness book," he said to the video screen.

Several high school males stood around a Space Invaders machine and passed a cigarette to each gaping mouth. One donned a black Motley Crue concert shirt. Inhaling his hit like a seasoned pot smoker, he closed his eyes and threw his head back, savoring the experience that he found so intense. Another with a faded blue Levi's shirt stared at a sixteen-year-old who slammed her fist against an Arcade Legends machine that ate her quarter. Spotting the same girl, Tommy walked over to observe her continuing action but not to offer any words of consolation. Carefully examining the young girl, he thought how lucky she was. Without knowing it, she was next to someone who was going to be so big, so important, that she would melt with emotion each time she recalled seeing him for the first time. Tommy was humbled by this thought and exited the arcade, satisfied that the future was not only bright but guaranteed. He knew that no matter what he did, his ascent was imminent, and it would be spectacular.

Exiting the arcade and spotting a recently constructed Spencer Gifts store, Tommy strolled over to it. Well, more like strutted. Sensing that his gait was off, he embraced a cinematic doppelgänger approach and watched himself from above, concluding that his posture was not at its peak, so he directed himself to stand more erect. And then there was the all-important swagger that was missing. Imagining central control whispering into his earpiece, he swung his arms in a confident way, making sure that the movement was not exaggerated. And then the hips. This is where it got tricky. He was not happy with what he saw, yet he knew that an aggressive advance would turn him into a caricature. Observing his sway, he cheated each step and turned himself into a runway model. Perfection.

Spotting an Uzi squirt gun displayed in a window crowded with other realistic looking toy guns, he gazed into the display and marveled at the piece. Not only was the toy scaled to size, but its black matte finish was a perfect match to the real firearm. Tommy appreciated authenticity, for he loved realism. Without hesitation, the unemployed man walked into the store, bought the gun, and left, marveling at the toy's light weight and how it complemented the clothes that he wore.

Chapter 5

There are advantages to being a minor; one of them is harassing an adult, all the while being protected by a legally celebrated tender age. Few would risk an assault and battery charge on a minor. Mike knew his limits and loved to test them. Raised a Catholic, the high school senior had an uncanny ability to infuriate people while at the same time placating them with an angelic face. No one could stay angry with him, for all it took was one flash of his covetous smile, and people would be disarmed. Although he never did anything horrendous or sinister, he loved to test the waters that allowed him to be somewhat naughty yet never out of control. No one knew this better than his parents, yet all they could nail him with was his mouth. "One day you'll get your comeuppance. Yes, you will. You mark my words. You will. You will," his mother foretold.

Although Ethyl could be a tad rabid, she could always be handled by her son's initiative. She might come home and discover that he had clipped the hedges without being asked or straightened up the kitchen's junk drawer. A room might find itself with a fresh coat of paint, paid by a teenager who lived off a meager wage, now working exclusively in the family business. He was a good son. A very good son—but he did like to have his fun.

Walking into the Nike outlet store, he was approached by an equally blond male who sported dark slacks, a referee shirt, and Nike court shoes. "Hi, can I help you?" he asked in his inquiring best, a piece of lettuce wedged between two front teeth.

"Yeah, I'm looking for some Listerine. Thirty-two ounce bottle."

The salesman stared at Mike and broke into a hyena-type laugh, the strip of lettuce fluttering with each emitted breath. "Yes, yes. That is rich."

Mike tried to make sense of the man but couldn't, for this was no act. He wanted to find mouthwash because he viewed a morning without as a disaster. Ignoring the gawking man, Mike walked by and examined a wall filled with every conceivable type of athletic shoe: tennis, walking, court, running, recreational, track. Each in various sizes, colors, and fashions, each graced with designer laces and metal eyelets.

"I want these. Buy them, or I'll tell grandma that you beat me."

Cruelly, Mike's fascination was interrupted by a small boy.

"Now, let's stay calm and use our inside voice. Now, these shoes cost $140. Now, Tyler. Don't you find that extreme?"

"Buy them, or I'll tell grandma that you beat me 'cause I won't let you touch me."

Man, if this were my kid, I'd stuff the brat on the highest shelf and leave, Mike thought.

"I want these. These," the child demanded.

The father held his hands up and then lowered them in a fashion designed to calm the boy, but the tyke would have none of it. "That's why I hate shopping with you. Mom's better. She doesn't argue 'cause she knows what I look good in. You don't know anything 'bout anything. Call mom and tell her to get here now."

Grabbing the boy by his shirt, Mike single handedly lifted the wide eyed child to an upper row of shoes and held him there as his father asked, "Ah, excuse me, but is there something I can help you with?"

Without taking his eyes off the runt, Mike responded, "No."

Becoming increasingly unsettled, the father continued. "Ah, excuse me, but could you please put my son down? We really must he going. There's a soccer match on cable that we've been dying to see."

The now whitened child's lower lip inched its way over its counterpart as Mike contemplated whether to drop the punk or throw him into a large cart filled with marked down fleecewear. Choosing neither, Mike brought the limp creature back to earth, pointed an accusing finger and said, "I like you. You're shrewd."

The child ran behind his father and choked out an unconvincing, "Thanks."

This was pure Mike. Grabbing a minor annoyance by the balls and twisting it to histrionic proportions. It's what he loved to do, and no one did it as well as him, for the graduate loved to play with the boundaries of accepted social mores. Why? Because he could—and because if he thought he could get a response, he would try anything.

Anything.

Oh, yes. Being well-built didn't hurt either.

Regardless of what some say, looks can get some people whatever they want; Mike could attest to this. He always had an army of teachers who tipped their judicious scales in favor of the handsome teen who flashed his Cheshire grin and took down anyone whom he perceived as a threat with eloquent ease.

As the father and son team bolted, a young woman turned the corner and approached Mike. She looked as if were born to be a cover girl for *Marie Claire*. Her soft, luminous skin and olive eyes, framed by brunette hair whose sheen was nothing short of breathtaking, made her fantasy material. Drawn to this vision who wore a trainee name tag, Mike began. "Hello. Hard day?"

"Why, no, sir. How about you?" she responded, trying in earnest to please the perspective customer.

Charmed by her high-pitched Suzy Creamcheese voice, Mike hit her with his beatific best. "I am fab, although do you know what would catapult me to a near orgiastic state? Listerine. You do carry it, correct?"

Twisting her freckled, twenty-four-year-old face in various contortions, the confused trainee tried to formulate a response, which made her appear even more captivating. "Great. Not sure about the origami, but—um, well, let's see." Her eyes darted about and then settled on the row of shoes in front of her. "Okay, we've got a sale on some of these." Pointing to a shelf of women's aerobic shoes, the girl tried to convey a sense of professionalism but instead came off as a special needs child.

Empathizing with the sales neonate, Mike responded, "No, not shoes. 'Stine. You know. Listerine." With that, Mike threw his head back and made an extended gurgling sound.

Baffled, the trainee bit two knuckles and said, "Um, I'm not sure." Shoving her name tag forward, her embarrassment was apparent. "This is my first day, and I'm still trying to figure out the store layout. I'm in the trainee training program, so I don't know where everything is yet, but I'll sure find out. Can you wait here for a sec?"

Nodding his head, she screamed, "Super," and fluttered down the narrow aisle brimming with colorful shoes. Mike tried to contain himself as he detected her off-key hum and joyous jaunt.

She was happy, and he loved happy. If he had his way, happy would be mandatory, and all malcontents would be sentenced to nonstop viewings of Marx Brothers movies until correction was attained. Although new shoes were the original matter at hand, it had been usurped by the Listerine quest, for once he secured the antiseptic, the journey to discover the real America could begin. Adventure. Discovery. Freedom. This was his song, one that would accompany him on his first vacation.

The Warner family had little time for travel. The family business kept everyone busy, including baby Michael. Graced with a thin, acrylic-like stream of drool, the infant increased business tenfold: he became the store's best advertisement. Compared to everyone from the Gerber baby to Sweet Pea, Michael enthralled the crowds with his sweet temperament and restful naps alongside stained dresses and soiled shirts. Old women claimed that he looked just like their first born while expectant mothers prayed that theirs would look like him. Michael was the toast of Lincoln Avenue, and his parents basked in the recognition that their creation generated.

And as he grew, so did the business. By the time he was twelve, the boy was acquainted with every facet of the business. He knew every customer, every salesman, every bad check, each advancement in dry cleaning technology. Everything.

Piped in elevator music brought Mike back to his surroundings as he detected a string-laced version of a Clash song.

"Unreal," he announced to the vacant aisle. Grabbing a pair of running shoes that were laced together, he stretched them until he transformed the left shoe into a fret board and the right shoe into a guitar's body, the taut laces becoming strings.

Massacring the words to *Should I Stay or Should I Go?* he let out a penetrating scream during the symphonic interlude and leapt onto a small, padded stool that now served as a stage monitor. Bouncing his head to the melody, he held the area captive with his manic energy and dynamic stage presence. Beads of sweat traveled down his nose and dripped onto the stained carpet. And to increase the dramatic performance, he fell to his knees and played to an audience of lower row footwear.

Sprinting around the corner, the trainee froze as she came across the one-man recital. Confused by a store that did not carry

Listerine, assistant managers who could not be found, and patient customers who were driven to amusements while waiting for answers that would not be favorable, she stomped her right foot and threw her hands forward. "Oh, forget it," she whimpered. "I'm no good in sales. I knew I should have listened to my mother and gone into fast food." Garnering the strength to approach her distracted customer, she inched her way to him.

Sensing that his immediate environment had changed, Mike looked up and saw the crimson-faced trainee make a friendly hand gesture that was cross between a wave and giving the finger. "Hi, again. How are you? Still good, I hope."

Saddened that he didn't have the opportunity to finish his performance, he replied, "Epic."

"Great." The high pitched word ascended to the corrugated ceiling, and Mike was positive that he had heard it rattle.

"So, did you find anything that you liked, sir?"

"Not really because I don't want anything but the 'Stine."

After hearing this, she pressed her eyelids shut and took a deep breath before opening them. "Well, I have some not-so-super news. You see, I couldn't find my supervisor or my supervisor's supervisor and, well, he only knows the answer because, well, you see, I don't. I'm really sorry, sir. I hope you're not too disappointed."

"Actually, I am."

"Oh, fudge," she returned, holding the oh for an unbearably long time. Her eyes filled with tears, and she stomped her foot for added effect. "Darn it all. I probably ruined your whole day."

Engulfed with a penetrating surge of compassion, Mike stood up and planted both hands on her slumped shoulders. "You know, this reminds me of something that Coach once told me. He said, 'Son, there're two paths that you can take to glory. The easy one and the hard one. It's up to you, but I'd take the hard one because once you get there you'll feel better that you worked so much harder for it. Remember, you have to sweat your way to get where you're going. Now, I know that some might not like sweat, but I don't care. Sweat's natural. It's human. It's what separates us from primates. You can swim in deodorant to cover up your sweat, but you're just fighting Mother Nature, and boys, she is not one to be messed with. So, elevate sweat. Embrace sweat. Make sweat your best friend. Go to bed in sweat and get even more sweaty as you dream of sweat.' So, do you know which path I took?"

Slowly shaking her head side to side, barely able to contain herself, she choked out an emotional, "No."

Staring into her entrancing eyes with the gentleness of a loving husband, Mike whispered, "The easy one. Our coach was a Nazi."

The trainee wiped away her tears with both hands and looked into Mike's eyes that were attached to his soul and a growing erection. "Wow, that was great. I can really relate."

"I knew you would. And I want you to remember this moment the next time life gets rough."

And with that Mike turned and proceeded towards the doors, awaiting his next adventure, and leaving behind a reborn individual.

Chapter 6

Traffic had ground to a halt because an obnoxious, mighty mouth television/furniture/appliance magnate had opened a store the size of two football fields, and its grand opening helped snarl the heavily traveled expressway. And if this were not bad enough for Tommy, he was now subjected to one of the entrepreneur's omnipresent radio commercials. Screaming at potential customers, the businessman alarmed radio listeners with, "This isn't just a super sale. It's not just a colossal sale. It's not just a humungous sale. It's a crazy sale! Crazy 'cause we're celebrating the opening of our new south side store at I-94 and Ryan. Two days of bargains that you won't believe—so unbelievable that they're trying to lock me up, so hurry before they take over and raise our rock bottom bargain basement prices. Ah!"

"I'll never be like that when I do promos," Tommy scoffed. "You need tact. Finesse."

An evening haze graced the concrete landscape as the last shades of daylight faded behind rows of apartment complexes and billboard signs that sported suntan lotions and Tennessee whiskey. Vacuous eyes housed within stalled vehicles looked forward, staring at the immobile lanes that moved in inch increments.

Feeling a tinge of melancholy, Tommy sighed, "Bob Dylan got stuck inside Mobile with his Memphis blues, and I'm stuck in Milwaukee with a temperature gauge that's climbing." Truer words have never been spoken as the unusually warm evening and stalled condition were taking its toll on a car that was having its own drama, for only one week had passed since Tommy had received bad news from a mechanic.

"Hey, bud. You've got a few problems that I listed here. First, your plug wires: shot. Second, your distributor cap is bad, bad, bad. Then there's your vacuum advance and your thermostat—I'm surprised you got through the winter 'cuz they need replacing real bad. All told, you're talking $130."

Any sum of money is too much when one doesn't have any, and Tommy was always broke, so broke that he had to borrow his car's down payment from his reluctant father.

"You want collateral? Dad, I don't have anything. Nothing I have is worth anything."

"I wouldn't say that, son."

"Well, what do you think I have?"

"Tommy, you came to me, remember? I didn't come to you. Now, this is business. You're never going to make it in life unless you prepare. Do you think a bank's going to hand over thousands of dollars without protecting its investment?"

"No, that's why I need you to cosign this loan."

"Cosign? Cosign? Who ever said anything about cosigning? First, you tell me that you need to borrow money for the down payment, and now I find out that my name's going to be on the loan in case you default? You're on a roll, son. A real roll. Do you have any other surprises you're waiting to spring on me?"

"I suppose I could stand some help with the insurance," Tommy replied in a cautious air.

"Insurance? Insurance? I'm supposed to pay for that, too?"

"Just until I get a raise."

"Raise? Raise?"

"Dad, you're repeating yourself."

"Damn right I'm repeating myself. This is my house, and I'll repeat myself any time I want. You enroll in college and within four weeks you chuck it because you're, you're—well, hell. I never did find out why you quit in the first place. Next thing I know, I'm getting up for work while you're watching *The Flinstones* in your boxers."

As traffic continued its glacial movement, Tommy watched as the temperature needle passed into the dreaded red zone, indicating that the engine was not too happy about the environmental conditions, warning the operator that something had better be done or severe consequences awaited. Stroking the brown vinyl dashboard that was designed to resemble fine, Corinthian leather, he said, "There, there. Stay cool. We're almost there."

But *there* was an elusive destination. The driver had no idea where he was going or when he would arrive. Because he had no close friends, it was not unusual for him to drive around after Friday's work buzzer blared, reminding its workers that the end of the day had arrived, and Monday was a short distance away. There was never time off work—only time separating each working day. "I know this is paying my dues, but when does the payoff begin?" he asked, staring ahead while absorbing the year that he had spent at a job he despised, his unremarkable days filled with mundane and repetitive tasks, each catalogued and critiqued by a downcast supervisor who answered to another and he to another.

Yet he no longer had to worry about his reviled job and despotic employer. That was now the past. He did, however, have to face his future.

With traffic gaining traction and Elton John's *I'm Still Standing* playing in his head, Tommy drove down I-94 feeling ambivalent, hoping that better days lie ahead, and that the magnetic powers of positive thought would escort him into the threshold of fame. He longed to experience future days that required him to maneuver his hectic schedule to fit the needs of charitable organizations that needed his assistance. UNICEF came to mind, and he was warmed by the belief that one day his very name would guarantee an event's success.

"Anything for the kids," he whispered. "Anything."

But memories of college forced their way into his mind, painful remembrances of his first meeting with his assigned counselor and the automatic response that he gave when asked what field of study he wished to pursue. "Chemical Engineering, I guess."

"What right did I have saying that when I flunked chemistry and got a D in basic Algebra?" he asked aloud.

The hard sciences had never held sway with Tommy. Ironically, the interest that he dismissed as filling time before his ascent to celebrity eminence was the one that he was best at: working with young people. Anyone who had ever seen him when he was a grade school hall monitor, watching over the younger ones, ready to protect them from any vestige of danger, knew of his gift. Later, while his high school classmates traipsed through various sexual/alcohol/drug experiments, Tommy spent his time assisting the Special Olympics, the reading skills lab, several kiddie theatre productions, and the junior league baseball team. Adults marveled at his ability to work with even the most temperamental of children and showed their appreciation by bestowing him with numerous awards and honorariums. Yet this was lost on him. His singular vision did not recognize the word alternative, much less compromise.

If one were to enter his bedroom, his awards would be stacked atop unopened bank statements that verified his meager finances. Next to the dresser was a life-sized Paul Molitor cardboard standup, the Milwaukee Brewer swinging a blurred bat through the parted air, the cutout's life-like qualities imposing yet extraordinary. Next to this would be a week's worth of laundry. Piles of faded jeans, blackened white socks, Jockey underwear, ripped T-shirts, and stained sweats lay clumped together like the aftermath of a lava spill. Tommy was in charge of his own laundry, so it was no surprise that it attracted the same type of attention as his other less glamorous duties, which translated into nothing. He dreamt and dreamt big, but any movement towards satisfying a goal was always sidetracked because of an innate inability to act.

A strong scent of hot, diluted antifreeze seeped into his nostrils and made him cringe with the realization that his car was overheating, and a mechanical rebellion was well underway. Spotting the Ryan Road turn off, he left his center lane and crossed into the right lane, ignoring a chorus of car horns and profanities as he cut off irate drivers with the utmost of ease, and passed onto the safety lane, guiding the tortured vehicle to the next exit and through a green light, allowing him to proceed to a large Park 'n' Ride lot that lay ahead. There he would be able to park his car, give it time to cool down, and figure out what to do next.

"Just a little more," he coaxed the sputtering vehicle. "C'mon, fella. A little more."

At this point the temperature gauge's needle was well in the danger sector colored with fire red shading. And just as Tommy secured a parking spot and reached for the ignition key, the car expired with a single lurch, a brief shudder, and a resigned sigh of relief. Climbing out, its owner walked to the hood and felt the radiator's hot gusts breathing on his fingers, warning him that he was not going to be happy with what he was about to find once he unlatched the engine's protective armor.

Large billows of smoke poured into his face as he opened the hood and peered into the vast landscape of mechanical invention that laughed when it saw the owner's twisted face and swinging arms that tried to fan the gathering smoke. In addition to the radiator fluid that he detected when driving, the sharp, pungent aroma of smoldering rubber held his nostrils captive as plug wires melted.

"That's nice. I'm stranded with a car that self-destructs. I don't have a job, and I don't have any money to buy an answering machine in case Hollywood calls. What a great day."

A tire emitted a soft, sustained hiss, and Tommy watched as the front of the car leaned to the right.

"Not happy. Not happy at all."

Leaning against the grill, the back of his shirt warmed by the makeshift steam treatment, he stared at the massive neon lettering that proudly spelled Nike, each letter enveloped in a majestic crimson hue. "Oh, what luck. A store that's still open. My life's a blessing. Joy to Man. I am so happy. What a fantastic way to cap a wondrous day."

And then the neon sign went dead.

"Motherfucker."

Few cars remained in the parking lot, and the rumble of the expressway made Tommy feel even more isolated. Scanning the scene, he tried to gain some perspective from the prevailing circumstance but was too tired and dispirited to craft a cerebral explanation for what was occurring. He didn't get it. None of it. Nothing made sense. The nineteen year old could not fathom how someone who craved fame so much could be locked in a losing battle with chance, himself becoming the captured pawn.

Tommy's newly acquired squirt gun sat in the front seat; its presence added a certain charm to a car littered with work clothes, a collegiate backpack, and discarded McDonald's bags. Walking back to the driver's door, he reached through the opened window and grabbed the gun, marveling at its compactness and the snug feeling it produced as the butt rested in the palm of his left hand. He twirled it around an extended index finger and smacked it several times, making it whirl though the air in a blinded flurry. As he did this, he locked his car, left the lot, and followed a service lane that led to the Nike parking lot.

"Wish I could whistle. Never could. Bet most people can. Probably a prerequisite in Hollywood. Even if I'm not the best vocalist, there might be a part that requires whistling. Maybe complementing a musical accompaniment that plays in the background. Maybe soloing.

Wonder who offers lessons?" he asked aloud as he continued to stroll and play with his toy gun.

"Bet I could be West Point material, with a little training. This tiny investment should come in handy when I land a military role that requires weaponry expertise. Although, I need to face it: the days of big ticket war movies are over. Still, need to make sure that I'm where I need to be. No one knows the future, and opportunity waits for no one," he determined, as he entered the Nike lot and headed to the store's front doors. "I need to make a list so I don't forget. Whistling lessons and rifle training. Need to jump on this before someone jumps in front of me and gets the part because he's more prepared than me." Yet before Tommy could utter another syllable, a earsplitting scream ripped through his eardrums, only to be followed by a crashing thump, the accompanying sounds of bodies falling, and the frantic sounds of at least one person trying to get up. Stopping dead in his tracks, he saw a woman in a referee uniform on top of a man, demonstrating every conceivable inaccurate way of swimming. The man lay motionless, the hysterical female's head turning to the left and right spasmodically as her arms swung in various directions, her feet kicking the asphalt parking lot.

"Gun—man—shoot—home," she cried.

As Mike had exited the store, he had been preoccupied with the mammoth wallet in his hands. Opening it and gazing at its substantial contents, he determined that this is what finances adventure. So, it was with alarm that he glanced up, only to see the frantic eyes of the salesgirl as she lunged at him, knocking him flat on his back, arousing every erogenous zone known to man. An elbow was wedged against his nose, but not even this could distract him from the excitement that this girl had bestowed on him. Recalling Erica Jong's timeless phrase, a zipless fuck, he grinned at the source of his pleasure and winked at the trainee who danced upon his loins.

Stars were now centerpiece in the evening sky, shining brightly, accenting the stately dark blue hue that colored the earth and allowed its inhabitants a chance to view the heavens and ponder what it would be like to travel to the farthest reaches of the imagination. A killdeer serenaded the three helpless humans while motorists traveled to homes that offered leather recliners and remote controls that were the lifeblood of everything from televisions to stereo systems.

"I'm too young to be tortured," the girl screamed as one of her kneecaps found its way to Mike's forehead. Before he could push her off, a foot burrowed in his stomach. Using it as a runner's block, she bolted off Mike and raced through the parking lot and onto a service road, past a tourist trap cheese store, and behind an adult bookstore that truckers frequented in between trips home. Her screams never abated and sounded as if they were a cross between a Southern Baptist revival meeting and the appliance magnate whom Tommy had heard earlier.

Shaking his head as quickly as a drenched dog, Mike tried to focus on the image in front of him, but the only one he saw was several men dressed alike, twirling something that looked like a black baton with a funny shape. Slowly, the several dissolved into one; Mike propped himself up on his elbows and concentrated on who he viewed and what had just occurred. He wasn't despairing over the situation. Rather, he felt it compelling and in a strange way provocative. Excitement followed him. He knew it, and the present situation only reinforced it.

"Is your back okay?" Tommy asked, leaning down. "The way you landed, I wasn't sure if you got totaled."

Staring directly at a gun that dangled in front of his nose, Mike asked gingerly, "Is this happening for real?"

"I would say so. What was with that girl? The way she was screaming, I thought you did something to her."

"Me? You're the one with the piece. Think that might have frightened her? Drr."

Glancing at the toy, Tommy replied, "I don't know why it would. There's a million of these around." Offering his hand, he helped Mike to his feet, the gun the sole object of attention to the graduate. "Car died, and I don't like hitching rides at night. So … yeah."

"Let me guess: you wanna use my car."

"Yeah. Like now."

"Um, my parents don't like me talkin' to strangers, but your piece speaks volumes."

"Just got it. Can make a crappy day less crappy. Know what I mean?"

"And you want the car."

"Well, you too of course. I'm not a thief. You have to come along."

"Right. And if I don't agree—no, don't answer that. I'm a reasonable guy. Friendly. Like to lend a helping hand. Just need to make sure the hand stays with the body. This body. So, no need to get trigger happy, pal. Like to make it to my next birthday."

"I just need your help."

"Hmm. Not what I had in mind. Criminal activity. Hostage. *Miami Vice* shit. Possible drug kingpin. Scary shit, my friend. Yet this is the real America. The new normal. Strange times we find ourselves, eh? Like what brought you here? And me here? Why did we meet, and what does it mean?"

"Ah, not sure what it means but …"

"Okay, okay. You win. You and your little friend. No need to go *Scarface* on me. You know, you're kind of like him. Just kind of a baby version with a Wisconsin accent. That kills me—and I don't mean that literally, so don't get any ideas. Everyone thinks everyone else has an accent but them—including us. You don't think we sound just like Southeners sound to Valley Girls, and Valley Girls sound to Man Mountain Mike, and North Shore Nancy sounds to an Eskimo gettin' it on? Course we do. We have an accent, doncha know. How's come you'z here? Aw, geez. I's forgots the sausages. Total Milwaukee. Hey, why'd you pick me? Have you been spying on me? Creepy. Although I do like video cameras. Like to see life being life. Know what I mean? Sometimes the objective becomes the subjective. Or is it the subjective becomes the objective? I don't know. Learned about it in philosophy class. Sucked."

"Look. I need to go. Like now."

"Well, of course you do. Everyone's in a rush, including you. Everyone needs to be somewhere, but why? What's the rush? Why not stop and count the concrete? When's the last time you did that? Count concrete slabs. Underrated activity. They come in all sizes, you know. You should try it. Just watch where you're driving when you do it. Almost ran into a garbage truck once. Huge green fucker. You know a lot of people think they're mob controlled, especially East Coast. I don't buy it, though. Hey, you would know. Know anyone in the business? Catch my last word? Business? My car's over here.

I suppose you want to drive, or I can if you want. I'll do anything as long as I'm back for my graduation a week from now."

"It's not going to take a week."

"Cool. No sex either. I have boundaries."

Unconsciously toying with the gun, Tommy pointed it at Mike's midsection with a finger poised on the trigger.

"Okay, okay. Anything you say, pal. Just be gentle. Hey, I pass no judgment. I've seen porn. You know some of those guys are impressive. More interested in the female tribe, though. So, don't get ideas. Or if you do, we talk first. Deal? We discuss. Communication is a lost art, you know. Speaking of knowing, or not knowing, did you know that nonverbal communication accounts for 75% of all human communication? Can you imagine? Did you know that? Freaky. Not as freaky as this, but close," the professorial seventeen year old stated, leading Tommy across the lot and to the rusted Pinto.

"Think I'll drive, if you don't mind. Settles the nerves," Mike said as he opened his driver's door. "Get in. Door's unlocked."

And with that, Tommy got into the car and pulled his door shut. Wrestling with his seat belt, he then saw a terrifying site: his door had no handle. Nightmarish headlines circled through his head. Every warning his parents uttered now crippled him with terror. "Ah, what's with the door handle?"

"Oh, that. Just a little trick to keep the good ones in."

Nausea made its appearance, and Tommy feared that he was sure to vomit. And as the car started and pulled away from the store, he put two and two together and realized that he was now a hostage, a willing pawn who was too stupid to see the warning signs and allowed himself to be sentenced to a grisly death. No wonder he was so anxious to help me, Tommy concluded.

"Hey, what's your name? I'm Mike."

"Tommy."

"You a grad?"

"High school?"

"Yeah."

"I graduated last year. Do you think we can head back to town? I'm gonna need a team to get me …"

"Shit, you don't need any help. You're a natural. You pulled this off like a seasoned pro. I think we'll have more fun with just the two of us instead of having some of your accomplices along. Bet they've got names like Vinnie and Hugo and Sanchez. Am I right?"

Setting his fear aside for the moment, Tommy's calling returned. "Actually, Hollywood is currently going with the name Chaz when portraying gangsters and thugs. It's rather continental, if you will. You only have to look at the evolution of criminal portrayals to see which direction the industry is taking," he posited in his erudite best.

Pulling out of the parking lot and on to the service lane, past the Park 'n' Ride, and to the interstate heading south towards Chicago, Mike glanced at the toy Uzi still held by Tommy and marveled at how exciting his life was. No one could match him with his unabashed appreciation of life's wonders. And if fear struck, he calmed himself with the knowledge that he could take out anyone, including a machine gun-toting youth, with a solid punch. Just as long as bullets weren't part of the equation, of course.

"North, I said. North."

"No, you didn't."

"Yes, I did," Tommy insisted.

"No, you didn't. I'm not in a nursing home. I have a memory. It's not like I'm sittin' here eating Portage, drooling on my bib."

"Porridge."

"Whatever. I can remember shit, Scar. Hey, that's what I'm going to call you from now on. Scar. I love that. Scar. Did you know that you should always give a dog a one syllable name? So, you're welcome, again, and feel free to thank me—now, of course would be the appropriate time."

"I just wanna go home."

"Are you crying?"

"No."

"Sounds like it. You're sensitive. Yet you walk around with what's in your lap—well, so do I. More like swing, if you know what I mean. Nope. Never had much competition in that department. I meant your little friend. Well, not that little friend. That black friend sitting in your lap—and please ignore the inadvertent racial overtone."

"Just take me back." But there was nothing back home. No job, no friends, and soon there might not be a life. His. Sweat glazed Tommy's face, and he realized that the best course of action would be one of willing compliance. He had no cards to play, no options, and the optimism that had once nurtured his soul was now at a premium and beyond reach. Resigned with the realization that he and the driver were embarked on an uncharted passage, Tommy threw his head back, pressed the gun against his chest, and exhaled one intense sigh.

Chapter 7

Detective Jonathan Peters had just turned thirty-one and was celebrating with his soon-to-be bride, Shanda. The two were spending an evening at Porter's Poke House, reminiscing about their profound thirty-five day courtship while planning a spectacular reception to be held at the local VFW hall. Visualizing his blushing bride jamming a fistful of carrot cake into his mouth triggered another image: the groom carrying his virginal, thrice engaged, bride over the threshold of the Motel 6 that overlooked I-94. He took his future husbandry duties seriously and viewed them as ones that required manly certainty and statesmanship; he would not disappoint. This made him even more amorous as he imagined the two of them as entwined as the expressway system. Jonathan felt a slight yet growing erection as he fantasized about bearing down on Shanda's padded midriff, producing sensations that neither had ever experienced, for both were unacquainted with the dynamics of sex. The closest Jonathan ever got was when he was a senior in college and dated someone who he later discovered was a cross dresser.

Always the gentleman, Peters took pleasure in opening doors, placing a female hand in his, and providing a quick peck on the cheek. His mild manner and lean six foot frame caught the attention of many, as did his striking black eyes that contained a child-like awe. His thick eye brows and long lashes were as inviting as his broad smile and deceptive confidence. Jonathan's occupation required a self-assured stance. He knew how to manage this; however, it was misleading, for a void existed within his soul, one so deep and profound that he was willing to risk almost anything if he felt it might correct this emptiness. And Shanda became his gamble. When it came to women, he listened to his father, Big Ben, a stout man who grew shorter with each consecutive year as his heart grew larger. "Never forget that a woman needs attention," the man reminded his second son on a weekly basis. "You need to pamper them. Pamper them like a witch's bosom."

Jonathan never figured out what that meant.

"Now, look at Tony," Big Ben continued. "Still sowing his oats, looking for the perfect girl, but we both know how conscientious he is. Watching over us and all. That's why we need to convince him that we're old enough to take care of ourselves. He worries about us, you know."

An aspiring hippie who wore tie-dyed bell bottom pants, battered cowboy boots, porkchop sideburns, John Lennon-like oval glasses, vintage concert T-shirts, shoulder length salt and pepper hair, a canvas belt graced with a marijuana leaf-shaped buckle, and a faded jean jacket, Tony was the antithesis of his younger brother. The eldest son's vocabulary was still filled with mentions of *the man* and other anti-establishment colloquialisms that are as irrelevant today as they were when they were first spoken decades ago.

And Shanda didn't like him one bit.

"Why doesn't he get a job?" she asked her fiancé. "All he ever does is smoke that crap and listen to those beat up records. You can't even dance to them."

Knifing his growth hormone-enhanced sirloin streak, Jonathan twisted his head like a baffled six year old and replied, "Aw, c'mon. He's my brother. Don't cut him down."

"Well, he doesn't make it easy. What will my family think when they see him at the wedding? Everyone'll be in their finest pastels, and what will he be wearing? An Impeach Nixon button."

"Regan," Jonathan corrected.

"Whatever," she dismissed.

Most engaged couples maintain smiles as they count down the days to their wedding day and navigate through marital preparations. But this was not the case with Shanda. She walked around with a brooding silence that labeled her difficult by her colleagues at the Allstate regional office. Her executive position required time, diligence, and above all human relation skills, the latter being the most ludicrous, for this woman was about as inviting as a social disease, and everyone could see that but Jonathan. Intimidating to the point of parody, even her immediate supervisor was too scared to remove her from her post. One glare from the woman who donned a bun so tightly bound that her eyes bugged out like a guppy made him seek refuge behind a closed door. Never one to mince words, especially when they were negative, the woman barked her opinions in a way that frightened her superiors and sickened her colleagues. Her less than pleasant deportment silenced even the toughest of critics, so she rarely had to engage in the type of corporate battles that engulf those who attempt to scale the ladders of success with backstabbing precision. Yet Jonathan considered her a solid, dependable woman who would satisfy his intense need for security and companionship, while others measured her officious, dour countenance as off-putting; her flattened face that resembled a cartoon character making contact with a frying pan didn't help either. And what of her insistence on sexual abstinence before marriage?

"Well, it is illegal in several states. You do know that, don't you?" Jonathan fumbled during a tiring argument over free love with his brother.

"Then do me a favor and remind me never to visit those places," Tony responded, his expressionless reply cracking his younger brother up. The older sibling made a comfortable living producing handmade tie-dyed T-shirts that he sold at Grateful Dead concerts. He cleared fifteen grand during a summer concert season, and his psychedelic bandanna business kept the winter months from becoming anything but lean. Then again, living with Big Ben made life easy. All the patriarch ever said was, "You keep doing what you're doin'. Count your pennies. Remember, it's not what a man makes but what he saves. Your mother's father used to tell me that."

"Yeah, well, he's dead and she's gone," he replied, the bitter words silencing the man who needed no reminder of a wife who had left him and their two young boys. No warning. No note. Just a sudden departure after seeing a PBS program that chronicled Chilean atrocities against its citizens. Ben blamed himself for his wife's abrupt departure, claiming his ignorance of politics caused her flight, but the only fact his boys understood was that their mother had abandoned them; this more than anything else disrupted Jonathan's image of what a family was supposed to be and dampened any interest he had in dating during high school and his early adult years. Tony's despair became equally tragic. He withdrew from social circles, encamped himself in the family house, and doubled his bong use to the point where he claimed that he could hear a tree breathe by pressing his ear against the bark.

"And if I have to listen to one more Grand Funk album, I'll bean the dolt," Shanda promised while attacking her Cow Poke special.

"More sour cream, my honey cup?"

"Don't you honey cup me, unless you want to hold an ice pack against something south of your belt line."

"I'm sorry, Shanda. You know how clumsy I am when I'm around you," Jonathan said in a dejected way. The two had met at a singles dance sponsored by a ladies auxiliary club, and it was love at first spill. Shanda backed Jonathan against a wall and slapped him after he spilled punch on her polyester pants suit, and from that moment on he never stopped admiring her ferocity.

"I tell you, dad. She touched a part of me that no woman ever has," Jonathan told his father after meeting the woman.

"I'm sure she did, son. Just make sure it's not the right side of your face next time. You know how easily you bruise."

Sure she was aggressive, but she apologized, and the two began their short, perfunctory courtship that culminated in a proposal that was accepted readily by the woman.

Stuffing half a buttered rye roll into her mouth, she complained, "And why doesn't your father do something about that counter-revolutionary? If Tony were in my family, my father would give him a good whoopin', give him a crew cut, and enlist him in the armed forces in two seconds flat. That's what he needs. Don't you agree, Jonathan?"

"Ah, well, I …"

"Are you telling me that you, a peace officer of this community, a role model for this nation's youth, accepts your brother's insubordinate, unpatriotic shenanigans?"

Trying to avoid a confrontation with a woman whose veins now protruded through her forehead, Jonathan replied, "My, this steak is juicy."

Meanwhile, six miles west, Big Ben and Tony were engulfed in an argument over the eldest son's bedroom condition. "Will you look at this? No woman in her right mind will ever marry you if you make her house cleaning appear more difficult than it really is. You have to make little piles, son. Baby piles here and there so the little lady doesn't get depressed, thinking that it'll take her all day to clean a room that's one big pile of mess. You have to space it out, leave a little here and there."

Tony looked through a haze of marijuana smoke and said, "Chill, Ben. Relax."

"Oh, Tony. Don't tell me that you're burning rope."

A vintage Gerard turntable spun a scratched copy of the Jefferson Airplane's *Crown of Creation.* Nodding his head to the title track's absorbing rhythm, Tony tried to ignore his father's admonishments, but they were hard to ignore.

"Tony, Tony, Tony. A boy as bright as you needs more fire in his life. Be assertive. Grab it by the horns and wrestle it to the ground." And with spastic physical motions that were supposed to mimic a lassoing cowboy, Ben backed into Tony's holy shrine.

"Hey, watch it, Ben. You almost knocked over my table." The stand that Tony referred to was the centerpiece of his bedroom sanctuary. On it sat an ornate incense burner, a copy of *Steal This Book*, a brass peace symbol medallion, a coiled snake-shaped ash tray, a small, cherry wood carved box filled with joints, and a roach clip with a multicolored, beaded canvas tail. "Be cool. Feel the beat and groove. Life's too short for a freak out."

Shaking his sixty-three-year-old head while caressing his hairless crown, Ben wondered why his eldest son led such a different life than his younger brother. How could Jonathan have assumed such a traditional occupation when Tony did not?

"So, what's up? I'm sure you didn't come in here for a hit."

"Oh, Tony. Don't say such things. What if your brother came in here and saw you smoking that?"

"Wake up, Ben. Little Bro sleeps in the third bedroom. He might be the long arm of the law, a puppet of the man, but he's not stupid. He's got a nose. As a matter of fact, I'll bet you he'd love to do a bong before he walks down the aisle with Poison Ivy."

Ben could not have been more exasperated over the thought that his eldest might corrupt his youngest. Trying to revive the stern paternal tone that he used to use on his boys, Ben warned, "Tony, you keep away from Jonathan, We've got a wedding on our carving board, and I don't want you high as a kite, causing a commotion. And I certainly don't want to find out that my two sons were breaking the law. That would destroy Shanda and ruin Jonathan's career. Do you hear me? We've got less than a week to get ready, and you can start by cleaning up this room. I don't want any eligible ladies scared away because you don't know how to trick 'em into thinking that you won't be difficult to clean up after. No siree bop."

Chapter 8

"Ease up, man," Mike advised Tommy, as thc man dug his fingers into the arm rest.

I'm not scared of this high school kid. I'm not scared of this high school kid, the nineteen year old repeated silently as if it were his refrain.

"This is a quasi-classic car. You could travel to the far corners of the world, and you wouldn't find one in this condition. It's got that lived-in look that communicates accessible yet refined. Know what I mean? Hey, wait a minute. Wait a hot fuckin' second. Know what? This is the type of car that belongs in Fourth of July parades. Why hadn't I thought of that before? How many times have you been to parades and saw a line of vintage cars right behind the Cub Scouts and in front of the fire trucks? Plenty. Plentyola. Speaking of which, what's with clowns on fire trucks? You've got the fireman driving, but there're these red nosed freaks jumpin' around on top. Why? And what's with the candy? Scary. Wouldn't let my kid eat clown candy. Nope. Not a chance. Never know where that Tootsie Roll was. So, no need to paw my car. Wonder if finger nail marks can be buffed out? Do you know? Not sure. Think they're permanent. So knock it off or lose 'em."

Tommy felt the bile rise.

"Kidding. I'm a peace lovin' guy. I wouldn't touch your digits. Weird word for fingers. Wonder where that came from? Like chicken fingers. Now, who came up with that? Show me a farm where finger-shaped chickens strut. Crazy. Wonder what they'd sound like? You ever been on a farm? I have. Not for me. More of a sports nut. That's why I dig peace. Even on the field I won't total an opponent. He's there to help me. Force me to sharpen my game. Expand my playbook Can't use the same moves each time in each game. Know what I mean? You play ball?"

Tommy looked at him with a sickly pallor.

"Yeah, sorry. 'Course not. But you know what I mean. So, with you appearing out of nowhere, it's kind of the same thing. This is not part of my daily routine, so I need to rearrange my thought process which in return rearranges my moves. Make sense?"

A small line of drool dripped down Tommy's chin.

"Face it, Tom Boy: we were meant to be. I'm not super religious, but why else were the two of us in that parking lot at the same time? I'll tell you why: predestination. I think we studied that in Humanities class. Can't remember. Don't care. But I do know that you are one brazen badass. How many others have the cojones to stalk a parking lot with an Uzi? Unreal. And Tom McGuire, he's this guy I went to school with. Nice guy. Kind of a tard, though, said that nothing exciting ever happens 'round here. Wish he were here to see this. Hostage. Great."

And then it hit Tommy: who exactly was the hostage? And why mention a toy gun?

"So, what's the plan—and don't say it involves goin' north. Been there. Just give me advance warning when you want me to turn and all that. Hate abrupt directives when driving. That's a female trait, you know. Janice Kensington, girl I used to date, although date is a stretch. She would call it dating. I called it incarceration. Hey, you ever done that? Incarceration? What's that like? You ever someone's bitch? Do people watch? Lights are always on, right? Not very romantic. What'd you do to end up behind bars? This?" Mike asked, pointing to the Uzi. "Closest I ever got to organized crime was when I ripped off a bag of Circus Peanuts from Walgreens. Those things are great. When's the last time you had some?"

"Wha'?"

"Circus Peanuts. Hello. They're these orange pieces that are supposed to look like, you know, orange peanuts. They're just bigger. Way bigger. Like *Land of the Giants* bigger. Think they're made of marshmallow with a bunch of dye. Excellent."

A major league headache settled in, and Tommy felt himself becoming faint. "Excuse me, Mike. It is Mike, right?"

"Yes, it is, Tommy. It is Tommy, right?"

"I'm still a little confused about why we're headed south."

"Great. We're back to this. Sure you're not menstrual?"

"Not sure what that's supposed to mean, but no."

"Yes, you are. I can sense it. You're just one big Y chromosome, messin' with my head, paradin' around with your gangsta beast."

"Males are X; females are Y."

"Exactly. Y are you so indecisive. See? Get it? Y? I score."

Turning to the driver, Tommy began. "Mike, I just want to go home. I don't want any trouble. Please. Just turn around. If there's anything I can do to help you, I will. I just don't want to get hurt. Please. Please, turn around. I promise to forget this ever happened. I'll erase everything about this incident, okay? Please?"

"Why would you need help? I am helping you. I've done everything you've asked. You wanted my car, done. You wanted me to drive, done. You trashed my armrest, done, although not cool. I'm a willing hostage. I'd didn't get all emotional on you. I didn't cry. I didn't rearrange your face, which I could in half a second. I did everything, everything you asked. What more do you want?"

"What?"

"How am I not compliant? What do you want me to do? Plead for my life? I don't think so. Sorry, pal. Not gonna happen."

"No one is holding you hostage," Tommy informed the youth.

"That's pretty good," the graduate laughed. "You are one good actor."

Mike had no idea what he had invited.

Proud that someone saw what Tommy considered his fine, instinctive flair for the theatre, he responded, "Yes, well, I've always considered myself a method actor. More Adler than Meisner. Excellent with timing. I also use it in my writing. As a matter of fact, I've got a project that I was going to start this weekend. It's a screenplay about two people whose love is so intense and passionate, that they never get it right. Kind of a contemporary *The Way We Were*."

"Never heard of it."

"Sure you have. Barbra Streisand and Robert Redford. Major film."

"If you say so."

"Come on. You never heard the title song?"

"Negatory."

Thrown by the lack of recognition, Tommy proceeded to sing the first two lines in his grating, off-key style, the same type that prevented him from singing with his high school rock band.

"No offense, man, but that song sucks, and you're no Robert Plant."

"I wasn't trying to be," Tommy pouted as he slid down his seat.

"Then who were you trying to sound like?"

"Barbra Streisand."

"Why?"

"Because she's the one who sang it in the movie. As a matter of fact, there're two versions: the one in the movie and the one that's on the non-soundtrack album."

"Two of them? Jesus. Double the pain."

Now, this was not the type of comment that Tommy appreciated. It was inconceivable to him that someone could not see the significance of another attaining an immeasurable degree of fame. "What do you mean, who cares? Do you know how she got her start? Do you know how long she's been around? Do you know how long she's been number one?"

"I don't care. She's still got nothin' on the lead singer from Bow Wow Wow."

Astonished, Tommy chocked, "Wha', wha' how can you say that? Haven't you done any research on the woman?"

"A little. She was seventeen when she was recruited by the guy who managed the Sex Pistols. Still has this awesome Mohawk that …"

"Not her. Barbra."

"Nah. Only stick with the classics."

Throwing his hands in the air, Tommy's Uzi bounced off the dashboard and hit the steering wheel.

"Hey, easy, Dirty Harry. I don't wanna get shot a couple dozen times before we reach the state line."

"My name is not Harry, and why would you get shot?"

"Sure you're Harry. Harry Callahan. Bet you don't know who he is."

"Of course, I do. Any student of the cinema knows that he's the character that Clint Eastwood portrayed in some of the most successful detective films ever released in this country and abroad," Tommy volleyed back in a curt, condescending tone.

"Gotta hand it to you, Tom Boy. You know your history."

"Yes, I do."

"So, I bet this thing isn't even loaded." Picking up the gun, Mike felt the warm plastic and considered how lightweight it was. And then it hit. "Is this a plastic gun? Where do they make these?"

"How should I know? You can buy 'em anywhere."

"Black market?"

"I don't know. I suppose."

"And where did you buy this one?"

"Spencer Gifts."

Realizing the ludicrousness of the situation, Mike moaned, "I got held up with a fake gun?"

"Held up? Held up?" Tommy asked in his animated best. "Why would you think that? I came to your aid. I heard the screaming and saw you on the ground, so I came over, helped you up, and before I knew it, I was the one being carted off."

"You pointed a fucking gun in my face. What was I supposed to think?"

"It's a toy! A stupid fucking toy that I got a good deal on. Some people walk around with cigarettes, others with cigars. I walk around with squirt guns. What's so weird about that?"

"Nineteen and a squirt gun? Can you say arrested development? Hello."

"Shut up. Exactly how stupid are you? Do I look like an armed felon? Do I look like someone who would risk freedom for this car?"

"Leave the car alone. It didn't do anything. And you shut up. Like now. I need to think." And as a coach bus passed the yellow Pinto, Mike asked in a mere whisper, as if his entire life had ended, "So, you never wanted to kidnap me?"

"Kidnap? Kidnap? Why would I want to do that? It's a crime. I could go to jail. How's Hollywood supposed to get a hold of me when I'm in the joint? And another thing. You were the one who kidnapped me. Let's not forget that little fact."

"I did?"

"Well, didn't you?"

"No. You were the one with the gun," Mike countered.

"Oh, yeah? Well, who was the one who didn't listen to directions and started driving in the opposite direction of where I wanted to go? Huh? Was it me? And what about my missing door handle. That's the oldest trick in the book. There was no way to escape. Of course, I thought I was being kidnapped. You lured me into a trap and wouldn't take me where I wanted to go."

"That is not true. Gun violence is rampant, but I took the high road. You should thank me for not fighting you to the death back there. I could have killed you. Just look at me and then look at you. I could bench press this car. Just take a look at my guns." And with that Mike rolled his sleeve up to reveal an impressive bicep perfected through intense daily workouts. "These guns don't run."

"Jesus, I'm stuck Ronald Reagan."

"And I'm stuck with Nancy."

"Hilarious."

"And I didn't buy these guns at a crappy store," Mike shot back, removing both hands from the wheel and pulling up the other sleeve.

"Of course, not. You're a real right wing, bench-pressing giver."

"I am, minus the right wing. My guidance counselor even said so in my college recommendation letter."

"Good for you."

"Yeah, good for me. Got into UW-Madison. No wait list, either. Just straight in. Bet you never got in there."

"No, I didn't. You're amazing. You're fantastic. You're destined to greatness, you stupid high school brat-packing jock."

Like a viper, Mike reached over, grabbed Tommy's shirt, and yanked him within an inch of his face. "Look, Tom Boy. You can call me anything, but don't call me stupid." And with that, Mike threw the baffled faux bandit against the door. "This is not good, Tom Boy. This is not good. Here I am, all excited about finding the real America, and you go and ruin it. My time is valuable, and you've wasted it. Time is precious, you know. It doesn't grow on trees."

"Bet you learned that in an AP class."

"Hey, watch your mouth. I earned a lot of college credit from those."

"Yes, dad."

"And you can lose the sarcasm." Silence filled the car as the expressway lights cast an orange glow, coloring Mike and making him appear like an intergalactic superhero. "Now, I'm bummed, and it's all your fault. You're a jerk, you know that? A real tease."

"I apologize for my shortcomings—not."

"Now, what am I supposed to do?"

"Turn around so I can get back."

"Why?"

"So I can get back."

"Why?"

"So I can get fucking back and fix my fucking car."

"Lotta fuckin', Tom Boy. Shouldn't swear so much. Shows a limited vocabulary."

"Pot, meet kettle."

"What's that supposed to mean?"

"It means, Mr. AP, that you are a hypocrite. You swear more than I do, yet you criticize me? I'll have you know Mike, Michael, Mikey, that my verbal skills rival those of Olivier."

"Who's he?"

"Barbra Streisand's husband, you stu … you wildly misinformed individual. Now can we go home or not?"

"Not."

"Not?"

"That's right. Not. You were the one who interrupted my trip, so I guess you're going to have to stay with me for the next week."

"What?"

"Yep. That's how long I'll be spending on my excursion. Then I have to get back so I can graduate."

"That's kidnapping."

"Said the guy who pointed a gun at my face and led me through a parking lot and into a car. My car. Which I'm sure is documented on a security camera. They have them everywhere, you know."

Dread incapacitated Tommy as he considered how the footage would appear to anyone who didn't know the details. "Then we need to go back so I can explain."

"Explain to who? A bunch of cops back there waiting to gun you down? How 'bout a soon-to-be trail of cop cars on our ass? Guns drawn. Helicopters overhead. President of the United States addressing the American people. Not happening—yet. So, until it does, you need to stay with me. I'm your best alibi. Your only alibi."

Tommy knew this was true. There was a screaming girl who might be able to ID him, and perhaps there was a security system. Perhaps not. Either way, he knew he was fucked. "And just what am

I supposed to do about my responsibilities back home? I've got lots of projects going on. And my car needs fixing."

"Fuck your car. It isn't going anywhere."

"And what about my parents?"

"They'll be there when you get home. And my guess is that they'll enjoy the break."

An unsettling sensation overcame Tommy. He knew that his choices were limited, but what bothered him most was that Mike had identified a simple truth: his parents would not miss him, and they most certainly would enjoy the break. With the Kenosha exit signs approaching, Tommy's ambivalence returned. And he knew that wasn't a good sign.

Chapter 9

A waitress donning a black leather apron approached the engaged couple's table. "How was everything?"

"Well, for starters," Shanda began, "my Cow Poke special was far from satisfactory. The salad looked like it was shipped from Pittsburgh without being covered. It was soaking wet and was brown. The tomatoes looked like they were grown in some Central American factory, and my relish tray was anything but satisfying. And as far as my meat goes, I've seen more tender backsides on creatures in the zoo."

The server rolled her eyes and turned to Jonathan. "And yours, sir?"

Afraid that he might incite a riot by acknowledging that his meal was fine, Jonathan looked at Shanda, then the waitress, and offered, "Ah, my spoon was a tad cloudy."

"There. A real waste of money. Don't expect to see us again, especially when we're celebrating important events such as a birthdays and anniversaries. And another thing: your $11.95 all-you-can-eat price is exorbitant. You'd better speak with your corporate head and revamp the prices, or you'll see your business go straight down the commode."

Still smiling, although it was about as natural as dental surgery without anesthesia, the waitress replied, "Thank you for coming. You can pay at the front counter."

"And where's the doggy bag?" Shanda barked.

"When the other waitress cleared your plates, did you ask her to save anything?"

"I most certainly did. Didn't I, Jonathan?"

Caught off guard, the policeman lowered his head and made a series of mumbles, sounding as if he were making saliva bubbles.

"See. My fiancé says that I did."

Gritting her teeth, the young woman replied, "I'm sorry if she didn't hear you, but your table was cleared five minutes ago."

"And where is she now?"

"She quit. That's why I'm here."

With an accusative finger pointed at the waitress, Shanda stated gravely, "That gristle would have been perfect for Snowball. There goes your tip."

Jonathan refused to look at either of the women, and instead concentrated on the scattered crumbs that lay on the stained table cloth. How he hated scenes, and no one excelled at them more than the woman he was to marry. Although he defended his betrothed to his family, even he had deep, nagging doubts about what he was getting into. Had he more confidence, he thought, he would break off the nuptials and find someone more to his liking. But he knew that decisiveness was not one of his hallmarks, so a resigned life was all that awaited him.

"You know something? Sometimes I wonder how you ever became a law enforcement officer. That woman is a prostitute."

"Shanda, please," the exhausted man moaned.

"Well, she is. What else do you call someone who gets paid by a criminal network for services dubiously rendered?"

"We're going." And with that, Jonathan pulled himself out of the padded booth adorned with longhorn steers and removed a $5 bill from his wallet.

"And what do you think you're doing? That better not be a tip, or I'll snatch it right up. That girl needs to be taught a lesson, and I intend on teaching it."

"For God's sake, Shanda."

"Don't you take the Lord's name in vain."

"All this over a doggie bag? Forget about your dog."

"I will not." Grabbing the five and replacing it with a penny, Shanda continued. "This is what she's worth. Maybe next time she'll remember to ask about table scraps."

An obedient silence followed as Jonathan's girlfriend exited the booth and led him out the restaurant. Once outside, he attempted to hold her hand, only to have it retracted to shield one of the woman's ferocious sneezes. Recovering, she swaggered to his car and waited for him to open the door. Once inside, she lowered the visor and peered into the vanity mirror, making sure that her spartan use of makeup wasn't overpowering.

After Jonathan went to the driver's door and got in, he glanced at Shanda, and that's all it took: an amorous sensation overpowered him. He leaned over, kissed the base of her neck, and slid his tongue up to her earlobe.

"Oh, my God," she screamed, a slap following.

Pressing a hand against his swelling cheek, he stared at the woman who dominated his life.

"That is pure pornography. I thought a snake was wrapped around my neck. Just who do you think you are, mister? I demand respect, and you'd better give it to me, or I'll give you your walking papers so fast it'll make your head swim. I'm no cheap show girl like that hussy in there. If one beer makes you this irresponsible, then maybe we should check you into a treatment center. I save myself for a husband my entire life, and you can't wait. Just like a spoiled child and a cookie jar. Well, I'm no Oreo, and you're certainly no glass of milk."

His romantic mood now soured, as was the beginning of yet another futile erection, he struggled to regain his bearings. "I'm sorry, Shanda. That wasn't proper of me."

"It certainly wasn't. And in a car!"

The ride home was uneventful, but the ensuing calm did little to mask the unhappiness that marked a man who was unable to live for himself. An annoying selflessness engulfed Jonathan. Because of his passive nature, any woman could tie him around a finger, and he knew it. Since his mother's departure, an intense need for security enveloped the lonely man and followed him through high school and college, soon escorting him into adulthood. It didn't matter who the girl was; it was only matter of time before she learned that he could be manipulated once the proper vantage point was discovered: his fear of abandonment. The striking policeman's edifice always gave way to his grave insecurity, and each girl tired of this weakness and left. All but Shanda.

Why don't I tell her that I'm not sure that I love her? he thought while driving back to Big Ben's homestead. All I ever do is cater to this woman, and I don't even think she's that good looking. Not that I'm a centerfold, but I know that I can do better. But I don't want to break her heart. She'd be angry, dad would be disappointed, and her entire family would want to kill me. No, I can't do it. Most marriages aren't happy anyway, right? Definitely. Happy endings only happen on television.

With that he continued through the suburban streets that led to his neighborhood and drove past the bountiful spruce trees that lined the subdivision's entrance, their fragrant aroma filling the night air; he remembered how magical they were, especially after a snowfall, for it made them dream-like and regal. And then he recalled the endless summer days spent scaling the massive trees with his brother, each boy in a race to be the first to spot their home, the only one he had ever known.

"Slow down, Jonathan. You're going too fast."

Shanda always claimed that he drove too fast; however, if there were ever a careful, defensive driver, it was her fiancé.

"One beer obviously impairs your performance. I'm contacting a therapist tomorrow. Better to meet a problem head-on instead of ignoring it."

At first he wanted to deliver a defiant retort, one that would make his displeasure crystal clear. One that would stop any further dispersions to his character. One that would establish him as a willing combatant who would not tolerate disrespect or hyperbolic nonsense. But he didn't. Instead, as was the case with this and any other woman he dated, he squelched his anger and retreated to a silent response.

"And I'm glad that you agree with me. Most men would hide their weaknesses and assume that the female was overreacting. But by your silence, I know that you're feeling guilty and ashamed of your behavior tonight; that's why I'm here. I'm the best thing that could have happened to you because I know what's best for Jonathan Peters. I know you better than you know yourself. And don't worry—you can write me a thank you note later. Just one phone call to a licensed professional, and everything will fall into place, and we can get on with our life together."

Pulling into his driveway, the couple watched a daily ritual: Big Ben running from window to window, trying to determine who had arrived. During high school, Jonathan and his football buddies used to drive slowly past the house just so they could watch the man dart about like a mechanical rabbit in a shooting gallery.

Getting out of the car and making his way to the front door, Jonathan was jarred by the blast of a car horn. Turning, he saw Shanda pointing at her door with a fearsome glare.

"I'm dead," he muttered as he walked back to the car. Opening the passenger door, he offered a monotone "Sorry," but was emasculated with, "If this is an attempt to insult me, it's working. Your behavior tonight is outrageous and unacceptable. For someone whose care society has been placed, I find your childish antics degrading and sophomoric. Now move it."

Brazen as ever, Jonathan thought.

"Oh, it's you two. How was dinner?" Big Ben's sudden appearance was a lifesaver for his son. Now the countdown could begin. First up would be Shanda's endless chat with his father, to be followed by intricate descriptions of how she planned on re-designing the house once Big Ben died, and finally the command for transport back to her apartment two miles away.

"Why, Ben. How good it is to see you," she said, embracing him in a fashion her fiancé yearned but never experienced. "Oh, forget about our dinner. How was yours? Did you have that chuck steak TV dinner that I picked up for you?"

"Yes, I did and let me tell you something, little lady: it was mighty tasty. You sure know how to please a man. Doesn't she, Jonathan?"

Under the auspices of eyes that could kill, he smiled at his soon-to-be bride and replied, "Yes, dad. She's a swell gal."

"Ain't she though?" his father laughed, slapping his knees like a sloppy drunk in an old Western movie. "Well, c'mon, Jonathan. Help the lady into the house, and let's have us a nice, long visit." Turning to Shanda, Ben added, "We don't get to see enough of you in this house, little lady."

Glaring at Jonathan as if to say, Now here's a real gentleman, she walked ahead of father and son into the house, allowing the screen door to close before either man had entered.

"I've got a spare broomstick if you wanna twirl." The unmistakable presence of Tony holding a pudding pop stopped Shanda dead in her tracks. In him, she saw everything that she hated: idealism, individuality, and contentment.

"Good. Why don't you get me one and yourself a job? Then I can brush your butt out of this house once and for all."

"Oh, good comeback. I see your wit is as keen as your fashion sense." And with that Tony walked over to greet his brother. "Hey, man. How's it goin'?" Giving his brother the hippie handshake, he continued. "Fraulein's in rare form. Maybe I can find some dust kitties for her to lick."

Normally, Jonathan would have chastised his brother over comments such as this; however, tonight was different. Nothing his brother could say would depress the policeman more than the thought that he was scheduled to spend the rest of his life with a woman who considered The Muppets promiscuous.

"Jonathan," she bellowed from the kitchen. "Where's the tea kettle? I want to make your father a nice, hot cup of Red Zinger."

Breathing in, attempting to control his annoyance, he replied, "Honey, don't you remember our discussion last week? Dad doesn't like tea. He doesn't like hot liquids."

The sounds of a slammed cabinet door and stomping feet produced pangs of fear in Jonathan. And then he saw what his dissension had wrought: the woman was charging towards him with a meat tenderizer hammer. "Why must you always contradict me and make me look foolish in front of your family?"

With the pudding pop now wedged in his mouth, Tony mumbled, "You don't need any help from my brother. You look ridiculous regardless of the angle."

"Tony, please," his brother pleaded.

Walking towards his target, Tony continued. "I should follow you around with a tape recorder so I can gather every idiotic comment you make. I could turn it into a greatest hits tape. Bet it'd sell a million copies. Two million."

"But that would take too much effort, for a freaky freak like you."

"Nah, you're easy—well, from what I hear, not that easy, which is a gift to mankind. So on behalf of our species, I thank you."

"Jonathan," she screamed. "I will not stand here and have you do nothing while your brother treats me like dirt. I want you to arrest him because I'm pressing charges."

"What?"

"You heard me. I'm charging him with harassment. He's causing great harm to my delicate mental state. Well, get to it. Throw on the cuffs."

"Honey," Jonathan whined.

"Don't you honey me. It's your duty as a police officer to protect the citizenry, and a terrible crime has been committed. Now, arrest him. I mean it, Jonathan. Arrest him now."

As if an epiphany had filled him with the light of truth, justice, and the American way, he announced, "No. He is my brother, and I will not do it."

"Is that right?" she asked. "Then I've got two words for you: date rape."

Jonathan's face paled as he saw the banner headlines. The suspension without pay. Television reporters. His family's humiliation. Himself homeless. His brother shoving a pudding pop in her face.

"Tony, Tony, Tony. How many times do I have to tell you not to play with your food?" his father chastised.

Shanda's deafening screams followed her as she ran into the bathroom. Slamming the door shut, she tore the shower curtain off its rings and threw it in the tub. Staring at her chocolate-laced face, she thought of every type of reasoned response: castration, the guillotine, lethal injection. But she considered these too humane, so she took an unlikely path and channeled her anger into something more creative and covert. "I know. I'll have the vice squad bust the creep at the wedding. Maybe that'll show Jonathan that when I say jump, he'd better ask how high."

The woman didn't ascend to the heights of corporate power by playing softball. Any hint of dissension was met with an iron fist, and those who dared stand in her way were eviscerated. Yet the very thought that her plan might ruin what was supposed to be a joyous day for all involved meant nothing to her, for revenge was the only taste in her mouth. Staring down her reflection, she wiped off the chocolate streaks and promised, "I will not sleep until that useless hippie is convicted and ends up sharing a cell with a bald, colored man."

"Shanda, it's me. Are you all right?"

"No, I most certainly am not. If you were any type of man, you'd put that criminal into custody, but you won't, will you?"

Afraid that a fist might sail through the closed door, he backed up a few steps and replied, "I don't think so."

As the door whipped open, Jonathan yelped at what he saw: Shanda's eyes shone with a ferocious glare that resembled a mutant in a carnival freak show. "I'd scream too, if I had to face myself for what I am: a negligent policeman."

And with that she brushed past Jonathan and walked into the kitchen where Ben was trying to lift the refrigerator. "Nothing like a little workout to keep the ol' ticker goin'," he groaned, his face flushed and sweaty.

"Why, Big Ben. Don't you think enrolling in a health club might be easier?" she asked.

"What for? I've got workout areas throughout the house. People go and spend a fortune on membership fees when they could be pumpin' appliances."

As Ben tipped the aged avocado refrigerator towards him, Tony breezed by, not giving his father's actions a moment's notice. Just then, the telephone rang. Looking to his son with pleading eyes, the man motioned for him to answer.

"Hello … Yeah, just a sec. Hey, Jonathan. It's that captain with the lazy eye."

Panicked, the policeman grabbed the phone and shielded the mouth piece. "This is my boss, Tony. Knock it off, or I'll be the one who suffers."

Tony merely snorted, brushed past Shanda, picked up his sandals, and walked into the family room.

"Good evening, Captain … Yes, I just got home. The little woman and I went out to dinner … Yes … Yes … Ah-ha … Oh, no. Do we have plates? … Description? … Absolutely … All right, first thing tomorrow … Yes, thank you … See you then … You, too. Bye."

"And just what was that about?" Shanda demanded.

"Sounds like a violent kidnapping at the Nike Warehouse. A girl was in hysterics, describing how she was almost shot to death by some punk with a machine gun. Seems like after she got away, he grabbed a customer who came to her assistance, held him at gun point, and then made him the getaway driver, using the poor guy's own car."

Dropping the refrigerator and watching it rock back and forth, Ben sighed, "Oh, Jonathan. That store is just a stone's throw from the beer depot. What's happening to our country? Has the entire world gone mad?"

A pregnant silence followed Ben's question, interrupted by the sounds of a videotaped episode of *Adam-12* that Tony was watching.

"I've got to meet with the Captain tomorrow morning and then interview the witness. She wasn't much help tonight. From what I was told, they don't have much to go on because she's too rattled. All they know is that someone was kidnapped, and the assailant had heavy artillery. No specific vehicle description or license plate numbers either, to make this even more problematic."

"Well, you'd better take me home right now so you can get proper rest. You've got a big day tomorrow, and you'll need time to sleep off your drinking binge. C'mon, let's go. Grab your keys. Chop chop." No more than two steps were taken before she stopped. "And you listen to me, Big Ben: stay away from that piano." And with that Shanda walked out of the house and to the car, waiting for Jonathan to open her door.

After dropping her off and returning home, he decided to, using one of his brother's terms, crash for the evening; however, he found a restful sleep elusive. A recurring dream pitted him against a large, prehistoric bird, one that kept him at bay in a large crevice, for just as the loin-clothed man garnered the courage to step outside his fortress and onto a ledge, the giant bird swept past him and pushed him back into his domain. As the dream proceeded, the sleeping man tossed about as his sweat-soaked body twisted in the rumpled sheets.

Sensing that he was falling backwards, Jonathan awoke just in time to slam his fist upon the alarm clock and catch himself falling off the bed, exhausted.

Chapter 10

Although he never had an ulcer, Tommy swore to himself that one had just formed. Never before had he ever felt this sick. It wasn't just that he had no idea where he was going or who this person was who was taking him somewhere. It was, quite simply, a feeling of virile hopelessness, coupled with an intense disdain for himself that produced the gastro misery that he was experiencing, for nothing sickened him more than the knowledge that he did not resist being taken by an individual who he considered to be an overzealous, thrill seeker who was having the time of his life.

"Hey, check this out, my man." Turning up the volume on his cheap car stereo, Mike treated his guest to a crackling fusion of distortion. "*Highway Star*. Deep Purple. The perfect cruising song. My buds and I love to cruise Wisconsin Ave on weekends and crank this baby. You ever hear of these guys, Tomster?"

"Of course, I have. Stop thinking that I'm unfamiliar with anything that's pre-Bon Jovi. You don't have the market cornered when it comes to musical knowledge, you know."

"I never said that I did. Just thought you were only into Barbra Streisand parent crap. Aren't we testy?"

"You would be too if your stomach was having a meltdown."

"No kiddin'? I used to get these death defying gut aches after …"

"Death defying. Please. Don't you mean excruciating gut aches? Unbearable gut aches? Crippling gut aches? Death defying. Makes it sound like your stomach works at a circus."

"And eats Circus Peanuts. Am I right? Am I right?" Mike thundered as his laughs made Tommy's unrest even more pronounced. "Okay, score one for Thomasina. As I was saying, I used to get these unbearable gut aches after eating too many Pop Tarts. Know how I got rid of 'em?"

Increasingly irritated at the person he considered an intellectual inferior, Tommy replied in his terse finest, "Let me guess: one bite at a time."

"Yeah, you got, Tom Boy. That's unreal. We think alike. We must have been separated at birth. Think of it. Crazy. Stork forgot that we were together and spazzed out, dropping us off at different locales. Oh, that stork. What a nut."

Sliding down the seat and holding his stomach as if it were about to burst, Tommy stared at the dashboard and tried to determine a means of escape. Traffic was now sparse, so obtaining someone's attention might be difficult. The guy's gotta run out gas sooner or later, the struggling teen thought. Once he does and we end up at a gas station, I could make a run from it. Or I could surreptitiously pass a note to the attendant. Nah, too film noire. I know—when he pays, I'll take off in his car. Perfect.

"Hey, Music Man. What's your favorite Deep Purple album?"

"None, when it comes out of a crappy system."

"Well, my apologies if it's not as nice as your disabled car back there, but this is all I have. Mommy and daddy don't exactly fork over tons of cash anytime I need new wheels."

Sitting up straight, Tommy asked, "Are you implying that my parents paid for my car?"

"I'm not implying anything. How would I know if you were telling the truth?"

"That is the most stupid, ignorant, nonsensical, inane, twisted from of logic I have ever heard. Are you doubting my credibility? You're a kidnapper. A common, petty, baby faced, rock 'n' roll thief."

"Hey, hold on there, Jackson."

"My name is not Jackson, Tom Boy, or anything else as far as you're concerned. You fucking kidnapped me, and you won't let me go, so don't sit there and pass judgment on my character, fuckhead."

Mike leaned over and grabbed Tommy's shirt, which brought a swarm of hands pushing him away, almost as if a karate movie in fast forward was being played.

"And quit grabbing me. Anytime you don't like something I say you latch on to me like some automated machine. What are you? Fuckhead RoboCop?"

Pushing him away, Mike sat silently for a moment and then began. "Let me repeat what I had explained earlier, just in case you're a slow learner. When I saw your little gun dancing in front of my face, I thought I was a goner, so I decided that cooperation would prevent me from getting my head blown off. This is my car, right? This is my time, right? Back there you interfered with the first vacation I ever got, right? So, who's kidnapping who?"

Stunned, Tommy shook his arms in front of his face and shrieked, "What? I try to help you, see if you're injured, assist you in your time of need, ask if you'd be kind enough to help me out, and the next think I know I'm headed God knows where with some high school senior who thinks that he's discovered the meaning of life because he knows who Deep Purple is."

"Yeah, and I bet I discovered them before you did."

A long, sustained scream filled the car as Tommy hit Mike with weak, sporadic blows. Pushing Tommy away with a single arm, Mike laughed, "Mike Tyson you ain't. Well, maybe Mrs."

"You're a real funny guy," Tommy dismissed while slipping into an even deeper funk, for nothing that he had ever experienced came close to the day's events. What am I supposed to do now? he thought. This maniac's driving me around, he's practically a giant, and I don't get why this is happening to me.

Rubbing Tommy's head in a comforting method, Mike said, "You know, Tom Boy, if you were a little more sociable, we might just have us a real good time."

As if a lightning bolt had struck, Tommy put two and two together and got five. "So that's it, huh? Now, you listen to me. I don't care how big you are or how strong you are because I'll fuckin' kill you before I'll let you touch me."

"What? You mean like sexually?"

"Yeah. Exactly."

"Ah, no. I don't think so. And not very original, either. You're just copying what I said back in the parking lot. Do you always steal people's ideas? Unacceptable. They have laws against that, you know."

"I have never copped another's idea. Never. I don't have to. My creativity comes from within, and I don't appreciate you suggesting otherwise. I stated a simple fact: you won't let me go, we're in the middle of nowhere, and you will never, repeat, never touch me. Got it?"

"You mean like this?" And with that, Mike poked Tommy in the shoulder, the unemployed man trying in vain to wiggle away from an extended index finger. "What're you going to do now? Call a cop? 'Officer, he's poking me. Wah, wah, wah.' Bet that'll send shock waves through the precinct."

"Don't get smart with me, Buster."

"Buster?"

"You know what I mean."

"Buster?"

"I've seen *Unsolved Mysteries*. I know what creeps like you do with young boys."

"Boys? You're older than I am."

"That's right, and I intend on keeping it that way, sicko."

"Sicko? What are you, an endless resource of stupid names?"

"Don't change the subject, pervert."

Grabbing Tommy again, Mike shouted, "Who're you calling a pervert, wimp?"

"You, you steroid poppin' molester."

"Get this into your head, Junior."

"Senior. I'm older than you."

"Well, if you weren't such a skinny fuck you'd look older. Now, get this straight. Number 1: I don't take steroids. Number 2: if you honestly think that you turn me on, that any guy turns me on, then you're flattering yourself. I was on my school's varsity football team since sophomore year. Did you hear that? Sophomore year. I had more girls interested in me than an Arab sheik, so don't start thinking that you've got some incredible body that turns straight men gay because you don't."

"Then why am I sitting here?"

"Because I'm trying to find the real America."

"Then why do you need me?"

"Because you had a gun and told me that you needed help. I figured if I didn't, my head would look like a Mouse Trap piece."

"Mouse Trap? Mouse Trap? This is, without a doubt, the dumbest, stupidest, nonsensical ..." And with that, Tommy became silent, unable to formulate a proper response that would express his frustration. Staring out the window and observing the sky's various shades of dark orange and blue blend together, forming a carpet that nighttime walks upon, the brooding man tried to determine what to do next. If it was the unexpected that nourished creativity, something he believed to be true, then he had found it. And with this realization, his mood changed. Yes, the day's events provided him with a fuselage of experience. Perhaps Mike's sudden appearance was nothing more than an elaborate pre-screen test designed to measure the dreamer's improvisational techniques. And what about the inescapable state in which he found himself? This could be nothing more than an endurance test that would train him to withstand even the most grueling travel schedules that Hollywood, the music industry, or the mammoth New York publishing firms would demand. Yes, even in the direst of circumstances, the man was capable of finding a grandiose design behind it all.

Be cool, he reassured himself. You might not know where this is heading, but everything happens for a reason. Maybe the forces of fame are conditioning me. Yeah, that makes sense. Why else would any of this be occurring? It does follow a logical yet circuitous path. I lose my job, make what might be my final appearance at the arcade before fame strikes, and now I'm racing around with some guy who very well might be my own Zen master.

"It's a good thing that I'm loyal to my Judeo-Christian upbringing; otherwise, I'd toss you like a salad. You probably never workout, do you? Man, if I were you, that'd be the first order of business each morning."

"Yes, but you're not me. I'm me, and you're you. Don't start telling me what I should or shouldn't do simply because you think I should."

"Just trying to help. Being helpful. That's what I'm known for—among other things."

"Yeah, I'm sure." Speculating what the best course of action should be, Tommy decided to play along and see where it took him. "You know what? You're right. You are absolutely correct. I do need to lift weights and get my upper chest built up if I want to be ready for my calling."

"Calling? Sounds religious. You plan on being an entertainment missionary?"

"No, I am not, and I will thank you to leave my outstanding working knowledge of that field out of your snide comments. I spent a great deal of time studying various professions and by ridiculing this task, you only make yourself appear foolish. Perhaps once you start college, if you actually do, you'll better appreciate my gift."

"Look, pal. I'm a Top Ten graduate—or I will be next week. Can you top that? What was your class ranking?"

"It pales in comparison to yours, not that it matters."

"Yeah, right. Everything matters to you."

"Said the high school psychoanalyst who knows a figure eight football play …"

"Figure eight? Figure eight?"

"And quit repeating yourself. You sound like my dad?"

"No kidding? Is he like me? That'd be unreal if he was. Were. Was."

"Were."

"Whatever. And let me fill you in on a little secret: you repeat yourself, too. So check this out. You do. I do. And your dad does. I tell you, Tom Boy. Maybe it's not that far-fetched that we're brothers. Think of it. There're an incredible amount of similarities, and now we have the daddy connection."

"Mike?"

"Yeah?"

"Shut up and turn up the radio."

"Hey, no problemo, bro. I knew you'd come around. Music's great. I love it. It's almost like heaven in an oval speaker. You sit back, look at the grill cloth, and suddenly everything takes on another dimension. Wow. That's almost like that *Outer Limits* dude: 'You're traveling in another dimension without sight or sound, void of noise.'"

"That's not how it goes."

"So, I left out the boring parts."

"And it was *The Twilight Zone*, not *The Outer Limits*."

"Oh, no. I know for a fact that it was *The Outer Limits* because my cousin used to collect *Outer Limits* bubble gum cards and made me memorize all the monsters."

"That might be, but the lines you butchered come from *The Twilight Zone*, hosted by Rod Serling, R.I.P."

"R.I.P?"

"Yeah, as in rest in peace. You did graduate from grade school, right?"

"He's dead?"

"Of course, he is."

"Gee. I didn't even know he was sick," Mike replied, one-way laughter filling the car.

"Please. That is the oldest joke in the book. I can't believe you said that."

"Timeless, eh, Tom Boy?"

"Whatever."

"So, Mr. Know-it-all. What are the correct opening lines of *The Outer Limits*?"

"*Twilight Zone*, and I don't know."

"What?" Mike asked, as incredulous as ever. "The champion of useless knowledge doesn't even know the answer but has the nerve to tell me that I'm wrong? What kind of pud are you?"

"I am not a pud. Secondly, just because I'm not sure of the wording doesn't mean that I'm incapable of recognizing a misquoted line."

"You sure do a lot of numbering when you get mad. Number one, number two. Secondly, thirdly."

"And I suppose if you were to say that the capitol of Maine was Oklahoma City and I challenged you, you'd claim victory because I couldn't name the proper city."

"Sounds fair to me."

Unable to continue the conversation, Tommy opened the glove compartment, secured a rag, and stuffed it into his mouth to stifle his screams.

"Hey, Tom Boy. I wouldn't stick that in my mouth. I accidentally ran over a squirrel last week and used it to wipe the guts off my tire."

Mike watched as Tommy's eyes doubled in size before he heaved into a discarded Cheetos bag.

"That-a-way, Jackson. Get the bad stuff out so you'll have room for the good. Next gas station, we're stocking up for a pork rinds chow fest."

Chapter 11

"Hey," the assistant manager shouted.

Mike looked out the gas station's front window and saw Tommy doubled over in the service aisle, vomiting in the windshield washer receptacle.

"If that kid gets any on the squeegee, he's dead meat," the twenty seven year old promised.

"Now, now. You know kids. Couple beers, and they're on their knees, confessing to mother toilet," Mike said, trying to soothe the man's inflamed emotions. Hitting the high school dropout with his infectious smile, Mike added, "Say, you know what sounds mighty tasty right now? Some barbecued pork rinds. You carry the Family Sow brand?"

"Sure do. One of our hottest sellers."

"Great. Where are they?"

"Two rows to your left, right by the Baby Heart beef sticks."

Seeking out his nighttime snack, Mike was sidetracked by a famous pink bottle that stared him down. "When Pepto's around, 'Stine isn't far behind," he sang. And there it was: his object of affection. "Well, here you are, you little devil. You have no idea the trouble you've put me through tonight."

As the assistant manager divided his attention between the retching Tommy and the serenading Mike, he advised, "You ain't gonna find those rinds in that aisle, fella. You're too far over."

"Got it. Just saw the 'Stine and was happy. Deliriously happy. Overjoyed. Damn near orgasmic."

What the hell is he talking about? the perplexed attendant thought. 'Stine? And as he pondered this, his fingers danced across the automated cash register. And then it happened: he hit the clear button; the gas purchase disappeared and was now nonexistent. "Son-of-a-bitch."

"Evening prayers?"

"Problem. Give me a second." Yet all the seconds in all of time would not bring back the now undocumented purchase.

"Got any cream soda? Nothing washes down Family Sow better than that," Mike yelled across the store.

"Cooler against the back wall," the man replied, distracted as hell.

Securing a two liter bottle, Mike juggled this with his Listerine, an extra-large bag of pork rinds, and a specially marked box of Fiddle Faddle that offered an exclusive toy. "You should have carts around here," he advised the man. "With all the great stuff that you sell here, people need a vessel to cart around their largesse." And with that, the teen returned and dumped his haul atop the counter, noting various items that were placed there to entice impulse buying. There were pipe cleaners, lighter fluid, Snickers bars, gum, scratch off lottery tickets, condoms, and breath mints.

Tabulating the amount while keeping a watchful eye on the high school youth, the assistant manager said, "Comes to $9.82, plus your gas."

Toying with the clerk in his unsurpassed facetiousness, Mike joked, "The only gas action goin' on out there is my buddy's digestive tract."

"Look, you little twerp," the man exploded. "Just 'cause I accidentally zeroed out your gas purchase doesn't mean you don't owe anything. Now, I want that money. How much was it?"

No evidence? Perfect, Mike thought. We're going to make out like bandits with this dude. "Sir, I know not what you mean. Sure, my friend is feeling a little under the weather, but don't you remember when you attended a high school graduation party and had a little too much to drink? The only reason I'm patronizing your fine establishment is because my friend and I require sustenance. Now, I ask: is there anything sinister about that?"

Although Mike thought he sounded convincing, the man would have none of it. "You listen to me, you little punk. I know for a fact that you owe me for gas because I saw it on the meter. Now pay up, or do I have to call the cops?"

Leaning across the counter, Mike grabbed the telephone and held it out, offering it to the man. "Here, take it. Come on, take it. Call them and say that a mean, disrespectful kid bought some gas and refused to pay. And when they get here, all I'm going to do is ask for evidence, like that high tech meter is supposed to provide. I'm sure the police, who are always busy on a Friday night, are going to be tickled when you tell them that you don't have any proof of a purchase, and the only documentation that exists is your belief that I'm lying. And who do you think they're going to believe? A high school football star who went to State and is caring for his gravely ill best friend, or an underpaid assistant manager who's trying to make a name for himself, who obviously made a mistake, and is too embarrassed to admit it? The ball's in your court, my fine fellow. What's it gonna to be?"

God, am I good, he concluded.

The man's nostrils flared as he spoke. "Boy, are you going to be one sorry bastard by the time I get done with you."

"No, I won't. I'm almost half a foot taller than you, and I'm not guilty of anything." Pulling back from the counter, Mike laid down a ten for the groceries and said, "Nice doin' business with you, pal. You're a real sport. Keep the change."

And with that, Mike grabbed his goods, left the store, threw the items in the Pinto, and walked over to Tommy; the attendant watched as the man was led away from the dispenser and into the car, the youth supporting the nineteen year old the entire time.

"Why you slick little prick," the man muttered. "You might think that you can stiff me, but you've got another thing comin'." Grabbing a pen and an empty carton of cigarettes, the vilified assistant manager scribbled down, Yellow Pinto. '72? Rust. 6618-UGV. Wisc. Tall male. 18? Football build. "Yeah, that's right, you little shit. You're gonna regret ever settin' foot in this place."

Meanwhile, Mike got in the driver's seat, started the car, gunned the engine, and attempted a burnout. But the car rebelled and lunged forward and quit, causing Tommy head to bounce off the dashboard. "Mike?" he moaned. "Haven't you done enough to me?"

Starting the car again and driving forward, he answered, "To you? You mean for you. We just got a tank of gas for el zippo. Comprende? Nada. Nothing, baby. Nothing."

"I know I'm not going to like this answer, but how did we get a free tank of gas?"

"Because my finely tuned mind never quits. I play all the angles. I see 'em before anyone even knows they exist. That's how," Mike boasted.

"And what does that translate into?" Tommy moaned, rubbing his forehead with one hand, his stomach with the other.

"That Bozo back there zeroed out the counter. As far as facts go, we never got any gas. God, I love computers. They're amazing devices, you know. They document your birth, death, school grades, taxes, stats. You name it, they do it."

"Are you telling me that you didn't pay our bill because you thought you could stiff the station?"

"Not thought, Tom Boy. Did."

"I should have made a run for it when I had the chance," Tommy half-lied. Although his nausea was still in full force, he was beginning to see the possibilities, regardless of how warped or off-beat this journey might be. If this is training, he thought, I guess it's better that I'm getting it out of the way now because that must mean that fame is around the corner. And this guy does possess a certain je ne sais quoi. "Mike?"

"Yes, my love."

"Number one, fuck you. Number two, do you have any idea where we're going?"

"Absolutely."

"And where might that be?"

"Wherever there's something interesting happening. Wherever there's a place where I can find out what makes this country what it is. You spend twelve years in school, and they never give you the essential facts; instead, they fill you up with stuff that's supposed to make you smarter, but it doesn't. All it does is occupy space and soon disappears, only to be replaced with more useless garbage. Know what I mean? When were you ever asked something truly important, like who are you?"

"I don't follow."

"That's my point. We're so conditioned that we don't even know what's critical and what's not. It's a joke; it really is, and I played their game better than most. You have no idea how many college scholarships I was offered based on me regurgitating everything they ever fed me."

Tommy stared at Mike and waited for his next indictment, but none came. What followed was silence, and the observer realized that the driver had bared a part of his soul, for just as he was about to dismiss Mike as the quintessential careless youth, Tommy caught a glimpse of someone he didn't think existed.

And he began to like what he saw.

"Are we going to drive all night, or are we going to find a motel? I'm pretty tired. Long day," Tommy said, his voice just above a whisper.

And in an even quieter tone, Mike responded, "Yeah. Time to find a pillow."

Taking the next exit, the driver guided his battered vehicle down a long, dimly lit road that at one time was used by pre-expressway travelers. A dilapidated motel sat to the right, scarred with overgrown shrubbery, a failing neon sign, a grass infested concrete driveway, and mangled lawn furniture.

"You sure you want to stay here?" Tommy asked.

"Wouldn't be pullin' in the parking lot if I didn't." Climbing out the car, Mike turned to Tommy and said, "I'm going in alone. Cheaper if I tell them it's only me. If I come back and you're not here, guess I'll understand."

The teen's melancholy tone made the passenger feel a slight tinge of regret, a feeling that he had been too quick in his judgment, and he was disappointed in himself for being so critical. He knew that it would be easy for him to walk away and hitchhike his way northward, but something held him back: the belief that perhaps the pair's sojourn wouldn't be that bad after all.

"So, if I don't see you again, take care," Mike offered the reflective man.

"Um—go check in. I'll watch your car," Tommy replied. And a warm feeling engulfed the man as a sparkle returned to Mike's irrepressible eyes.

"Great. Be right back."

The motel's lobby was in worse condition than the building's exterior. Large strips of wallpaper were either missing or dangling from the wall. Spotting a desk bell, Mike rang it twice and waited for someone to appear. When no one did, he yelled out, "Hello? Anyone here, or should I just grab a key, leave in the morning, and call it even?"

Before he knew it, a small woman donning a babushka swaggered into the lobby, a small glass of liquor grasped in her blue-veined hands. "Try and rob me, and I'll slice you open and use you as fly paper."

Mike was in love.

"Need a room. Cheap, please, 'cause I need to conserve my resources. I'll be covering a lot of miles over the next week, and I don't want to run short," the graduate explained.

The elderly woman looked at her customer, took a long swig of her drink, swashed it about her mouth, swallowed, burped, and replied, "You people're always lookin' for a bargain. What's the matter, boy? Run away from home? Make off with mom's silverware?"

"Just her afghan. So, how much is the room?"

Staring Mike down, the woman reached behind her and secured a key; she tossed it onto the desk and grabbed a pen, never once wavering in her attentive glare. "Sign the register first."

Mike stared at her and stifled a laugh, as the woman looked as if she had just walked off the set of an Iron Curtain mini-series. Printing the requested information on the faded form, he pulled out his billfold, overflowing with his abundant cash reserves.

"You're in luck tonight, Mr. High Roller. One room available. Single. Nineteen dollars."

"That I can handle," Mike declared.

"Thirty for you and the mystery person in your car."

The youth was about to challenge the assertion, but the woman's unibrow proved intimidating. "Of course. Wouldn't want the little lamb to freeze out there."

After paying the woman and listening to her stern warning that checkout was 11:00 AM and not a second later, he walked back to his car and the awaiting man. "I supposed I should say 'grab your bags,' but I know you don't have any. We'll stop at a K-Mart tomorrow and pick up some ace traveling clothes for you. Ready?"

"Yeah, I guess."

"Don't guess in life, Tom Boy. Know."

"Yes, Pappa." Yet Tommy considered this advice profound, and he promised himself that he would remember it for future use, possibly in the screenplay that he planned on writing.

Once inside the room, both men stopped dead in their tracks and looked around. A large, black sewer pipe ran over a double bed that was caved in. A faded painting of a pheasant flying away from an aiming hunter hung on the wall, frameless. Below it sat a three legged end table with a lamp graced with a ripped shade. And then there was the bedspread. Adorned with a map of the United States, someone had taken a magic marker and drawn caricatures of tourists engaged in various sexual positions. A couple in Florida, naked except for their large brim hats, were in the missionary position and sang out, "Don't get dicked. Floridas got the best licks." A female pair lay across Utah 69ing under the phrase, "Mormons do it better."

"Ah," Tommy cried. "That's disgusting."

"Lighten up. Think of it as folk art."

"They missed a possessive in Florida."

Mike stared at Tommy for a moment. "And that angers you?"

"Yes, it does. And the women's breasts are totally out of proportion."

"It's a cartoon."

"More like slander."

"Because they have two gal pal Mormons?"

"Don't like women being on the receiving end of hate," Tommy stated.

"As opposed to men."

"As opposed to anyone. I'm part of the Rainbow Coalition."

"Any unicorn members?"

"That is so racist. Unbelievable."

"Calm down, Tom Boy. You're not running for political office, and I promise not tell anyone that we slept huddled against each other in a cheap motel. Man, I love this bedspread. Hysterical. I'm talking this when we leave. Gonna use it in my dorm. I'll never part with it. I'm going to stipulate in my will that it be used on my deathbed—during the Last Rights. Way too cool. This is American humor in its purest form. Little sass mixed with a touch of naughty. Priceless, baby. Price—less."

"Glad to see making fun of people keeps you entertained. If you were a lesbian, you wouldn't think this is funny."

"I am a lesbian. Proud member of my tribe."

"How are you a lesbian?"

"'Cause we both dig the same female parts. Not too bright, are you, Sparky?" Motioning for his traveling companion to move, Mike proceeded to fold the bedspread in his meticulous best.

Impressed by Mike's diligent skill, Tommy asked, "How'd you ever learn to fold like that?"

"My parents own a dry cleaning store. It's been in the family for a long time. You grow up around this stuff, and you start picking up pointers. Not that I want to do this the rest of my life, but it does come in handy once in awhile."

"Like when you steal something."

"I'm not going to steal this. I'm simply gaining custody. I'm no criminal. Hello."

"Got it. Probably what Al Capone used to say. And with that, I'm going to bed. Turn off the light when you're done doing whatever it is you plan on doing."

And with that, Tommy pulled his T-shirt off, yanked off his shoes without untying them, and tossed his socks in a corner. After unfastening his belt and removing his jeans, Mike cried out, "Jesus. Do you ever eat?"

"Yes, I eat. Could eat you under the table. So, I'm not overweight and don't have a gut. I consider that a blessing."

"I suppose," Mike returned. And then, as if lightning struck, he continued. "Hey, Tom Boy. You're right. Did you know that Stallone reduced himself to four percent body fat when he trained for *Rambo*? You, my friend, have the right idea. Why didn't I think of it? With the proper training, you could be bigger than Rocky. Think of that."

God, this guy's right, Tommy thought. Once I get a contract form the West Coast, they'll hire a trainer to work with me, and I'll end up with a body that'll be the envy of all. Content with this musing, he climbed into bed, satisfied that the future was indeed bright; within moments, he was fast asleep, and Mike soon retired also. The bed's dramatic indentation caused each occupant to roll into the other, but the evening's events produced a deep sleep that awakened neither.

As the morning sun poured through the frayed curtains, Tommy awoke to find an arm resting comfortably across his chest, and it wasn't his own. Glancing at Mike, he viewed the youth who possessed a contented, serene look and tried to remove his arm without awakening him; however, each time he tried, the arm made its way back to its original locale. Frustrated by this response, Tommy turned to his side, only to have the arm drop down his back, resting close to his underwear.

"Fuck it," he said to himself and drifted back to a sleep that was more restful than any other he could remember.

Chapter 12

The perfunctory morning staff meeting was being held in the precinct's basement due to a City Hall-mandated beautification plan that called for Jonathan's station to be remodeled. As interior designers brushed past him, each holding numerous color swatches and paint charts, the exhausted man walked through the corridors in a daze, still thinking about the morning phone call that Shanda had placed.

"And I'll contact you later today once I make the necessary arrangements for your treatment, so don't worry about anything, Jonathan. That's why I'm here: to do your worrying while you get well."

She can't be serious, he thought. She can't.

"Hey, Jon. How's it goin'? Looks like you had a rough one last night," a co-worker said in passing.

"You have no idea," the disheveled policeman replied. After walking down two flights of stairs, Jonathan entered the temporary meeting room and secured a seat.

"All right, gentlemen," Captain Manning began. "With the exception of one case, it was a pretty quiet night, but we've got, and I hope to God that I'm wrong, a potentially lethal situation. We received a 911 from a young female who claimed that a man armed with what she believes to be an assault rifle approached her in the Nike Warehouse parking lot and assaulted a customer who came to her defense, allowing her to escape. Information about the suspect is sketchy, but we do know that he is in his late teens/early twenties and escaped in an older model compact car, probably yellow. Now, this might be coincidence, but late last night we received another 911, this one from a service station attendant who reported that two young men made off with a tank of gas without paying. Fortunately, he took good notes and ID'd the vehicle, its plates, and gave a detailed description of the driver. We don't know if there's a connection between the two incidents, but Peters is going to find out. Jonathan, for heaven's sake, be careful. If these incidents are related, one of the suspects is well armed, and I need you in one piece. You'll report to the War Room, and I'll brief you further with what we've gathered thus far. Questions?"

"No, sir," Jonathan replied.

"The rest of you?" the captain inquired. "Good. Now, everyone will be receiving an APB on the car shortly, so keep your eyes open: they just might save your life."

The meeting was adjourned, and Jonathan proceeded to the upstairs briefing room, one that resembled something in the Pentagon. Large, acrylic maps, each marked colorfully with Southeastern Wisconsin's major arteries, lined a wall while banks of computers sat opposite them, each connected to a national network designed to provide law enforcement personnel with immediate updates.

After glancing at what was accumulated thus far, Peters turned to his superior and asked, "How reliable is our female witness?"

"Shaken, but I think she's fairly stable considering what she went through."

"And Raymond Tanner, the assistant manager at the gas station?"

"Not much to tell you other than what I said earlier, Jon. Some teenage males ran off without paying for their gas. I just want to know if the driver is the one who was taken hostage. According to Tanner, the passenger remained outside and appeared sick. Sounds like a cover to me. If this is our suspect, my guess is that he was watching the hostage closely, to make sure that he didn't do anything suspicious, and remained partially hidden outside, so Tanner couldn't ID him."

"Interesting," Jonathan said. "Maybe there is a connection. I'll need to speak with him after the girl. Could you ask Carole to make arrangements to bring the girl in?"

"Already done. She'll be here at 1:00. Wanted to give her time to rest."

"Understandable."

And just as Peters stood and collected the file, the Captain offered, "Jon. Be careful. You've got a bride waiting for you."

"Yes. Thank you. You have no idea what that means to me." But then again, neither did Peters, for he found it increasingly difficult to sort his conflicting emotions. Sure, he maintained, Shanda was perfect for him. Sure she provided an anchor to his life. Sure she was self-motivated. She even liked him.

Liked, he thought. Liked? What about love? Does she love me, or am I another managerial conquest? Someone who is attained and then placed in the work completed file. And what about me? Do I love her? Hell, I don't even know what love is, but we are engaged, so I must love her. Right?

"God," he mumbled after exiting the War Room and walking towards his office. "Why do relationships have to be so complicated?"

"Pardon?" an office staffer asked.

"Ah—nothing. I was just thinking out loud."

"Bet it's a girl," another chimed in.

"Yeah. Fiancée."

"Fiancée? How romantic," a middle aged woman added. "When's the wedding?"

"Next weekend."

"Bet you're scared," she continued. "Who wouldn't be? I've been married twice and believe me, it doesn't get any easier. There's something about those vows that floors me. They're so final."

"Yeah, final," Jonathan agreed, appearing as if he had just seen a ghost.

"Have a good day," the woman shouted as he continued on.

"Thanks. Good night."

"Night? In the morning? Strange. Must be a Virgo. They're all screwed up," the woman concluded.

Jonathan arrived at his office, retired to his desk, and stared at his file. What would possess anyone to hold up another in such a visible location? he considered. And what about this girl? Wonder how credible she'll be. And the gas station attendant. What about him? Securing the man's home telephone number from the file's first sheet, he dialed and looked out his window, transfixed. Two cardinals, one male and female, danced in front of his window and appeared to be watching him. Their effortless existence mesmerized the man as he observed how their majestic forms hung in mid-air, the male's crimson color and the female's brown shading holding the man spellbound. They looked directly at him, wings batting at imperceptible speed. Amazing, he thought. In perfect alignment.

Together. Unforced. Easy. "Who the hell is this?" the male voice hollered into the phone.

And the birds disappeared.

"Detective Peters, sir. I'd like to ask you a few questions about the accusations you made against the pair who allegedly made off with a tank of gas without paying."

"Allegedly?" the man returned. "I was there, remember? I know what I saw. They made out like little bandit bitches and made me look like a fool. I want those bastards busted."

"Yes, sir, but first I'd like some information, specifically how they carried out the alleged crime."

"Look, they were sharp. They knew exactly what they were doing. One pretended to be sick while the other distracted me and made me clear the gas purchase."

"What was that?"

"I accidentally cleared out the register that lets you know how much gas a customer got."

"And you claim that one of the two made you clear the total?"

"Yes, he did, all right. Played mind games and distracted me, like black magic or some shit."

"And how was this accomplished?"

"By talking his fool head off about pork rinds, potato chips—I don't know," he replied angrily. "He just did, and before I knew it I'd cleared the total."

"So, he never actually forced you to do it."

"No."

"Did he have a weapon?"

"Not that I seen."

"Did he act suspicious?"

"Yeah, real weird-like."

"And how was that?"

"I'll tell you how: he was too friendly. No one that ever comes in here is that nice. Believe me, it was part of his strategy. Shine a big smile and make me do what he wanted."

"But you say that he never physically forced you to do anything, isn't that right?"

"Well, yeah, but he did it. Somehow. Probably some jiu-jitsu black magic shit."

Jonathan knew that this line of questioning was getting nowhere, and that this individual would also have to come in to make a formal statement. "Once again for my notes, sir, the alleged perpetrator never threatened you, told you to zero out the total, didn't do it himself, didn't have his companion do it, and the only evidence you have that these individuals filled up their vehicle and left without paying is your word."

"Yeah, what more do you need? I'm a bonded employee. I go through training. I know what I'm doing, and if you don't catch these creeps I'll have to cover the loss."

And just as Jonathan was about to terminate the discussion, a co-worker handed him the vital stats about the car in question.

Michael William Warner, Jonathan read. "Seventeen," the policeman muttered.

"What?" the assistant manager asked.

"While you were talking I was handed a printout of the vehicle's owner. According to this, the car is a '72 Ford pinto, and its owner is seventeen, 6' 1," 175 pounds. Blond hair and blue eyes."

"That's the fucker. He's the one. Now, nail the fuckhead and tear his nuts off."

"You're sure?'

"Yeah, tear those fuckers off and …"

"Sir, that kind of language doesn't help."

"Stuff them down his throat …"

"Sir, please."

"Stir fry the fuckers and …"

"Sir, please listen and refrain from the profanities. This might be the person you speak of, but it doesn't sound like you have any firm evidence that a crime occurred. All we have is your word and the fact that you correctly copied down someone's license plate number."

"What?" the attendant exploded. "I try to do my civic duty, and all you try to do is tie me down with facts and proof? Well, fuck me."

"That won't be necessary, sir; however, I would like you to come in and make a formal statement. We'll investigate and see if any laws have been broken."

"Yeah, right. The only thing that's gonna go bust is my wallet, all because of that high school punk."

* * *

After arranging for the man to make his statement, Jonathan began drafting questions for his female witness, but before he got too involved the telephone rang.

"So, how do you feel, Jonathan? A little nauseated, possibly? A little groggy after an alcohol-induced binge?"

"Hello, Shanda," he responded, sounding as if he'd just been impaled. "How are you?"

"I'm fine now because I just made the necessary arrangements for your road to recovery. You'll report to the Christian Way Treatment Center tomorrow. It'll be hell, Jonathan, but seeing that you got yourself there, you'll have to get yourself out. And you don't have to thank me now because this is why we're together. This is what until death do us part means. Any questions, or do you need to vomit?"

Shaking his head, wondering if he were still asleep, he replied, "Shanda, what you've done is admirable, but I think you're overreacting. Now, if you don't mind, I have a lot of work that needs my attention."

"Not as much as this does," she countered.

Gritting his teeth, Jonathan responded, "I have to go. I'll talk to you later."

"Now, you listen here: do I have to march over and talk to you man to man?"

"I'll deal with this later. Now, if you'll excuse me, I have a damn busy day ahead of me."

"Don't you cuss."

"Goodbye."

"I'll be right over in …" Jonathan heard as he hung up. I ought to have my head examined, the exasperated man thought. Where do I come off thinking that I'm headed towards a perfect union with someone like that?

Several hours passed, each filled with diligent research and painful self-reflection, and now the questioning of the female witness was at hand. With legal pad in tow, Jonathan walked into the interrogation room and was struck by the young woman's beauty. Her innocence soothed his tortured heart, and a smile made its way to his face.

"Good afternoon, Miss Arthur. How are you today?"

Fidgeting in her metal folding chair, she responded, "Fine, I guess."

"That's good. May I get you some coffee? Water?"

"No, thank you. My mother tells me that it isn't good for me. Coffee. Even though it has water. I drink that. Just not in coffee."

"Right," Peters agreed, attempting to hide his Styrofoam cup behind him. "First, let me say that we're all grateful that you've taken the time to come down to the station after the trying events of last night."

The girl didn't speak but nodded her head.

"Now, there are some questions that must be asked, and they will be transcribed into what we call a formal statement. Once this is drawn up, we will ask you to read it carefully and, if you find it satisfactory, sign it. Do you understand?"

"Yes, sir."

"Fine. Let's start at the beginning."

"I was born on a snowy day in February. My …"

"No. Not that far back. Last night's events please."

"Oh, okay, but it's kind of hard to know when it started, officer. See, this really nice guy came into the store looking for Listerine."

"You mean the mouthwash?"

"Yes, that's right. I didn't know if we carried it or not because I just started working at the store and wasn't sure where everything was. So, I went to find my boss, but I couldn't find him either. After I told this customer the bad news, he thanked me and left."

Handing her an enlarged Xerox of Mike's driver's license picture, Jonathan asked, "Is this the man you're referring to?"

"Yes," she replied, choking back tears. "That's the saint that tried to help me."

"Good. Now this next part is critical because I have to find out exactly what then happened."

"Well, he gave me this really good pep talk."

"Pep talk? Regarding what?"

"Football and Nazis. It was powerful. I was so moved that I decided to quit my new job. It was closing time anyway, so they weren't inconvenienced. And as I was going to my car, I saw this horrible looking man walking towards me; that's when I noticed his gun. I started screaming and ran, but the customer had just walked out the store, and I ran into him, but I got up and got away, but he didn't, so he got captured, and I didn't," she cried.

Jonathan was thrilled with the ironclad evidence: Mike Warner was indeed the same man at the warehouse and the gas station. "And then what happened?" he asked, monitoring the tape recorder's voice levels.

"I don't really know. It happened so fast. I ran away and didn't look back until I was just outside the parking lot; that's when I saw the two of them getting into this beat up, old yellow car."

"An older model Pinto perhaps?"

"I think so. I'm not sure. I don't know cars too good."

"But it was an older car."

"Yes."

"Yellow."

"Yes."

Now that another major point had been verified, Peters knew that one additional piece of information was critical to his investigation: the identification of the gun-wielding suspect. "Good. You're doing fine," Jonathan reassured the girl. "Now, what I'm interested in is a description of the man who approached you in the parking lot, the one with the gun."

"Oh, he was horrible looking," she cried. "Just horrible. Like a skinny version of the Terminator. He's probably being mean to that brave man who saved me."

Anticipating a major break, he pressed on. "And this man holding the gun. Tell me how big he was. Did he have any unusual physical attributes? What about his age, race—anything you can recall."

"Well?" Twisting her face into various contortions, she struggled to formulate a response. "He was male."

"Yes. And what about physical size?"

"I don't know. It's hard to say. At least as tall as my brother."

"And how tall is he?"

"Well? Maybe a little taller than me."

"Possibly 5' 9," 5' 10?"

"I guess so."

"What about hair."

"Well groomed."

"No, I mean hair color."

"Well? Dark, I think."

"Dark brown? Black?"

"Well? I guess."

"Race?"

"White," she stated confidently. "I know for a fact that he was white."

"Good. Age?"

"I just turned …"

"No. The age of the suspect."

"Oh. Um—maybe my age, but I can't be certain."

"So, he looked youthful."

"Yes."

"Youthful in appearance."

"Yes. Well rested."

"And you mentioned a weapon. A gun. What kind was it? Handgun or …"

"An Uzi."

Baffled by her sudden certainty, Jonathan asked, "How can you be so sure?"

"Officer, I've seen every episode of *Miami Vice*. I know my firearms."

Thirty more minutes of questioning ensued before Jonathan was satisfied that he now had as much information as the girl could provide. Although he knew that he didn't have anything concrete on the suspect, he was confident that the APB issued earlier in the day would garner the necessary break that this case required. After all, he didn't need anything hanging over his head while walking down the wedding aisle, he determined.

Nothing, that is, but the nagging question: what am I getting into?

Chapter 13

Panic struck Tommy as he looked about the stage and didn't recognize any of the assembled rock musicians who looked back at him. A hushed crowd held its collective breath, and the man knew for whom they were waiting. A large array of instruments sat in front of him. There were banks of synthesizers, an RMI harpsichord, a Hammond B3 organ, and a nine-foot Steinway grand piano. As a soft blue light enveloped him, the daunted man grasped for meaning—anything that would explain what he was supposed to play. And then, as if an inner light were guiding his very soul, the musician brought down both hands onto the Hammond organ and orchestrated a stunning glissando, bringing the crowd to its feet as they cheered the recognition of one of their favorite Tommy Alvin-penned compositions.

The rest of the group listened to their colleague color the hall with impressive riffs that were envy of any keyboardist and nodded their heads in affirmation that Tommy's recent Rolling Stone cover story was no fluke. A blinding spotlight hit the man and followed his electrified fingers caressing his various instruments. Here was an individual who bent notes and created a wholly unique, multi-layered sound that revolutionized contemporary rock music. Those pressed against the stage roared their approval while their fellow brethren lit the darkened hall with a dazzling shower of light produced by matches and disposable cigarette lighters.

Tommy rapidly built two harmonic scales against each other by playing them on separate keyboards; the roar of the crowd was now deafening as throngs screamed their approval, and within seconds one of his bandmates ran to him and wrapped an appreciative arm around the acknowledged hero's shoulder.

"God, you're good," Mike whispered into the dreamer's ear.

Jumping out of the bed and stumbling into an aged dresser, Tommy shouted, "That's not funny, Mike. You shouldn't do that. Jarring someone out of sleep can cause sleep apnea and cardiac address. Everyone knows that. You want me to have a heart attack? You want me sprawled on the floor when they discover my dead body? You always ruin everything."

"You're right. Wouldn't want to be the cause of sleep apnea, which I believe is snoring. No, sir. Wouldn't want to be its catalyst. By the way, impressive boner."

And with that, Tommy looked down at his massive erection and covered it with both hands. "Nothing happened, and you know it."

"Calm down, Horse. Give your ego a rest—and somethin' else a rest, if you know what I mean. And fix your hair. Major bed head. You look like a cockatoo."

Glancing in the mirror, Tommy found the assessment accurate, as his hair was parted on the left and looked as if it were glued to his head while the hair to the right was spiked in two opposing directions, as if they were at war with each other.

"Loosen up. I was kiddin' 'bout the hair. I dig it. Uber punk. Crazy hair, dude. Crazy. Very cool. Bet you could start a new fashion trend. You, my man, just might be a trendsetter."

"Well, not sure about that," Tommy added, feigning modesty, all the while picturing himself at Fashion Week.

"Yeah, totally. Think of it. You could be on *Entertainment Tonight*. My guess is you live for that shit."

"Of course. Who wouldn't?"

"Not me. Could not care less. Note the phrasing, my fine writer. Not could care less. Could not care less. Too many people mess that up. Now *NFL Tonight*. That's different. Book me, baby. Book me." And with that, Mike arose and began his morning ritual: stretches. He closed his eyes and tilted his head to the right and snapped his fingers five times to chronicle each second. He then moved to his left and repeated the action, his eyes pressed shut as if in a trance, his concentration flawless. He then lifted both arms above his head, joined them, and moved to the left and then the right, his muscular body growing more defined with each extended arch. Tommy watched in awe.

"How often do you work out?"

"Every day. Used to use a Weight Flex I got for Christmas but got bored. Not a fan of gyms, either. Too many posers. Too much preening. Like a mating ritual. Fuck that. Just do my stretches, watch what I eat, and do a lot of push-ups. Only gym I need."

"Impressive. You should be proud," Tommy replied, more than a tad envious and hoping not to sound that way. Walking into the bathroom, he viewed himself in the cracked mirror, each feature on display under the harsh florescent tubes that lined the ceiling. Running his fingers over his face, he felt the whiskers that needed shaving and saw teeth that needed cleaning. He then remembered that he had nothing with him, not even the barest of basics. "Oh, God. I'm going to have to share a toothbrush. Gross."

"Hey, Tom Boy. You sleep talkin' again? Kept me up all night with your chatter. Talk, talk, talk. Thought I was sleeping with a myna bird. You do know what that is, don't you? It's an exotic species with sleep apnea."

Tommy opened the bathroom door and leaned against its frame. "Michael? Do you think I could borrow your toothbrush?"

"Michael? So formal. Especially after I shared myself so freely with you last night."

"Not funny."

"And why do people always say borrow? It's not like borrowing a book or a CD. You intend on using it, so why not just say, 'Michael, my Adonis. My mouth feels like someone changed their car oil in it. May I use your toothbrush? I promise to clean the gunk off when I'm done.'"

"And a pair of underwear, if I could."

"You are one needy bastard."

"Yes, I am, and let's not forget how I got here."

"You know I didn't bring that much with me, and underwear doesn't grow on trees."

"I'm trying to be polite. Do you think you can help me out, or am I to spend the rest of your little vacation smelling like your jock?"

"Tell you what I'm gonna do," Mike said, walking over to the nineteen year old. "I'll let you use my toothbrush, Crest, and 'Stine. I'll even give you this pair of underwear that I'm wearing."

"I'd prefer a fresh pair, please."

"Needy. Very needy. Not much of a camper, either. Okay, have it your way." Mike then walked over to his blue and gold high school gym bag that sported a white crucifix with crisscrossing electrical bolts and dumped its contents onto the bed; Tommy stood in amazement at how little there was.

"Mike, I only see two pairs of shorts, a couple socks, some personals, and a T-shirt or two."

"Yeah, I travel light. Here."

Catching the tossed underwear, Tommy continued. "You did say that we'd hit a store today, right? There's no way we can make it a week with this amount of clothes."

Mike looked at Tommy as if he had just been presented with a cherished wish. "A week the man asks? One week? He's alive! Alive!"

"Answer please."

"Alive!"

"Tiresome."

"A store? A store that's alive!? Absolutely, Tom Boy. I'm rolling in dough, and I've got the family graduation bash coming up. That'll be good for at least a grand."

One thousand dollars? Tommy pondered. Is this guy joking? All I got when I graduated was a stale Sara Lee coffee cake, a clock radio, and $15 from my aunt.

"Tell you what, Frankenweenie. Why don't you jump in the shower—that's alive!, and I'll straighten up."

"You're going to clean the room?"

"Yeah. Remake the bed. Straighten up. Make everything nice. Don't wanna be a slob. Then I'll shower, and we'll hit the road."

"When is checkout?"

"When we checkout."

"Oh.

"Ah."

The Saturday morning sky was a cloudless blue; the temperature was already in the high 70s. Getting back on Hwy 41, Mike looked about the vast countryside and tried to imagine his state looking differently. He couldn't, for the graduate loved how the rolling hills of green coalesced into open pastures that climbed into peaks highlighted by various wildflowers.

"Look around you, Tom Boy. Can you picture our beloved state ever becoming a condo parking lot?"

Tommy shuddered at the thought. "God, I hope not. You don't think it's possible, do you?"

"Hard to say. I'm so used to seeing concrete back home; sometimes I wonder if that's the way everything'll be one day."

Once again, Tommy was struck my Mike's reflectiveness. "You know what, Mike? I think you're a little more down-to-earth than you let on. Maybe that outrageous bit you always advertise doesn't tell the whole story."

"Ah," he dismissed with one wave of a hand. "You're the beast. I'm only along for the ride."

"Even though you're driving."

"What can I say? Fate. So, where do you want to go today?"

"This is your adventure. You're the one in search of the American spirit or whatever you said."

"The real America. Close, though. What about Iowa? People of the land. Farm folk. Wide open fields of grain."

"We have that here."

"Yeah, but I've never been to Iowa."

"And I've never been to Oklahoma, but I have no pressing need to go there." Reaching over, Tommy turned on the radio and fished through the stations, never providing each with more than a two second audition. "Can't you be a little more specific about what you're hoping to find?"

"Unreal," Mike blared, knocking Tommy's hands away. "Violent Femmes. You ever heard of them?"

"I'm from Milwaukee, too. Of course I know who they are. They're hometown heroes. As a matter of fact, I ran into their drummer at Oriental Drugs once."

"No kidding? What'd you say?"

"Nothing. I just saw him, and that was that."

"What?" Mike asked in amazement. "You saw Victor DeLorenzo and didn't say anything to him? What are you, nuts? Do you have any idea how many people would kill for the chance to talk with him?"

"Yes, I do. That's why I didn't want to bug him. If there's one thing that my research has shown, it's that celebrities don't appreciate being accosted by fans," Tommy stated in his erudite, self-assured way.

"Research? What kind of research was ever done on the Femmes?"

"Not on them specifically, but I've gone to great lengths scrutinizing the famous and how they got there. I could go on and on about what I've found. How Bon Jovi became friends with Cher when he worked as a janitor at the same recording studio that she was using. How Pink Floyd was discovered at a psychedelic club called 69 in London. How Dustin Hoffman got his break while living in a cold water flat in New York. The way I look at it, the more I know about how people got to where they are now, the easier it'll be for me to get there."

"What? Where?" Mike asked, trying to keep the car from veering onto the shoulder.

"To the top, of course. Where else?"

"But how do you plan on getting there?"

"I just told you: by studying how others got there."

"Sorry, bud. You lost me. One more time. So, you study like an animal. Then what? What field do you plan on breaking into?"

"That's easy. I've got this screenplay that I've been tossing around for a couple years. As a matter of fact, when we stop to get some clothes, I want to pick up a notebook so I can finally commit it to paper. Once I sell the rights to it, they'll be a negotiated part in the contract that allows me to play the lead once filming begins."

"You mean you're going to have the main part in the movie?"

"Right."

"How?"

"I just told you. It'll be negotiated in the contract once the screenplay's sold. That in itself will provide my launch into stardom."

Swerving in and out of his lane, Mike tried to make sense of the plan laid out. Maybe he's right, the graduate thought. People get discovered in plenty of ways, so why not this guy? "So, what's your play about?"

"Screenplay," Tommy corrected. "Not play. The former is for the screen; the latter is for the stage."

"Whatever," Mike dismissed, his interest now dashed.

Irritated by the man's flippant dismissal, Tommy asked, "What do you mean, whatever? There's an important distinction here. You wouldn't call a car's engine a motor, would you? You wouldn't call a zebra a horse, would you?"

"Tanya Roberts did in *Sheena Queen of the Jungle*."

"That wasn't the name of it."

"Then what was it, *Jeopardy* man?"

"I don't recall."

"Shocking. Are you this way with your friends? Anytime someone says something, do you challenge him even though you don't know the answer? You know, this is a repeat of last night. You should be concentrating on social skills instead of this Hollywood crap."

As if a sacrilegious indictment were levcled, Tommy gasped, "Why you dangerously misguided, insensitive tween. Don't you know that it's rude to criticize another's career?"

"Yes, I do but seeing that it's not your career, what harm can be done?"

"A lot," Tommy maintained. "You can cripple someone's creativity, their individuality by degrading their profession."

Drifting into the opposite lane and jarred back by an angry motorist's car horn, Mike shot back, "You know what? You never did tell me what you do for a living—and don't give me any of this crap that you're a wanna be hangin' around a Nike outlet store, hopin' to be recognized."

"I'm in between jobs," Tommy replied. "I fulfilled my service at the factory that I was stuck in since college."

"Get off it. You're too young to be a college graduate."

"I never said that I was," Tommy replied. "I dropped out so I could devote my energy to my career."

"The one you're aspiring to."

"Exactly."

"Well, that's a lot different than claiming that you're a working writer, or whatever you said."

"I never said …"

"Okay, inferred."

"What is your problem, Mikey?"

"Look, Mr. Writer. Don't call me names. The last guy who did that is now drinkin' Gatorade through a straw."

"Oh, how original. Maybe you should be the writer. You employ every known cliché in your everyday speech."

"As opposed to my every other day speech. That doesn't even make sense. Hello."

Continuing west, the rusted Pinto made its way across the state, distancing itself from the mammoth expressway system that links Milwaukee and Chicago. Large, family-owned dairy farms peppered the peaceful, bucolic scenery. Herds of brown and black Guernsey cows glanced at the passing motorists before returning to the business of grazing, ignoring humans who try so hard to find the importance of life, yet never once determine what creates it.

Although a K-Mart never made itself available, a large convenience mart caught the attention of the two sparring travelers and, after a seemingly endless battle over fan etiquette and semantics, the pair decided to visit the store.

Walking into Smart Mart, Mike was met by a towering hound dog with a large Slurpee cup grasped in his paw. "Hey, is this supposed to be Pluto?"

"Of course, not."

"No, you're right. I know for a fact that this giant dog is not Pluto. I have no idea who he is, but he definitely is not Pluto. Only an idiot would think that. A real dolt. Most certainly mentally retarded."

"Sounds about right," Tommy dismissed and walked past.

Aisles of motor oil, breakfast cereal, and napkins were lumped together in a hapless method that made his apparel search confounding. "Why would they have a paint roller next to adult diapers?" he muttered. And just as his head was about to burst after spotting tuna and discounted snow shovels next to each other, he heard Mike's stirring cry.

"These are unreal. Hey, Tom Boy. You've gotta check these out. They're perfect."

Following the direction of the voice, Tommy found Mike holding up a pair of T-shirts, both of which read, *I'm Too Hung*. "And if this doesn't tickle your funny bone, there's this one."

Tommy didn't believe anything could be worse; he was wrong. "Mike, I'm not wearing anything that says, *I Swallow*."

"Why not? This is a riot. Come on."

"No."

"Well, they've got a whole rack of other gems. Take your pick. It's on me."

Flipping through the selection, Tommy found shirts that featured a large, stenciled mosquito with the words, *Wisconsin State Bird*. Others offered *Where the Hell is Dickeyville*, *Party Animal*, and *Fueled by Beer*. Bypassing these and opting for numerous plain, blue

T-shirts, he proceeded to gather three double packs of underwear, six pairs of socks, three Budweiser Bermuda shorts, a singe tube of Aquafresh, a toothbrush, Right Guard, and a large dispenser of dental floss."

"My goodness," Mike began. "Aren't we frugal when we don't have any money of our own? Not."

"Said the felon."

"Said the let's-spend-other-people's-money man." Knocking Tommy into a stack of beach towels with one quick push, Mike added, "Just fuckin' with ya. Buy whatever you want. We've got an entire week of discovery in front of us."

Hesitating, Tommy wasn't sure if he wanted to verbalize what he was thinking, but went for broke. "Don't let this go to your head, but in an offbeat way, this is kind of nice of you. Kind of. When you overlook the kidnapping thing and, well, you know, everything."

"I never kidnapped you, and you know it. I thought I saw something that I mistook for something else, and for the umpteenth time, you don't have to stay. Take off if you want to. If you want me to drive you back home, fine, I will. I'll bring you anywhere you want. But I'm tellin' you. It'll be more fun to stick with me. You don't even have a job anymore. Live a little, Tom Boy. Get wild."

After paying the $40 bill, Mike sang some off key indecipherables, tossed the overflowing plastic package in the back seat, climbed into the car, started it, and then grabbed the unemployed man, as if he were thunderstruck by the gods. "Wait a minute. Wait a major minute and a minor fugue. Brainstorm. Huge. Colossal. Nuclear fusion-like."

"I've never been more frightened."

"We're going to the heart of the Wisconsin industrial base," Mike proclaimed. "We're going to Janesville, home of GM. Remember: what's good for America is good for GM, and what's good for GM becomes excitement for us."

Gazing past Mike and at the oil-stained parking lot, Tommy replied," Thrilling."

Chapter 14

"Tony, Tony, Tony. How many times do I have to tell you that cookin' is women's work? If they see you slaving in the kitchen, they're going to get the wrong idea and spend their days eating bonbons," Big Ben said while surveying the various pots sitting atop the range, each brought to a rapid boil.

"Mellow out, Ben. I'm working on my tie-dyes for the Dead."

"Oh, Tony. I don't think loved ones want to see these on their dearly departed."

"C'mon, man. The Dead. Grateful Dead. They're going to be at Alpine Valley in two days, and I'm completing my stock. You've seen me do this countless times; they're in town every year."

"But why are you cookin' 'em?"

"Because that's how the dye sets. Don't you remember the bowling shirt that I did for you last Father's Day?"

Raising his upper cheeks as he squinted, Ben tried to place the shirt of which Tony referred.

"C'mon, Ben. You told me that your entire team wanted one. You've got to remember. How many other people do you know who have an apricot tie-dyed bowling shirt with the Woodstock logo on the back?"

"Oh, that. Now I remember. That little bird sittin' on the banjo neck."

"Guitar," his son corrected. "But you're getting better. Last week you told me to take off my Jimi Henderson album. That's the closest you've ever come to Hendrix."

Excited, Big Ben added, "Florence's son, right?"

Staring at his father, Tony answered, "No, Ben. Jimi's black and dead. Florence is white and getting whiter."

"Oh," the older man replied. "She's not well, huh?"

"Let me put it to you this way: Wesson Oil and *The Brady Bunch* don't mix."

Returning to his brew, the counter culture entrepreneur stirred his creations with a long wooden spoon while humming the '60s anthem, *Eve of Destruction.* A sharp odor permeated the house as the boiling cauldrons created wears that padded the man's tax-free existence that went unnoticed by the IRS.

"Now, Tony. How much longer are you going to be? Shanda's coming over for dinner, and you know how disagreeable she can be when her blood sugar's off."

"Hang on there, Ben. You get on me because you think I'm cooking food for a member of the female clan, and now you're worried that you won't have time to fix supper for one of its members? At least I think she is. That moustache of hers is fierce. Maybe she's a he/she."

As if reasoning with a five year old, Ben replied, "Tony, I'm doing everything I can to shape you into the fruit that females like to pick. Now, Shanda's not interested in me. It's your brother who's caught her eye. She could care less if she sees us in the kitchen, but never let a woman see you doing her work, or it'll be the last thing she'll remember."

"Thanks, Ben," Tony said, placing a pomegranate-dyed hand on his father's shoulder. "I'll remember that next time I get hitched. In the meantime, I say we throw a trough in the living room and let fate take its course. I'll even pitch in for her feed bag."

"Feed bag? In the living room? Well, now you're just being silly." And with that, Ben walked out the kitchen, positive that it would be a long time before his eldest son marched down the wedding aisle to an awaiting bride.

As Ben pondered Tony's plight, Jonathan examined Mike Warner's driver's license photo and wondered if the words In Memoriam would be placed next to his graduation picture in the next yearbook. Would there be an entire page filled with images of the youth documenting his four years of activities? In a few moments, the policeman was to meet with the teen's parents, and he prepared himself for the couple's emotional state. How would I react if it were my son? he thought. What must go through a parent's mind when he's told that his only child has been kidnapped at gunpoint and his whereabouts are uncertain? Is it the sheer fright of the unknown, or a numbing terror of each passed day without resolution that reduces a parent to a shadow of what he once was?

Jonathan's telephone brought him back. "Detective Peters."

"Well, there you are. I just wanted to make sure that you were at work and not some saloon slamming down weekend specials.

Saturday is the real Sabbath, you know, so don't get any ideas about hiding out in one of those caves because I'll find you, and you know I will."

"Excuse me, but the Warners are here," an office staffer informed him.

Quite out of character, the irritated man responded, "Shanda, I'm in the middle of a difficult day, and the last thing I need to hear right is you babbling about a whole lot of nothing. Now if you'll excuse me, there are parents who need my help. Goodbye."

Unable to hear her response, he took a deep breath and went into the interrogation room where the Warners sat; there he saw the large father and fidgety mother who looked down at her dress, unconsciously stretching its fabric.

"Good afternoon. My name is Detective Peters; I'm in charge of this case. Before we begin, I just want to tell you how much I regret the circumstance of our meeting, but I'm quite confident that with the information that you'll provide today, we'll have your son back soon. I know you've already been briefed about his car being identified south of here, so I'll move on to other areas that I need help with."

"Is my son dead, officer?" Mr. Warner asked.

"We have no information indicating that, sir," Jonathan responded through a tightening throat. Although he'd been trained in grief counseling, a shared feeling of pain engulfed him, and he worried that anything other than a calm, stately appearance would further inflame the couple's anxieties.

Without looking up, Mrs. Warner began. "There was a gun involved. What makes you think someone crazy enough to kidnap a seventeen year old wouldn't use it on him?"

"I don't know how else to say this other than I have a gut level feeling that there is more to this incident than we know, and that's why you're here. Perhaps you know something, no matter how small or inconsequential you might consider it, that will assist our investigation."

"Oh, for God's sake," Mike's mother exploded, her eyes directly on the policeman. "This is my son we're talking about. My only son, my only child. It's my life we're talking about. We come home and find a note saying that he's searching for America or the real America or whatever he said, and the very next day we receive a call from your department telling us that our son was kidnapped by some lunatic in a parking lot. I'm not a well person. Our family business keeps me going Monday through Saturday, and I don't need to be told that I need to spend more time with my son, so save your breath."

"I was not suggesting that, Mrs. Warner." Yet the woman's act of contrition humbled Jonathan, for she had just offered a painful truth for all to hear, and to him nothing was tougher than facing an unpleasant reality.

Mr. Warner remained silent, refusing to acknowledge his wife's revelation. In him, Jonathan saw a man ruled by a woman, incapable of asserting himself, which struck a nerve that the detective tried to ignore. "Sir, I'd like to ask you something, and it might be uncomfortable, so please take your time."

"Certainly," Mike's father responded.

"How would you characterize your relationship with your son?"

"I'm not sure what you mean."

"Well, are you close?"

"Officer, my son goes to school, plays loud music, does his homework, is involved in every conceivable extra-curricular activity, dates, and never talks back. Does this sound like a person that a father would have trouble with? He's a model son; he's as close to perfect as you get. You have to find him."

Jonathan felt the increased pressure in his eyes and knew that they were turning red. "Mr. Warner, you mentioned that Mike dated. How frequently?"

"Once in a while. He never dated anyone steady."

"What about his male friends. Was he close to them?"

"As much as high school boys are, I guess. Detective, we don't have the largest house, so Mike did his socializing away from home most of the time. He never even got that many phone calls because anytime he planned something with his friends, he did it at school, or at least that's what I always assumed."

"And don't start looking at his friends like they're behind this. They're fine boys, fine. Tell him, Bert. They love Michael and would never do anything to harm him."

"Ethyl, please."

"Actually, I must ask some rather difficult questions concerning his relationships. If any of these are painful, I apologize." Swallowing hard, he began. "Are either of you aware of any fights or disagreements that he had with his friends shortly before the abduction? Any friction over a girl? Jealousy over anything? Grades, tests?"

"How many times to I have to tell you? My son is loved by his friends. They look up to him like a brother, and you're painting them as a pack of animals. Make him stop, Bert. Haven't I been through enough without having to listen to this?"

"I meant no disrespect, Mrs. Warner, but if we're to locate your son, you're going to have to consider these questions, even if they seem arbitrary or useless. Even if they hurt."

"Why are we spending time talking nonsense when you should be out there looking for my son? How many times do I have to tell you? He never had any problems with his friends or anyone else. Isn't that right, Bert? Tell him."

"Ethyl, please. Let the man do his job."

"Mrs. Warner, I understand that you and your husband own a business."

"Yes. Dry cleaning."

"And it's doing well?"

"For two generations, my family has made a comfortable living."

"Thank you. Mr. Warner, is there any reason that any of your customers, competitors would have to vent their anger against you or your …"

"Absolutely not," Ethyl interrupted. "We've been in the same neighborhood for forty years. We're friends with everyone. There's not one person out there who would have any reason to get back at us. We run an honest business—if you really want to know who the criminals are it's those chains that move into a city and drive out the independents. If there's any kidnapping to be done, we should be the ones carrying it out, not the other way around."

"Ethyl! Enough." Mr. Warner pressed the palms of his hands onto his head. "You'll have to excuse my wife, officer. She's been under a great deal of stress since yesterday. We both have. It's not uncommon for her to make unfortunate comments under pressure."

Thirty-five minutes later, the interview concluded, and Jonathan was still at a loss as to why Mike Warner had been abducted and who the perpetrator of such a baffling disappearance was. Staring at the youth's picture, the investigator wondered what was running through the graduate's mind. Fear? Terror? And then he questioned if the captive were still alive. "I don't even want to think about that," he whispered as he put away his files and exited the office, ready to head home for a Saturday afternoon cookout.

The late afternoon traffic was light, and Jonathan had little difficulty weaving his Ford Taurus through the city's maze of streets. Burger King billboards lined the concrete passage ways along with various anti-drug campaigns left over from Nancy Reagan's numerous crusades. Although Jonathan's upbringing kept him well-insulated from those less fortunate, he did witness the misery of neglect on a daily basis with his job. A steady stream of petty thieves made their way through law enforcement's bureaucratic corridors and almost always returned after committing yet another ridiculous theft.

Jonathan often wondered how much money was spent on the country's slick Madison Avenue drug campaigns and how much more good could be gained by channeling that money to treatment centers, job training corps, and health classes targeted to grade schools; however, he knew that the '80s political climate produced a Washington-manufactured hysteria that he considered more self-indulgent than magnanimous. Even his co-workers were surprised by the way the detective balked at the conservatism with which his profession is identified. Whether it was interceding on a suspect's behalf to protect him against what Jonathan considered harsh treatment or simply voting for a candidate not endorsed by his union, the man stood tall and refused to be bullied by any of his colleagues.

Now, if I can only stand up to that woman, he thought. And as he arrived home, there she was, arms crossed, military stance, on the front stoop; from her expression, he knew that she was not pleased. "Jonathan," she began. "Your brother has the entire clothesline covered with those stupid hippie shirts of his, and they're dripping coloring dye. The lawn looks like a cabbage patch."

Not wanting a confrontation, the drained policeman replied, "That's how they dry. You don't want him to put the shirts in the dryer, do you?"

Taken aback and still reeling from his earlier treatment of her on the phone, she demanded, "What has gotten into you? You've been treating me like some common housewife, and I don't like it. I knew this was bound to happen once you scoffed at my attempts to assist you in your time of need. And by the way, the treatment center wants you there ASAP."

"Damn it, Shanda. When are you going to stop worrying about me and move on to other things, like our wedding? Aren't there any preparations that require your attention? You're driving me crazy with this relentless therapy talk. I've got a kidnapping case that's consuming me, and all you do is make matters worse by complaining about my brother, me, and God knows who else."

"Well," she said, taking two steps forward. "I have never been treated so rudely by anyone in my life. If I try to help you, it's because I want our life together to be productive and problem-free. If that isn't to your liking, then maybe we should cancel the whole thing."

Now you're talking, he thought. "Shanda, I don't want anything cancelled," he lied. "I just want you to give me some breathing room because it's getting pretty difficult with you always thinking that you know what's best for me. I'm a grown man. If I need any help, I'll let you know."

Twisting her body back and forth like a spoiled child, she relented and walked into the house, but then backtracked, her eyes laser-like on Jonathan. "And what about those creations in the back? I don't want my bratwurst tasting like a flower child."

"Jesus Christ," he uttered under his breath.

"Don't you cuss."

"Jonathan," Big Ben called out. "I thought you'd never get home. How's that kidnapping case? Have you nabbed the sucker yet?"

"No, dad. I spoke with the seventeen year old's parents today, but nothing broke."

"How are they doing? They must be heartbroken. If one of my boys was taken away from me, I don't know what I'd do."

"Sometimes I wonder why anyone would want to bring children into this world today. A woman's not safe in her own house anymore, your kids are easy prey when they're out, there're so many guns on the streets that people are treating them like fashion accessories. It's a complete mess," Jonathan replied.

"And if that's not enough, some kids never grow up and cause all sorts of problems for everyone else," Shanda added.

Appearing at the front door dressed in frayed, cut-off jeans, sandals, and a psychedelic bandanna wrapped around his receding hairline, the shirtless older brother hovered behind Shanda. "You need to cut back on your red meat, Morticia. You're almost tribal."

"Tony," Ben scolded. "We don't have tribes in the suburbs."

Staring at his father after hearing Shanda emit a deep grunt, Jonathan knew that the evening was going to be long, so he decided that the only means of escape was to concentrate on the Warner case.

Chapter 15

Janesville, Wisconsin is a feast or famine town, almost entirely reliant on General Motors. Located thirty miles south of Madison, Wisconsin's state capital, Janesville is a bedroom community composed of mostly high school educated, blue collar citizens. When Detroit prospers, this municipality is one of the first to experience the sweet sensations of growing pains; however, each time a hiccup is felt in the Motor City, Janesville is the first to be labeled DOA. The city's downtown area is a who's who of closed businesses, both large and small, for few are able to withstand the ever-changing economic conditions, so they fall victim to the dynamics of Ergonomics and vanish with little fanfare.

Visitors are hard pressed to find small, family owned businesses; instead, shoppers must rely on large corporate enterprises that inflate prices to pad a conglomerate's ego. Gone are the neighborhood barbershops and hairdressers; in are the $7, twelve minute styling establishments that are housed in malls located on the outskirts of town, the ones where pronouncements are advertised on formatted radio stations, buttressed by light, catchy pop jingles and a bubbly female voice over.

Main Street is a patchwork of faded, brown papered window fronts and distressed businesses struggling to make payroll and the next month's lease. In front of these, children play hopscotch next to trees planted alongside sidewalks, both neglected by a financially strained city government.

"What a depressing sight," Tommy commented as the two drove the downtown thoroughfare. "And we came here to see this?"

"Yep. Look around you, Tom Boy, and witness the decline of small town America. And don't be so critical. My guess is that each of us lives in our own little GM town in some way."

Mystified by the comment, Tommy asked, "What does that mean?"

"Nothing represents America like GM, right? Look around you. What do you see? A decaying relic of what was once a booming city. But then the big boys started playing hardball, and this is what happens when they go undefeated."

A United Auto Workers food pantry sat near the street light where the travelers were stopped. Over the entrance, a hand painted sign greeted members. “Man, let’s get out of here,” Tommy pleaded. “There’s nothing around here to see except a dying city. This is beyond depressing.”

“Take it easy, Tom Boy. These people could just as easily be you or me.” As the sympathetic driver gazed at the few pedestrians who were out and about, he sensed that each possessed a certain distance, the unsettling look of resignation. Those confident, hopeful faces that he was accustomed to seeing back home were absent in these people. In them, he saw expired confidence and unresolved problems that he sensed would only become worse with each downward turn of the economy. “Let’s get something to eat. Add some dollars to this place.”

The Golden Gate restaurant was anything but golden. Cloaked in various shades of barn wood red, the establishment resembled a stereotypical vision of the old South. Prune-faced men and women sat at undersized red and white checkered tablecloth tables, each neatly aligned yet leaning precariously. Bib overalls and horn rimmed glances were as plentiful as the piped in country western music. Counter service was available to those who didn’t mind resting on ripped cushions, stuffing escaping though stark lacerations. And if this weren’t atmospheric enough for the youths, silence befell the eatery once they entered.

“Is it my imagination, or is everyone staring at us?” Tommy mumbled under his breath.

“They are, but maybe they’re reading our Chakras.”

“In that case, we’re dead.”

A young waitress approached the front door and stared, as if gauging the youths, silent as an executioner.

“Hello, and, no, I’m not Tom Cruise. We’d like a table for two,” Mike stated.

“If there’s one available,” his partner added.

“Not from around here, are ya?”

“Nope, but we’re mighty hungry, little lady.”

Oh, God. Here we go, Tommy thought.

"Yeah, whatever you say, little man. Follow me," she commanded, walking towards a back table.

"Works every time, Tom Boy. Just have to know the lingo."

"Stupid and arrogant?"

"You're no fun."

The adolescent waitress led them past the gawking masses and seated them. "Do ya know what ya want?"

"Ah—could we see a menu please?" Tommy asked.

"We ain't got none."

"What was that?"

"No menus here."

"Huh?"

As if her entire existence was being questioned, she replied, "Do ya think I'm lyin'? No menus. We only serve the basics."

Sensing that he'd better stop his line of inquiry, Tommy replied, "Excellent."

"Well, how the hell're we supposed ta know what you've got if we ain't got one of them there menus?" Mike queried.

Positive that they would soon be shot, Tommy said a quick Hail Mary.

"Just tell me what ya want. Menu's always the same. Hamburger, cheeseburger, fries, Coke. So, what do ya want?"

We're in Southern Wisconsin, and she's talking as if we're in Alabama, Tommy determined.

"Okay. We'll each have two cheeseburgers, two fries, two Cokes, but hold the pickles. Hate the suckers. So does my brother, here. No fried onions either. Gross. Raw onions only. And no ketchup. Just mustard."

The waitress leaned over and directed Mike's attention to the sticky condiment basket caked with grime. "That look like I'm the one who's supposed to mustar' your burger?"

"Just sayin', pumpkin," Mike replied.

"Do it yourself. I'm not your mother," she answered as she walked away, passing a trucker with a Confederated flag on his worn Levi's jacket.

The restaurant's clientele returned to their meals and conversations. Red capped country boys mixed with factory hands and complained about the current state of affairs and what the hand of fate had dealt them, cigarette in one hand and a fork in the other, their demeanor defeated and resigned.

"You know some of these people remind me of the guys I used to work with," Tommy informed Mike. "It's like work is their entire life. When it's great it's only fine; when it's bad, it's lethal."

"So, what did you do before you fell into the writing trade?"

"I spray painted Christmas tree stands and screen door handles. You know those silver tubes that prevent the screen door from slamming shut? I did those, too. Five thousand per hour."

"Five thousand?"

"As God is my witness. And when the orders decreased, they moved me to packaging."

"Sounds industrial."

"Oh, yeah," Tommy replied. "Meet your quota, or you're out. Talk about shitty work conditions. No protective gear. No face mask. I'm positive that my lungs are lined with silver paint."

Rubbing his forefinger against the table's smooth edge, Mike offered, "School would have been more exciting than that. Why didn't you do that? I thought every suburbanite went to college."

"Tried it. Engineering. Didn't work out," Tommy replied in a mere whisper.

"Drag," Mike responded, attempting to make eye contact with Tommy, but the unemployed man looked away.

"Doesn't matter. If there's anything the experience taught me, it's that I don't need a bunch of professors teaching me what I already know."

"So, you're a closet engineer who needs no additional insight or training? Cool."

"Don't be snarky."

"Snarky? Now I'm a fish?"

"Don't be a dick. How's that?"

"Much better."

"What I mean is that I already possess knowledge gained from common experience. No amount of liberal arts classes will further define what motivates society and my place in it."

"And engineering is absorbed like osmosis. All anyone needs is to think and, therefore, is. Amazing. Why wasn't any of this in the student brochures that I received? Damn."

"Well, trust me, Mike. I know what I'm talking about. There's nothing that college can teach you that you don't already know. Do you really think that a writer needs to go to college? What can he possibly learn?"

"Um, how to write. And what happened to engineering? You are one hard monkey to follow."

"Yeah, well—never mind. That's none of your concern. So, what are you going to study?"

"Osmosis."

"Dick."

Silence befell the ponderous teens as they listened to clanging silverware, muttering patrons, an irritated cook complaining about her son, sizzling burgers, drivers gunning their engines before peeling off, and an aging soda dispenser that choked as it struggled to fill a large glass. Mike heard a man boast about the raccoon leg he found chewed off in one of his many traps while Tommy eavesdropped on a pair of elderly women who talked about Jesus and Elvis.

But before the teens could compare notes, a tall, middle-aged, wiry man walked into the restaurant. "Danny," the young waitress yelled as she ran to him and threw her arms around his waist, appearing as if she were embracing a long-lost father.

"Hey, Deb. How're these ol' cows treatin' ya?" he asked, his hands firmly on her ass. The object of her affection had bright red hair that was parted down the middle with what appeared to be Saudi crude. His lanky frame was offset by full biceps bursting out a plaid shirt with rolled sleeves, a pack of Camels nestled in one. "Ya got time for a little hooch?" he asked loudly enough for the entire restaurant to hear. A quick glance through the place only added to his down home performance. "You know I can't keep my hands of ya," he drawled, slapping her backside for added effect.

"Not now," she fawned while prying herself away. "Customers."

"Well, get goin' then," he instructed. "Never keep a hungry man waitin'."

And as she secured and then deposited two Cokes in front of Mike and Tommy, the object of the waitress' desire strolled about in a style that resembled something between a strut and a stumble.

"Oh, Jesus. Kit Carson's on his way."

"I got this one, Tom Boy. I speak cowhand."

"That's what I'm afraid of. Just don't be a smart ass. Everyone in here's probably friends with everyone else."

"Hey, boys. How're they hangin'?" Danny greeted the two as he approached their table. "None of you's is from here. Am I right?"

"Nope. Milwaukee," Tommy replied as he tried to look every which way but the inquisitor's.

"The big city, huh? How's come you's guys came all this way? Family?"

"Li'le vacation, that's all," Mike replied. "We like ta see what's out there," he added while pointing to the front window. "There's a whole world waitin' ta be had."

"I'm with ya, mister. My name's Danny. What's yours?"

Offering his hand, the driver replied, "Michael, and this here's Tom Boy, my best bud," which took Tommy aback. As he looked at Mike, the graduate smiled back, his eyes welcoming. Intoxicating. Warm.

"Nice meetin' ya both," Danny said, shaking each man's hand as if they were visiting dignitaries. "We've got us a fine li'lle town for ya both, an' I hopes ya have a great time visitin'."

Trying to sound as much a good old boy as possible, Mike continued. "So tell me, Danny. Just what the hell do ya do in Janesville that rattles your balls 'til they bark at the moon?"

"Goddamn, boy. You're a man after my own heart," Danny said, slapping the youth on the back. "We get us a couple cold beers an' a couple hot ladies an' party down like there's no tomorrow. How's that sound ta ya?" he directed at Tommy.

"Ah, great. Sounds, ah—great. Yeah."

"But I s'pose you two knows all sorts of hot tricks from back home with all those fine lookin' city girls, eh? Eh?" A nefarious chuckle supplemented an elbow jammed against Tommy's arm, which he pulled away.

"You bet, Danny," Mike insisted. "We got 'em comin' by the bus loads, if ya catch my drift."

"I sure do. 'Round here they come like cattle," he bellowed.

"Jesus," Tommy moaned.

"Danny, are ya botherin' those boys? You leave them be. Last thing they wanna hear is you carryin' on," she added as she deposited the travelers' meals.

Caressing the upper portion of her legs, he replied, "I's just bein' friendly, that's all. Now quit your worryin'. Ain't good for the baby."

Oh, God, Tommy thought. No way can these two be married. She's way too young. "Baby?"

"That's right," Danny said, patting the girl's stomach. "Seven more months, and I'm gonna be a daddy."

"Just in time for yer birthday, I'll bet," Mike added, facetious as ever.

"Hey, that's really good," Danny replied. "But not my birthday. Deb's. We just cel'brated my fortieth. Quick, get my cane," he yelled and teetered as if he were in a convalescent home.

"Yes, sir," the pregnant girl added. "Doctor thinks it might be born on my birthday—it's real close to Christmas. Wouldn't that be something? My baby bein' born on either my birthday or Jesus'. I couldn't ask for a nicer present for my seventeenth."

Dumbstruck, Tommy asked, "You're sixteen?"

"All year. Well, almost," she added.

A crippling sense of sorrow overcame Tommy as he tried to absorb the numbers. When her child was her current age, the mother would only be thirty-two. And if her offspring followed the same pattern as his mother, this waitress would be a grandmother by age forty-eight, and most likely a great-grandmother by sixty-four. Angered by the calculation, Tommy asked, "And what do your parents think of this?" His words came out sharp, each syllable propelled as if it were a weapon designed to never take prisoners.

"Oh," she beamed. "They're real happy for the both of us. They woulda preferred if we'd waited 'til I graduated, but they're gettin' ready for Danny ta move in. They really likes 'im."

"I works with her dad at the mixin' plant. We make those concrete blocks you build basements with. He's a real ol' boy, I'll tell ya. He parties like the rest of us. Most people don't even b'lieve that he's thirty-three. He's a wild kinda guy."

"I bet," Tommy replied, depression gripping him.

"You guys students?" Deb asked.

Pointing to Mike, Tommy replied, "He will be in the fall."

"Tech school?" Danny asked.

"College. I'm graduating from high school next week."

"Is that right? And ya came all this way for the heck of it? That's nice. That's real nice, isn't it, Danny? Most folks just drive right through town, but ya stopped. I like that."

"You bet. We got us two fine ol' boys here, Deb. Two reg'lar hell raisers, ain't that right, boys?"

Tommy looked at Mike and saw the unintelligible look on his face. It wasn't as if Mike found the situation amusing. Far from it. He too was alarmed by the matter-of-factness in which the couple basked, their lack of concern or fear over what their actions might produce. Staring down at his untouched plate, the graduate had lost his appetite and glanced back at Tommy, hoping that he too was ready to leave.

And he was.

"Damn. Forgot to leave the key at the hotel when we checked out. We'd better bring it back, or I'll be charged."

You can do better than that, Tommy thought.

"Wanna call from here and tell 'em you'll be right over after …"

Tommy jumped up and replied, "No, can't do that. There's no phone at the hotel. One of those cheap ones outside town. We're kinda economizing."

Pulling out a twenty, Mike handed it to the waitress. "This should cover it. Keep the change."

"I can'st do that. Your bill's not even half that," she protested.

"Put it towards, the baby, okay? Buy it something nice."

Following his partner, Tommy left the restaurant; the soon-to-be parents watched the departing pair and silently thanked God for what they considered a windfall.

Once Mike climbed into the car, he sat and stared ahead, thinking about his early life and how his parents cared for him. The family gatherings came to mind as did his bountiful birthdays, Christmases, St. Nicholas Days, and all the other moments that were fortified with unwavering paternal love. What kind of life can a child have under those conditions? he thought. Sure the parents seemed okay, but how can a child care for another child? And how much does that guy make? When I told her to keep the change his eyes almost fell out.

"You okay?" Tommy asked, careful to avoid any hint of intrusion.

"Think of it, Tom Cat. You and me driving around, not a care in the world, blowing off money like it's going out of style and counting down the days until I get more, and those two back there are figuring out how to rearrange that little girl's bedroom so they can make room for her baby. Doesn't make sense, does it?"

Tommy saw the pain that Mike grappled with and tried to determine how to best deal with the driver. "No, it doesn't. Sometime we don't know how well we've got it until we run into people who'd trade places with us in a second."

"But don't you see, Tom Boy? Those two wouldn't want to trade places with us because they're happy. Isn't that weird? They're so fucked up that they think their way of life is typical. Can you imagine what that child of theirs is going to consider normal? God, it's so depressing. So hopeless."

As Mike started the car and commandeered it through the downtown streets, he was soon stopped at a railroad crossing, and a long caravan of train cars rolled past the aged Pinto, each railcar sealed tightly, hiding its cargo. Alongside Mike's vehicle, small boys did wheelies on their bikes, the youngsters flying in the air each time they dove off their toys, only to land a few feet from the moving train. "And what about them? This whole city seems like one big accident waiting to happen. In a couple years these kids'll graduate from high school, no doubt possessing minimal skills, and they'll all line up at some assembly plant, if it's still open, or a concrete mixing paradise, hoping to land a job. Once they get that, they'll get a wife, a car they can't afford, a house that'll bankrupt them, and finally divorce papers. And by then they'll only be twenty-two. Maybe this is the real America," he concluded.

Tommy was depressed over this bleak assessment of American culture but was also captivated by the insight that Mike had just provided. Don't tell me this is the same guy who I've been with for almost a day? the passenger asked himself. Because if it is, something significant has just been revealed. Hoping to snap Mike out of his discouraged state, Tommy said, "Hey, Mike. Wanna get a twelve-pack? It's perty hot, and I's buildin' up a mighty thirst."

"Glad to see that a little Danny rubbed off on you, but I don't drink."

"Neither do I, Squirt Gun, but I gots a hankerin' for a couple cold ones. So, whata ya say?"

"I say affirmative."

And as the train passed and children proceeded to drive across the tracks, Mike gunned the Pinto and produced his finest burnout yet. The car sailed across the metal rails and tossed the two about as they laughed over the hasty choice.

"You're gonna kill us," Tommy counseled.

"Unlikely yet possible."

With grain silos to the left and an abandoned strip mall to the right, the two sailed down the road and basked in their carefree existence and the late spring temperature.

"Hey, Minute Man," Mike began. "How are you going to buy the beer? You're not twenty-one."

"I look legal, don't I?"

"To a farsighted, elderly woman perhaps."

"Then you come with me. Strength in numbers."

"Look, Tom Cat. If you'd have a hard time passing for twenty-one, it'd be next to impossible for me. I put the baby in baby face."

"Well, come with me anyway. In the rush of our buying spree this morning, I forgot to get a notebook for my screenplay. You get that, and I'll grab a 12-pack."

"What happens when you get caught?"

Smiling at his accomplice, Tommy responded, "I'll blame everything on you and tell them that you kidnapped me."

"You know what, Tom Boy? You're getting more like me each second."

"Frightening thought, isn't it?"

Chapter 16

Piggly Wiggly's parking lot overflowed with weekend shoppers who were lured by the store's Giant Truck Load sale. Scores of parents stood beside a large semi-trailer and waited their turn to walk away with a couple eighty pound bags of water softener salt and corn meal.

"Check it out. Moscow invaded Wisconsin, and we're the last to be told? Unacceptable. Had I known, I would have brought a pet bear," Mike announced.

Resembling the docile, obedient Russian formations that Americans saw on the evening news, the Janesville consumers stood in a queue, talking amongst themselves, children safely in tow, and moved ahead to the hawking salesman who offered a brand ten cents cheaper than another stacked neatly on the store's shelves.

"Why would anyone put themselves through this?" Mike asked.

"You're the one who wanted to seek out America. Isn't it obvious? Yanks love a bargain, even if it's only an illusion."

"Want some?"

"Nah, my water doesn't need more softening. Let's head inside," Tommy replied.

Walking into the store, the pair marveled at the screaming children and battered parents who ignored their offspring and focused instead on the staggering totals that were calculated on the state-of-the-art registers. High school baggers hurried about, arms flying through the air, attempting to pack as many goods in as few bags as possible. "One hundred fifty-four dollars and thirty-three cents, please."

"That'll be $64.99, sir."

"Eighty-eight fifty, please."

"Sixty-three even."

Each pronouncement echoed throughout the checkout area as a bank of cashiers tried in vain to keep up with the crushing consumers, the pulse of the store felt by all.

"You ever work in one of these, Tom Tom Club?"

"These variations of my name would dazzle a second grader."

"Be nice, and I'll buy you a coloring book."

"You do that. What kind of beer do you want?"

"Like I say: I don't drink. Never have. Drug free, alcohol free."

"How virginal."

"If you say so. Which brand is considered good?" Mike asked.

"Not much of a drinker either, but seeing that we're from Milwaukee we should go with Miller. They make good commercials."

"And that, of course, is the definitive way to determine the finest beer. Okay. Might as well patronize a hometown product. I'll grab it. You get the notebook."

Tommy agreed, and the two proceeded to amass a sizable college ruled notebook, a bag of Munchos, two large boxes of Cherry Pop Tarts, four Slim Jims, napkins, a *Little Mermaid* coloring book, a jumbo 64-count Crayola box equipped with a crayon sharpener, and a 12-pack of Miller. Easing their way into an express checkout lane while ignoring the glare of suspicious shoppers, the two came face-to-face with that most powerful of individuals: the checkout clerk who would pass judgment on the validity of the purchaser's age.

"Morning, guys. How are you?"

"Ah," Tommy stumbled. "Fine. How are you?"

"I'm fine, too." And as she grabbed the next item to scan, she stopped and pressed it against her dark blue smock. "*The Little Mermaid*? I love *The Little Mermaid*. Oh." With her eyes now closed, she grasped it as if traveling to her special place. "I have to get one before I leave. This must be new. You're the first one to purchase it that I've seen."

"He's a pioneer. That's what he is," Mike added.

Placing the coloring book back to the counter and scanning it, she looked at the youthful Mike and then grabbed the 12-pack. She didn't just eye him. She surveyed him and then moved on to Tommy. "Need to see an ID."

"Ah, wallet was stolen last month, and I'm still waiting for my replacement license. I can show you my university ID, if that'll help," he told the college age girl, trusting that she would bypass the offer.

"Okay, let's see it."

"Oh, no," he moaned. "Man. That was stolen, too. Stolen with my other wallet. Don't even have my social security card to show you."

The girl smiled, ran her fingers through her shoulder length blonde hair, and scanned the final item. "That'll be $26.23. You do have that, don't you?"

Pulling out his wallet, Tommy replied, "Oh, sure. That I've got." But looking into his empty wallet, he remembered that he didn't have any cash. Making eye contact with the girl, he said, "Ah, guess I forgot to cash my paycheck. My friend has money, though."

Mike smiled at the girl, put his arm around Tommy's neck, and pulled him close. "You'll have to excuse my brother. He's been a tad absent minded since he got back from the war."

"And which one would that be?" the clerk asked.

"Ottawa."

"Not sure I've heard of that war," she played along.

"Yeah, not many people have. Little skirmish we had with the Canadians. Lasted 'bout four minutes."

"Just four, and all that damage to your brother—or was it your friend?"

Sensing that their cover was now blown, Tommy interrupted. "Mike, mom gave you money for school supplies, right?"

"Ah, no, because it's summer."

"Yes, and you have to attend summer school because you flunked gym class because you wouldn't shower with the other boys."

"Yes, and that's because they ran away screaming when they saw how hung I am."

Tommy turned to the girl and said, "It's cute that he thinks that."

Mike leaned over and flashed his million dollar smile to the clerk. "Shell shock. Pay no attention to this poor afflicted man."

Not to be out done, Tommy pushed aside Mike and added, "Please don't judge him harshly. He's never gotten over his botched circumcision."

"Love for this to go on, boys, but I've got a line. So, I need some money. Like now."

"But of course, my little aperitif," Mike said. And with that, he pulled out his ample wallet and paid the amused clerk.

"Thank you very much, gentlemen, and have a good day."

"We will," Mike replied, pushing Tommy forward and out the door. "We, my friend, are gold. Solid gold. Platinum. That was sheer brilliance in there. She knew what we were doing. That girl just wanted a good story, and we provided it. That was incredible. We should do stand-up. I'm hysterical, and you could be the straight man. So, how do we go about this? Your research must have come across this at some point. Do we go to New York, or is L.A. the place to be right now? Chicago? Don't know. No idea. But it would be fun. Where would we stay in New York? The Y? Nah, that's more up your alley. You and the Village People keeping house, although I do like the stache on that leather guy. Never quite understood it though. What's with all that leather? Must get hot. And that Indian. What is his story? That headdress is too much. Whatever. We'll figure it out. Amazing. You know that girl could've busted us high and dry. Do they call the police for that? My parents would freak. We're very law abiding. Fly the flag. Wash the sidewalk. Crime is not part of my vocabulary."

"Pause for irony."

"Pause for shithead. So, where do you wanna go?"

"Home?"

"Fuck, no."

"Then let's find a place to stay. Hotel and then a park? Nice day for a beer bash."

As the two continued their odyssey through Janesville, they both considered a simple fact: they were enjoying each other's company. For Mike, this wasn't surprising because he liked everyone. But for Tommy it was a different story. He knew that there was no logical explanation for him having such a good time other than being with the person who introduced himself so unconventionally.

"You know once we check in, you can call your parents and let them know what you're up to. They're probably wondering where their working class son is."

"No, I can't do that," Tommy replied with a hint of panic.

"Why?"

"They went up north for the weekend," Tommy lied.

"Well, then you can get a hold of them Sunday night."

"Yeah, that's a good idea," the deceptive man agreed.

Next to the I-90 on-ramp sat an economy motel. With its long, expansive single story frame, the dwelling invited truckers and motorists to rest before continuing their trek to Madison and the northern portion of the state. Although few cars and trucks were parked beside the motel, it wouldn't be long before the no vacancy sign flashed its neon message, for the resting spot attracted capacity crowds nightly due to its reasonable rates and ideal location.

After an uneventful check-in, the pair unloaded the Pinto and investigated their room. "Not bad, Mike. I'm impressed. This is a heck of a lot better than what we had last night."

"Sure is. And look. I know it must break your heart, but we have separate beds."

Tommy laughed a little over this and pulled his recent purchases out of a plastic bag. "You know what, Mike? A good writer is never afraid to place himself in situations that many wouldn't. Helps create real characters. Living, breathing people with a past. Filled with joy, ambition, fear, and inhibitions. Writers come from all walks of life, you know, and from all parts of the country. Did you know that Faulkner wrote *The Sound and the Fury* on the back of an oil barrel when he worked in a factory?"

"No. By the way, who's this Faulkner chap? Some comic strip dude?"

"Yes. One of the finest."

"Thought so," Mike joked, being all too familiar with the Southern novelist. "Guess if you want a creative mind you've got to place yourself in unusual situations. I'm tellin' ya, Tom Boy. This was meant to be. We need to get wild, do the unexpected. Worst that can happen is we die."

"Pleasant thought. I'll be sure to include it in my screenplay."

"So, what's this script going to be about?"

Selecting each word carefully, Tommy sat on Mike's bed and began. "It's not so much what it's about. It's more like what it's not about."

"A-ha. Eat some 'shrooms when I had my back turned?"

"What I mean is that it's not really important what the screenplay's about because I'm using it as a star vehicle for me."

"News flash: story counts."

"Not necessarily. It has more to do with timing. For instance, I could've chosen song composition, but I didn't. My screenplay'll be my meal ticket."

"I'm lost. So, now you're a writer/engineer/songbird?"

"Not exactly. More like a Renaissance man."

"A-ha. Think you caught their plague."

"If you're going to make fun of ambition, then we'll talk about something more up your alley, like cutting classes and skipping to the front of the lunch line."

"Okay, okay. It's just that you're hard to follow. I'm only an honors graduate, so you need to take it slow. So, what instrument do you play?"

"I don't."

"Oh. Then you're a singer."

"Nah, not much of that either."

"So how, pray tell, are you going to perform a song that will make people take notice?"

"I'll find a famous group to record it," Tommy stated, self-assured as always. "Lots of groups do covers."

Confused, Mike remarked, "Tomster, you're annoying me. None of this makes sense. Do you actually believe that someone like Tom Petty's going to record one of your songs simply because you say it's good? How would you even put it down on paper if you don't have any musical knowledge?"

"I do. I know a lot about the history of the recording industry. Ask me who founded RCA. Go on, ask me. I can tell you what ASCAP and BMI stand for. I even know where the old A&M records in Hollywood is."

Frustrated, Mike countered, "That doesn't mean shit. What does any of that have to do with writing a song, giving it to a star, and then becoming one yourself? Nothing."

"Why are you yelling? Shut up. You haven't even graduated from high school. Where do you get off criticizing me? I've had more world experience than you."

"No, you shut up. You're only a year older than me."

"And besides, I just told you that I'm concentrating on my screenplay, and that has nothing to do with music."

"Or engineering."

"They all blend together, Mike. You'll learn that as you get older. Life is a collection of experiences that merge together to create a whole—an entire …"

"Abyss?"

"Forget it. I'm not explaining myself as well as I should. Let's have a beer."

"Now, you're talking. What kind do you want?"

"How about the only kind we bought?"

"Just checkin' to see if you were still conscious." Tossing a can to Tommy, Mike grabbed one for himself. "Did you ever see *Blue Velvet*?"

"Of course. Dennis Hopper. Superb."

"He was the crazy guy, right? Remember when he offers that kid a beer, and he asks for a Heineken? Hopper stares him down and yells, 'Heineken? Heineken? Pabst Blue fucking Ribbon.'"

Tommy marveled at Mike's imitation and broke out laughing. "You're a pro, Mike. You know that? That was pitch perfect. You almost scared me: it was that good."

"What can I say, my doubting apostle? You're not the only actor in these here parts."

"Really? Explanation please."

"Nothing much. Grade school crap. Sixth grade, to be precise. I was one of these weird twins: Feeslie and Meeslie. Forgot which guy I was. All I remember is that we had to wear these strange costumes. My grandma made mine out of old green curtains."

"Like *Gone With the Wind*."

"Don't know. Never saw it. Anyway, I had these huge, sagging sleeves that came down to my knees, and I had to walk around like some Oriental guy, you know, shuffling around in my shoes, making this scraping sound. Pathetic. And racist. Can you imagine? And it was a Catholic grade school. Got an A in the class, though. Your turn. Dazzle me with your theatrical experience."

"That would be hard. Was never in a play. Auditioned for one once. But that was in high school, and you know things operate there. Everything is who you know and if you hang around the right people. That's why I never got depressed or anything. Instead, all I ever did was promise myself that one day I'd come back for one of our class reunions, and everyone would recognize me for what I was: famous. Real famous. So, when I was a junior, I ended up joining a rock band, but we never went too far."

Confused with what he had just heard, Mike asked, "Wait a minute. Two minutes ago you said that you didn't play an instrument. Now you do?"

Tommy stopped for a moment and got a faraway look in his eyes. Without the slightest hint of evasion, he said, "That is so strange. When you asked me earlier about what I played, I honestly thought that I didn't play anything. Weird."

Drinking his beer, the man became silent and looked ahead with a hollow expression, causing Mike to wonder what must be going through his friend's mind. Was he erasing something too painful to remember, or did he simply forget an inconsequential moment in his life? "Ah, fuck it. You just had a momentary lapse of reason. Happens to me all the time. I remember when I couldn't remember my locker comb after Easter Break. So strange when that happens. Or your telephone number. How many times were you left standing there, looking like a spaz 'cause someone asked you for your number, and you couldn't remember? And those stupid student numbers that they assign for college? Got mine last week and was told that it was critical that I commit it to memory 'cause my entire existence would center on those digits. Weird, huh? So bogus."

But Mike knew that Tommy had gone somewhere, perhaps a place that provided answers and brought him peace, so the graduate sat back on his bed and drank his beer, hoping that his new friend would soon break his stony silence.

Newly arrived neighbors poured into the rooms surrounding the two young men and rattled the confines with confusion and verve. Children shouted questions to their parents while they in return questioned each other about the location of swimming suits and checkbooks. Mike listened to the unmistakable sounds of bodies jumping on beds and parents warning that the ceilings were low enough for significant pain. Yet the children continued, and Mike's irrepressible identification with their enthusiasm brought back memories of his nine-year-old tanned body scurrying through neighbors' yards, chasing his friends and relishing every second of it. Glancing at his still silent counterpart, Mike wondered what this person's life was like. Was he happy? Secure? He didn't know and wasn't confident that the time to inquire was now; instead, the graduate finished his beer and grabbed another from the 12-pack that now sat at his feet.

"God, I feel like there's a wheat field in my mouth," Mike commented.

"Hops. You're tasting hops."

"Oh, yeah. I should know that."

"Comes from years of watching commercials."

"Welcome back, Tom Tom. You ever tour a brewery?"

"Not in town. I did the Coors tour in Colorado, but I was with my parents, so it wasn't that great. Besides, like I said before, I'm not much of a drinker. This is my christening into the world of 12-packs."

"You know what? It's weird that neither of us ever toured a brewery in Milwaukee. We both grew up there, but we never did what countless visitors do daily. Isn't that bizarre?"

"I suppose. You ever been out west?"

"Oh, no. I wasn't kidding when I said this is the first vacation I've ever taken."

"Thought you were being dramatic."

"Nope. My parents were always busy with the store, so we didn't get out much."

"Didn't they have an employee who could've watched the place?"

"Nope. After grandpa died, I came along. Besides him, my parents were the only employees. Still are. I help out once in awhile, but Bert and Ethyl handle the store singlehandedly. Pretty impressive, eh?"

Tommy nodded his head while leaning down to grab another beer.

"We're closed on Sundays, so any traveling has to be done between 5:00 PM Saturday and 7:00 AM Monday: you don't get very far when you're working under that kind of time restraint."

"True."

"When I was in eighth grade, my dad used to take me to the Packer games, but the drive pretty much killed him because he was always so tired from the work week. So, we ended up watching the games on TV. My mom would make this incredible popcorn with Parmesan cheese sprinkled on top. Good, good, good. She'd always be fixing a feast while we watched the Packers wail on the Bears or whomever. Right around the start of the fourth quarter, dinner'd be ready. She is one good cook, my mom. Incredible. Little neurotic, but I guess we all are in some way. Even you, Tom Cat."

"Maybe," Tommy replied. "Sounds like your home life was pretty good. You know how lucky you are, don't you?"

"Yeah, but so are you, although I think mom and dad should've invested in some weights for you."

"Yes, I'm well aware of your opinion. I stand as your inferior on the Adonis front."

The two leaned back in their individual beds and stared at the yellowed ceiling. "This could be a movie, Tom Boy. Any second Godzilla's foot'll come crashing down on that Buick parked next to our car."

"And all the people will be running out of the hotel, thinking that they can outrun the mighty beast from the east."

"But they can't because the fire-breathing creature'll toast them like a piece of rye bread."

"And their mouths'll still be moving after they're done speaking," Tommy laughed. "You're pretty creative, Mike. Play your cards right, and I'll let you work on the screenplay with me." Tossing the notebook to Mike, he pitched it back.

"No, thanks, Tom Boy. You're the writer. I'm just a beer drinking simpleton who gets off watching behemoths wolf down people."

Getting up, Tommy stopped and looked down at Mike. "You don't want to watch any TV, do you?"

"Nah. You're more interesting."

Genuinely moved, Tommy responded, "Thanks. No one's ever said that to me."

"You are. I've met a ton of people in my time, but you take the cake. You're a regular superstar waiting to happen. I'm not sure how you're going to get there, but it's a trip listening to you. It really is."

"Then let me hit you with this little plot line I've been tossing around."

"Is this for the screenplay?" Mike asked.

"No. Novel."

"And when's this supposed to happen? After the screenplay's done or after your acting debut?"

"Somewhere in between. The way I look at it, once I get my foot in the door, nothing'll stop me. So, picture this: you have this one guy whose entire life fills the novel. Every conceivable aspect of his existence is covered. College, marriage, kids, everything."

"Birth?"

"Yeah."

"Grade school?"

"Yeah."

"Then you should say so."

"I did. I said everything."

"But you started with college."

"I know. Whatever."

"Kind of important, don't you think?"

"You're interrupting my flow, Mike."

"Just sayin'."

"Yes, you are. Got it. So, when it comes time for the guy's death which, by the way, will be incredibly moving, he'll be screaming and crying and—cut. The very next thing the readers will find is two parents hovering over a crying infant. One reaches down into the crib, lightly pats the baby's head, and the other asks, 'What do you think's wrong?' The other will look up—and this is great—and say, 'Oh, nothing. Just a bad dream.' Get it? The baby just dreamt his entire life, and the reader doesn't find out until the end. Pretty good, eh? The ultimate surprise ending."

Mike leaned forward and asked, "That's it?"

Thrown, Tommy replied, "Well, yeah. What else do you want? A car chase?"

"Might help."

"What?"

"Just thought there'd be more. Is your friend Barbra Streisand going to provide a song?"

"How can you top a man's entire life experienced by an infant in a dream-like state? It's otherworldly."

"Just think there could be more."

"Like what? His family tree?"

"Now, you're talking. It'll give it a nice twist. Kind of like the beginning of the *Conan the Barbarian* series."

"Oh, give me a break, Mike. Don't even compare those stories to this. What I'm talking about will revolutionize the world of fiction. I'll be a contemporary Joyce. You have heard of him, correct?"

"*Ulysses* is my middle name, you condescending wordsmith." Just as there were no holes in Michael's education, what he excelled at was something that Tommy would have benefited from most: a keen observer of character. And not the type found in novels. "Thomas, put down your choo choo train and consider this, okay? Don't you think that you should concentrate on one career before planning a couple others?"

"You don't think I'm capable of doing any of this, do you? Come on, Mike. Answer me. There's no reason to be afraid. I'm not going to get violent. Let's hear it."

"I didn't …"

"You don't think I have what it takes, do you?"

"Of course, I do," Mike answered in a doubtful tone.

"That's convincing. Real convincing, Mike. You should go into law. With that act of yours you'd have a 100% track record. One hundred percent failure, that is. There's not a jury in the world that would buy that crap of yours."

"I'd only be practicing in the US. The world? Way too ambitious. More up your alley."

"Shut up, counsel. If I wanted any more of your cheap, stupid comments, I'd have asked." Downing his beer and grabbing another, Tommy gulped it down. "You always have to ruin everything, don't you, counsel? Nothing's sacred to you. Not a person's privacy, dreams. Anything. You must be a real pleasure to live with."

Upon hearing this, Mike followed Tommy's lead and grabbed another beer, gulping it in four boisterous swallows. "I never said anything that was supposed to put you down. I just asked a simple question that seemed logical."

"To who?"

"Whom."

"You're seventeen years old. What do you know about life?"

"A lot, Tom Boy. I know a whole lot. I'm a Top Ten graduate. I took both the ACT and the SAT and scored in the top six percentile. We went to State, and I almost made the winning touchdown."

"But you didn't, did you?" Tommy asked.

"No, because some 230 pound fucker kneed me when I went for the ball. But I still got my picture in the Milwaukee Journal. Front page. You ever done anything like that? Have you ever been interviewed by anyone?"

"Not yet, Mr. Hall of Famer, but my time's coming. Every news organization in the world's going to want me, pal, and don't you forget it."

"How could I? I'm sitting here with Robert Redford Hemingway, drinking away a Saturday afternoon, and being insulted by someone who thinks success is achieved by sending in cereal box coupons. Man, you are fucked up. I've never met anyone like you—but come to think of it, maybe you do have something. Now, try this on for size: why don't you write about this weekend and cast Pee Wee Herman as yourself once you sell the film rights? I do have the proper order, don't I? Book first, movie later? Isn't that the master plan you keep yappin' about? Jesus, you remind me of those old cartoon characters. They're always screwing around in a kitchen, a stack of dishes falls on their heads, and the next thing you know a bunch of geeks are sittin' around, flappin' their mouths that have plates wedged in 'em. Come to think of it, you'd be the one with coffee cup earrings, and I'd be the one footing the bill!"

Flying across the bed and straddling Mike, Tommy gripped his hands across the graduate's throat, screaming, "If it's money you're after, I'll give you what I owe you."

An unopened beer can smashed against the rabid man's temple, causing him to twist in pain, beer foam dripping down his flushed face and onto Mike. Falling to the floor, Tommy reached up to grab the bed but failed.

Mike jumped to action. "Aw, shit. You okay, Tom Boy? I didn't mean to hurt you. Let me lift you up. No, on second thought stay there. I'll get a doctor. Wait. Move your head and see if it's cracked. Stop. No—I got it. Lie there and remain still. I know CPR, so you won't die. Learned this in football. The assistant coach's uncle used to play back in the day and one of his teammates broke a rib, so they decided that we all needed training, which made no sense to me, 'cause CPR is for the heart, not a broken bone, although I'm sure there's a link somehow. Maybe the circulatory system merges with the skeletal system. Not sure. More of a chemist. Organic."

Slapping the frantic hands away from his face, Tommy climbed from between the two beds and looked at Mike head on. "I'm leaving. Don't stop me, or I'll make so much noise that the neighbors'll think there's a murder goin' on here." Climbing up and teetering a bit, Tommy walked to the door and opened it.

"No," Mike pleaded, jumping up and dashing to the door, forcing it shut. "I'm sorry. I just snapped when you attacked me."

"Get out of the way, Mike, or I'll kill you."

"I will after you hear me out."

"I asked you politely once; I won't a second time."

"No, Tom Boy. You don't understand. You can't go. You have no idea how important it is that you stay with me."

"Get out of my way, Mike."

"No, I won't. All my life I always got everything I ever wanted because everyone thought I was perfect. Everyone loved me at school. My parents thought I could do no wrong. All the neighbors went wild over me, but inside I knew that something was missing. I always had this feeling like maybe I wasn't real, or everything was some kind dream—almost like that book you were talking about writing."

"The one you made fun of."

"Yeah, but I only did I because I didn't know how else to react. You hit a nerve. No one's ever done that before. Everyone's always looked to me to lead the way and do this and that, but for once it seemed like I ran into someone who called his own shots and didn't care about anything else but reaching his goals, no matter how out there they appeared. That's new to me. Don't you see? For once, I'm along for the ride, and I like it, and if I say stupid shit, hey, I'm sorry, but don't go. Please. Don't make me have to go it alone now. You spoiled me, Tom Boy. I'll never be able to find someone as crazy as you."

Tommy looked at the man and pondered the options. He could just stay and continue living as he had the past day, or he could leave flat broke and somehow return home, a place that seemed increasingly distant and foreign. "If you ever waste another beer, I'll walk."

Beaming as if Christmas had arrived early, Mike smiled and replied, "I promise."

"Shake?"

"Only when I work with live wires."

The two sealed their bond and continued work on the remaining beers. Although Mike was the first to doze off at the ripe hour of 6:00 pm, Tommy's imagination fueled him to a creative frenzy. Grabbing the notebook, he wrote voraciously until the approaching darkness lulled him into a fitful sleep.

And as the two travelers dreamed of fantastic places and surreal images, a sixty-three-year old woman thanked a trucker who had provided transportation all the way from Denver.

"And if you ever need a place, call me. My husband's name is in the Milwaukee directory."

"You got it, Alma."

"Take care."

"I always do, Mrs. Peters. I always do."

Chapter 17

The large winged creature swooped down and caught Jonathan by the shoulders, hurling him through the mountain's cresting corridors and into a camouflaged nest filled with wailing adults, each crying out for a protective parent.

"No," the alarmed dreamer screamed, awaking himself and those in the house; Ben was the first to arrive.

"Jonathan, did you crack the case or your head?"

Tony was next. "Bad trip?"

Apologizing for the disturbance, Jonathan thanked each and assured them that everything was all right. But he knew it wasn't. The night's dream was simply a replay of one that had haunted the anguished man since his mother's departure. Never one for psychologists or therapists of any sort, the policeman attributed this recurring vision to nothing more than perpetual adolescent anxiety, a term that he had coined.

Thinking about the woman who had abandoned him when he was eleven, Jonathan tried to remember every detail about her: the delicate style in which she carried herself about the house, always moving with hesitance and sadness; her resourcefulness in making ends meet yet never allowing her children to do without; her unwavering commitment to a racist-free America; and the resigned expression she wore anytime she saw successful women on television, realizing that she would have to leave her family if her dreams of social independence were to mature.

"You're not listening to me, Ben," Jonathan remembered his mother telling his father. "I can't be a daughter, wife, and mother anymore. I need me. I need to discover the reason why I was put here. Why can't you see that?"

But he couldn't. None of them could. So, she left, writing daily to her children, then weekly, monthly, and then the letters stopped. Soon, rumors circulated that she was off to South America with a group of middle aged Unitarians to live by the ruins and wait for alien beings. But the family would have none of it. They knew the woman was too smart to become a cultural distortion; they also knew that she would not return until she had found what she believed she was missing. And most painful of all? That they were not enough for her to stay.

Looking over at the framed picture of himself and Shanda that rested on the nightstand, Jonathan considered that maybe his life wasn't meant to get any better, and that happiness was only measured in degrees. We're all happy, I guess. Maybe some more than others. Wish I were more like them, he thought.

Depressed, Jonathan picked up the phone and telephoned his fiancée, not the type of activity that she appreciated at five in the morning.

"Hi, Shanda."

"If this is an obscene phone call, I'll tell me husband! He's a policeman and has a gun that'll turn a buck into a doe with one quick pull of the trigger!"

"Shanda, it's me. Jonathan."

"Well, why in God's name are you calling me at this hour of the morning? You scared me half to death, and now I can feel a worry line forming. Just how exhausted do you want me to appear at our wedding? My father has spent a fortune on one of the top photographers on our street; if his money goes to waste, you're going to reimburse him out of the separate bank account that I have taken the liberty of establishing for you."

"I only wanted to talk."

"We'll talk, all right, when I get over there in a couple hours for Big Ben's brunch. Now, goodbye!"

"Bye," he said to a loud click. Getting up, he sauntered out his room and into the kitchen where he made a pot of Mr. Coffee, an early wedding gift from his department. Making his way to the front door, he opened it, expecting to find the Sunday paper. Instead, he found his neighbor's cocker spaniel gnashing his teeth on the supplement section.

"Hey, hey. You can't do that. Stop it," he commanded to the canine marauder; however, the animal refused to obey and growled at the robe-clad human. Grabbing the paper, Jonathan engaged in a man/beast tug of war. The dog dug its teeth deep into the Quaker Oats coupons while the cop grasped them and the accompanying Parade Magazine insert.

"Jon Jon."

Turning, Jonathan saw Ben standing in the doorway, nearly naked except for his Michigan State University boxer shorts that crept up like hot pants. "You sure look cute playing with this dog. Maybe I should get you one for the wedding. Guess you miss not having a pooch around after all these years."

"Dad," Jonathan strained, still in combat with the dog. "We never had one."

"Oh. Maybe that's why you miss it so."

Lifting the paper up to his waist, Jonathan attempted to shake it out of the elevated dog's mouth. Twisting its head back and forth while clawing the air with its paws, the dog relented, dropped to the ground, and took a quick leak on Jonathan's feet before scampering away.

"For God's sake," the humiliated man cried. "Why don't those blessed neighbors keep that dog tied up? What do they do? Let it roam the streets at night?"

"Makes a darn good watchdog, if you ask me." Exited by an idea, Ben added, "Maybe we should all get dogs and let 'em patrol the streets at night. Bet no ganster'd come around here to kidnap anybody." Confident that his son would give this insight considerable attention, Ben walked into the house to begin work on the Sunday brunch, a weekly ritual that featured his famous waffles, aptly named Ben's Famous Waffles.

After wiping off the saliva residue on the paper and fanning his wet ankle with the sports section, Jonathan walked into the house and, after cleaning up, retired to the family room, only to find Tony wide awake, cleaning his water pipes.

"Tony, put those away. You know what I think of them."

"Yeah, I'm with ya. We both hate streaks," Tony responded, not in the least distracted from his polishing duties.

"And don't let Shanda see them. She wouldn't understand."

"What I don't understand is why you're hooked up with that chick. Man, with your looks and position, you could get any woman you want."

Touched, the policeman responded, "Thanks for the vote of confidence, but you're wrong about Shanda. She is a very, ah—oh …"

"Exactly. Words fail to describe."

"Solid. Yes, solid as a rock."

"So's a glacier, but I wouldn't want to crawl in the sack with one."

"Tony," Jonathan protested. "You know I don't like talk like that."

"Why not? We're all guys. We know where the parts go."

"Well, let's just say that your gift of openness allows you to discuss these things much easier than me."

Lifting a long-stemmed, rose decaled pipe up to the morning sun that streamed through the room's bay window, Tony said, "Interesting that you didn't deny."

"There's more to a relationship than that. When you get married, you'll find out how important trust, honesty, and dependability are to a relationship. Leave passion to the young."

"Spoken like a nun."

"No. Spoken like an adult."

"No, spoken like a man who's in dire need of a blow job."

"I have no idea what you mean," Jonathan said in his evasive best, while flipping through the real estate section.

"C'mon, Jon. It's nothing to be ashamed of. Carnal knowledge is as important as a password to a computer system. A man who cracks that exhibits courage and conviction—as well as a raging hard on."

"I'm afraid I don't agree," the anxiety-ridden man responded.

"Wanna know three words that keep me up at night? Your Wedding Night. C'mon, bro. Tell the truth. You ever try out the merchandise?"

"Please, Tony," his brother begged.

"C'mon, man. No need to be bashful. We're brothers. Nothing wrong with discipline just as long as it's what you want, and it's not being forced on you by someone who's a closet dominatrix."

"Stop it."

"Probably has a dungeon. Gonna make you eat hardboiled eggs. Spank you with a leather paddle."

Setting the paper down, Jonathan looked at his older brother and tried not to laugh. "Think of it, Tony. Here we are. My older brother living a life that fell out of favor after the sixties, and me, the long arm of the law. Who would have figured? Most brothers are at each other's throats their entire lives, but us? If ever there were two who should be, it'd be us."

"But we're not, are we?"

"Nope. Never in a million years. You're still my big brother, and you'll always be there for me."

"That is a fact. So, when Vampirella goes all bondage on ya, you know where to go."

"Yes, I do. Now, knock it off."

Tony went back to his spring-cleaning duties and then added, "Probably has a collection of anal plugs waiting to use on you."

"Stop it."

"No lube, either."

"Enough."

"Sorry, but it's true. She freaks me out. Children run away crying when they see her coming. Animals bolt. Skies darken. Earthquakes. My God, the earthquakes."

Tony watched as his younger brother tried his best not to fall into hysterics. The older sibling's irrepressible joy was something that Jonathan always wanted. Nothing fazed Tony. Nothing and no one. He was as fearless now as he was when he was in grade school, watching over his younger brother, totaling anyone who gave the youngest any trouble. "Think mom'll come?"

The question came out of nowhere and threw Jonathan. "Ah, not sure where this came from, but to answer your question: don't know and don't care. And how would she even know? Fuck her."

"Jon. Come on. She's our mother. You don't mean that."

"Yes, I do. Who takes off and leaves her children and a husband behind? Emma does. That's who. Look what she did to us. Look what she did to dad. He's never been the same. You know what replays in my head? Hearing him cry when I was in bed. Eleven and hearing your father cry. Just imagine what that does to a boy."

"Maybe mom didn't have a choice," Tony replied, his voice a blend of defensiveness and melancholy.

"Emma's choice was to leave me. Us."

"Interesting that you don't call her mom."

"She didn't earn it. And by the way, you call dad Ben."

"He asked me."

"When?"

"You weren't the only one who heard him in that condition. I walked into his room to see if I could help. Couldn't. Never saw a man cry before. Sat down on the bed, and he told me that he'd never felt more alone. It was right before I started high school. Barely able to shave and trying to help a grieving man. You know he blamed himself, don't you?"

"Yeah."

"I tried to comfort him the best I could. That's when he said he needed a friend more than ever and asked me to call him by his first name. Just stuck."

"Why didn't you tell me?"

"You were too young. We both were. No way I was going to lay that on you."

The hand-held mixer filled the house with its high-pitched whine, the beaters hitting the aged red ceramic bowl that had been with the family since the boys were in grade school.

"Do you think any of this is why you're with Post-Nasal Drip?"

"No. Don't think so. Not really."

"I detect reticence."

"No. I just know that she'll never leave me. Walking away from anything is not part of her vocabulary."

"An untreated STD won't leave you either, but I don't want one."

The comment brought a smile to Jonathan. "You know she's not that bad."

"Yes, she is. Hey, guess what? Guess what I'm giving you for a wedding gift?"

"Sure you want to tell me?"

"Yeah. Hate surprises."

"Okay, what is it?"

"Two tenth row, dead center tickets for tomorrow's Dead concert at Alpine Valley. Great, huh?"

The thought of Shanda attending a rock concert mortified the man. Sure he was humbled that his brother would produce such a cherished, close-to-the-heart gift as this; after all, the Dead were Tony's lifeblood, his cultural sustenance. But his fiancée in a sea of tie dyed, time tripping, pot smoking music fans?

"Great seats. Couldn't believe we got so lucky with the mail order."

"We? Oh, so you'll be with us?"

"Of course. Think I'm gonna give up the opportunity to see Boxcar Bertha writhing in pain at a concert? No way."

"What about my schedule?"

"Fuck your schedule. You're usually home by late afternoon. Leave an hour early. You're on call anyway. If something breaks, it breaks. You'll deal with it. But my guess is that you need this more than I do. Time to open your horizons."

How am I going to break this news to Shanda? the detective asked himself. She barely made it through the Ice Capades because she thought the female skaters were too racy. "This is kind of you, Tony. It really is. And I know this must have cost you some serious money. The Grateful Dead. Not my typical Monday fare, but maybe that's what I need. Shanda, too."

"She'll hate it. That's one of the reasons that I bought them. It was either these tickets or a blender, but this is way safer. Can you imagine her with one of those? Your Jim Dog would be an endangered species if you ever pissed her off."

Amused by his brother's colloquialism, Jonathan laughed, feeling secure with his immediate environment. The industrious Tony, the diligent Ben. A sun-filled family room, and a hefty Sunday paper.

Making it through the front section, the metro portion, and the sports pages, Jonathan fell asleep in his chair as his brother went into the kitchen to assist Ben. "How's it goin', man?"

"Oh, hi, Tony. You and your brother have a nice talk?"

"Always. Need some help?"

"Yes. Need to set the table, so you need to move those T-shirts. My goodness, how many did you make?"

"Three hundred."

"Well, I hope those people appreciate a product well-made. That's one thing I taught you boys since day one: take pride in your work, and your work will take care of you."

And Ben's edict rang true for both his boys. Few Grateful Dead vendors could compete with the finely styled designs that the thirty-four year old created. The breathtaking, multi-colored explosions that leaped from the shirts held viewers spellbound. "I'm going to make a killing this year, Ben. I only paid $1.50 per shirt, wholesale, of course, and they bring in $25 each. And this year I have two helpers."

"Good, Tony. But I don't want you wearing yourself out and not having any energy left for a nice looking girl who captures your eye."

"No need to worry. Jon and Elvira will help me out. They just don't know it yet. Got them two tickets for the concert. Great, huh?"

Ben stopped beating the eggs for the quiche, cast a stern look at his son, and said, "With the two of you working together, there's nothing that you can't accomplish. Nothing."

"I agree, my man. Maybe this little taste of free spirit will rub off on him. Then he can dump you-know-who and move on to better conquests."

"Oh, I don't know," Ben stated, shaking his head. "Shanda's got him by the shorties."

"Why, Ben. Did you just agree with me?"

"Now, stop that," Ben pleaded, wiping the newly formed beads of sweat from his brow. "You caught me off guard."

Several hours passed as bacon fried, muffins cooled, quiche baked, and a large pitcher of orange juice chilled. Exhausted, Ben retired to the living room and turned on his favorite program, *Jesus Christ: Another Fundamentalist.*

"Tony, come watch Brother Lee kick Brother Bob's butt. Last week they almost got into a fist fight over Noah's Arc."

Every Sunday, Big Ben sat glued to the TV, amused by the two hosts and their religious histrionics.

"Ben, you shouldn't be watching that," his eldest scolded. "Let's not forget about the time we thought you were having heart palpitations."

"But, Tony. It's so exciting. This's better than *Roseanne*. One of 'em even looks like her."

"Then just stay calm. You'll ruin the brunch if you die."

As if a profound statement had been made, Ben replied, "You're right, Tony. You're right. What would Shanda think if she saw me lying on the floor with my feet sticking up?"

Staring at his father, Tony replied, "Ben? Were you hitting the bird seed again?"

Unable to follow his son's joke, Ben looked blankly at him and then shifted his attention to the program.

"Welcome, friends ..." Brother Bob began.

"Yes, yes. Jesus loves you so," Brother Lee interrupted, much to the chagrin of his co-host.

Excited, Ben blurted out, "Oh, here they go, Tony."

"Yoo-hoo, I'm here," Shanda announced as she entered the house. "Big Ben? Where are you, you little gourmet?"

"Shanda's here, Jonathan. Wake up. Your honey walks."

"Well, of course I do, Big Ben. You are such a card."

"Come in and sit right next to me," Ben insisted.

Noting what the family patriarch was watching, Shanda commented, "Oh, Big Ben. Why are you watching this trash? Don't you know that *The Old Time Gospel Hour* is better?"

"Shanda?" Jonathan asked, barely conscious.

"Yes, it's me, and I'm exhausted after that little prank of yours this morning. Do you know what your son did to me, Big Ben?"

"Stole your purse?"

"Of course not, but he terrorized me in the early morning by posing as an obscene caller. Now, just look at me. My eyes are all puffy and tired looking."

"There's always surgery. You can start with the eyes and move down to the rest of your body," Tony responded, classifieds in hand.

"Very funny, Tony. I'm surprised to see you up at this hour. You must get up early to do your drugs." Seeing him walk away with his newspaper section, she added, "The classifieds? Don't tell me that you're planning on getting a job."

"No, just gonna line the chair that you'll be sitting in for breakfast."

Flabbergasted, Shanda pleaded, "Big Ben? Big Ben? Are you going to let that son of yours talk that way to me?"

"Shh. Lee's 'bout ready to bust Bob's jaw. What a show!"

Fully awake now, Jonathan got up to kiss his fiancée and wish her a good morning. Instead, all he was greeted with was a firm, "Oh, get away from me and brush your teeth. You remind me of one of those zoo monkeys that stinks to high heaven."

"Planning a family reunion," Tony called from the kitchen.

"Never you mind, you felon-waiting–to-happen."

"Sorry, but I just woke up," Jonathan apologized. "But I've got some great news. Tony is giving us our wedding present a little early. We're now the proud owners of two excellent tickets for tomorrow night's Grateful Dead concert. Isn't that thoughtful?"

Shell-shocked, Shanda asked, "Jonathan, are you out of your mind? Do you expect me to sit with a bunch of spaced out, drug crazed hippies listening to some acid rock group, getting my eardrums blasted into oblivion?"

"Don't forget about the sodomy."

"Stop it, Tony. Shanda, please," her fiancé pleaded.

"And what about the treatment center? They're expecting you tomorrow morning, and I don't think they're going to be thrilled when they find out that you'll be going to some free love festival."

"If that's your concern, don't worry," Tony said as he re-entered the room. "One look of you naked will cause the masses to bolt."

"Tony, that's enough," Jonathan scolded.

"Man, when they came up with the term piece of ass they had no idea that you were coming down the pike; otherwise, they would have coined it piece of black hole."

"Oh, stop that, Tony," Ben chided. "You've been watching too many episodes of *Nova*."

"Jonathan! One more insult from this waste of space you call a brother, and I'm leaving. Do you hear me? One more."

Alarmed that his brunch might be ruined, Big Ben jumped in. "Oh, don't do that. There're so many plans that still need to be worked out. We've got the rehearsal dinner, the wedding, and what about tomorrow night? Tony'll have to train the two of you on proper sales techniques, right son?"

"Ah, Ben. Don't think right now is the best time to discuss this," Tony responded.

"Sales techniques? Jonathan, what in God's name is Big Ben talking about?"

"I don't know." Prepared for the worst, he asked, "Tony, were you planning on us helping you sell your shirts tomorrow before the concert?"

The eldest son looked at the trio's probing eyes and replied, "Hey, how 'bout a rousing episode of *Green Acres* before brunch?"

Chapter 18

The first sensation Mike noticed as he awoke was the pain produced by his left leg, dangling over the bed and twisted in the opposite direction that he lay. Then there was the rancid odor emanating from his mouth; a moment's panic ensued before he remembered what produced the foul taste. And then there was his stomach. Not since he was tackled in a pre-season game had his abdominal area been in such pain. "Oh," he moaned, hoping that his deep bellow would stir his friend to consciousness. It didn't. Looking over at Tommy, Mike saw the fully clothed teen with a Bic pen clenched in his right hand and a notebook resting on his chest.

So, that's the famous screenplay, he thought. Let's see just how good this guy really is. Rolling off the bed and balancing himself on tentative feet, Mike reached over and lifted the notebook off his companion's chest. There was no resistance.

"Well, where's the title?" he asked while combing through the opening pages. Although there was none, he sat back on his bed, pushed his pillows behind him, and began reading.

FADE IN:

A large body of water sits in front of a full moon. Stirring music plays as TWO CHARACTERS look passionately at the scenery.

FLASHBACK: A YOUNG MAN watches in horror while his arm is severed by a large sawmill blade. He SCREAMS.

BACK TO SCENE: The same two characters that were first seen reappear. Close-up. We see that the man is the same one who got his arm cut off.

MARK

I don't think I've ever seen anything so beautiful in my life.

FRAN

The lights are incredible, aren't they?

MARK

I wasn't talking about them. I was talking about you.

FRAN

I know you were.

MARK

So why the icy stare, beautiful?

FRAN

It's so hard. I haven't been with anyone since, since …

MARK

You don't have to say it. I know all about the abortion.

FRAN

(Struggling)

It wasn't just that. It was the way the orderly touched me.

MARK

(Enraged)

You never told me that. Why, I'll kill him.

FRAN

Oh, Mark. How could I possibly tell you when I knew that the only person you yearned for when we were together was my sister.

MARK
(Dramatically)
That (pause) is a lie.

FRAN
No, it is not. It is the truth.

Mark wipes away tears.

MARK
Why? Why? Why can't we just forget this crazy world and start over again, like we were before. Before, before, you know.

FRAN
I know. The tidal wave.

MARK
(Courageously)
It was hell.

FRAN
I was terrified.

MARK
I was aghast at the situation.

FRAN
Your arm wrapped around me, your legs wrapped around the palm tree, keeping me from being dragged out to an uncaring sea.

MARK
I don't think I ever told you, but that was the first time that I realized that I, I (BEAT) loved you.

FRAN
(Shocked)
What?

MARK
Yes, it's true.

FRAN
(Confused)
Oh, oh.

MARK
I wanted to tell you, but I couldn't.

FRAN
But why?

MARK
Because, because of my, you know, my problem.

FRAN
(Shocked)
You know your missing arm never mattered.

MARK
(Anguished)
That's because you are a woman!

FRAN
Oh, Mark. Mark. You must have been tortured worrying about it, Mark.

MARK
You have no idea. It's a miracle I'm still alive.

FRAN
(Lovingly)
And I thank God that you are.

MARK
But does it really change anything? So much has happened since the accident.

FRAN
Life is grim.

MARK
It blows.

FRAN
But there's always light at the end of the tunnel for those with hope.

MARK
You're such an optimist. I wish I could share that special gift of yours.

FRAN
We almost did.

MARK
Yes, but that was before (CLOSE UP) Danny.

FRAN
(Close UP)
Danny.

FRAN & MARK
Danny.

MARK

I'll never get over him.

FRAN

Neither will I. I still lay away at night, unable to sleep because the memory of his head caught between the crib bars is so real.

MARK

(Pounding his head with his fist)

Why? Why?

Fran grabs a hold of Mark and buries her head in his chest.

FRAN

Oh, Mark. What have we done?

Mark continues to pound his head with his only fist.

MARK

What have we done? What have we done? Not nearly enough. That's what we've done.

FRAN

Do you think we'll ever get over this?

Music builds to a climax and peaks.

MARK

Not as long as you're chasing after that astrophysicist.

FRAN
(Angrily)
So, we're back to him, are we?

MARK
Yes! Yes!

FRAN
How many times do I have to tell you that he's only a friend.

MARK
Say it as often as you like, but you forget that I saw the two of you at the planetarium.

FRAN
What you saw was nothing more than a student with her teacher, searching for gamma rays.

MARK
Ha!

FRAN
Oh, what difference does it make? You won't believe me anyway.

MARK
You're right because you're a conniving, little vixen.

FRAN
And you're an ass!

MARK
A what?

FRAN

An ass!

MARK

(Close up)

An ass?

FRAN

Yes!

MARK

(Exploding)

Go to hell!

Fran slaps Mark. Stunned, Mark slaps Fran with his only hand. They both engage in a pensive stare as swelling music begins.

MARK (CONT'D)

I'm sorry.

FRAN

So am I, my love.

MARK

Why do we do this to each other?

FRAN

I don't know. Why can't we be like the lovers on 42nd Street?

MARK

Because it's all my fault. I had a lousy childhood. Do you know what it's like to share a bedroom?

Mike screamed upon reading the last line and kicked his feet in a child-like frenzy, pounding the mattress with his hands, the screenplay flying in the air. "Unfucking real," he cried. "This is incredible!" Leaping from his bed and jumping on the awakened man, Mike continued. "You're incredible, Tom Boy. Sure I had my doubts when you started all this crazy shit 'bout doing this and that, but you're good. You're really good. I'm the first to tell someone when I'm wrong, and I was wrong about your talent. Know what Coach used to tell us when we were behind in a game? He'd go, 'Boys, if you don't butt some heads and win this game I'm gonna do some huntin' of my own.' And now I've finally figured out what he meant: you either win in life, or you'll become the hunted. Get it? I sure do."

Still stunned after the abrupt awakening, Tommy looked at his rambling cohort and said, "Mike, you're sitting on me. Your underwear's halfway down your hips, and you're straddling me."

"Play your cards right and you might see more, big boy. You're a star. A superstar. People'll be throwing themselves at you once this comes out. We should be celebrating. I still can't get over it. I'm friends with someone who's destined to be one of the greatest comics of our time."

An uneasy feeling overwhelmed the aspiring artist when the word comic was used. What is this guy talking about? he asked himself.

Leaning over to his bed, Mike grabbed the notebook and shoved it in front of the disheveled teen. "This is probably the finest satire of those soapy romantic movies that I've ever read, not that I've read a lot of screenplays, but you know what I mean. I go to movies; I know what's hot, and this is. You've got the gift, Tom Boy. Now run with it and make a touchdown for me and the boys."

"What boys?"

"Yeah, you're right. Fuck them. For me then."

"Give me the script," Tommy said in a low, angry voice.

"What?"

"Give me the script."

Mike complied and placed it in his friend's outstretched hand. "You get hit with some new ideas? Yeah, by all means take this and keep working. When you're on a creative roll, nothing should stand in your way. Nothing and no one. You do what you need to do, and I'll be on my bed, silent. Not a word. Not even sign language. Nope. Won't hear a word from me. Want me to give you time alone? Just let me know. Anything you want. Anything that'll allow you to continue working on this. Excellent. I'll even stand guard outside the door so no one bothers you. Cleaning lady tries to enter, her ass is grass. So, go to. Nothing, repeat, nothing will get in your way."

"Including a senseless high schooler who doesn't know the difference between tragedy and comedy?"

"What? I thought you'd be happy that I was crazy over something you wrote. It's good, Tom Cat. Real good."

Sitting up, Tommy leaned forward and breathed into the man's face. "It's not satire. It's not comedy. It's a love story about two people who never get it right."

"Get outta town. You're pullin' the ol' weasel."

"No, I am not pulling your weasel, your big ten inch, or whatever else you ignorant adolescents banter about in your stupid locker rooms."

"Hey, hold on there, Jackson."

"I know you're too young to recognize literary subtlety, but the least you can do is respect an artist's privacy and not dig through his first draft like some obsessed fan. And I'll thank you to not reveal my plot line to anyone once we get done with this little journey that you insist that I accompany you on. Good ideas are hard to come by, and I don't want some hack making off with my creation."

Jumping off the bed, Mike paced the room. "Wait a minute. Are you telling me that this is not some type of comedy that you're working on?"

"God, you're quick. I can see why you're a Top Ten graduate."

"So, Fran and Mark aren't exaggerations?"

"Of course, not. They're real people faced with real life and its accompanying complexities. Do you think there's anything funny about getting your arm cut off by a large blade?"

Frozen in his tracks, Mike turned to Tommy and replied, "As opposed to a small blade? Yeah, if it's presented the right way. Of course, I do."

"Then you're sick."

"So, you didn't purposely make the dialogue into a parody of those love stories, boy meets girl, boy loses girl?"

"No, I did not."

"So, instead, you've come up with boy meets girl, boy loses arm, baby loses head, bitch slap ensues, and you claim that I'm sick?"

Jumping off the bed, Tommy sprang to the near-naked man and shouted, "You are the most insensitive, ridiculous, banal, idiotic nothing I've ever met. The woman just lost the love child that she bore, and the father is torn apart by the circumstances that prevent the couple from achieving a happy life together, and you think that's funny? You think I'm trying to be cute? I'll have you know that I cried when I wrote that dialogue. I wept like a baby and was worried that I was going to wake you up and be subjected to the same type of moronic comments that I'm listening to now. God, you're stupid."

The insulted youth grabbed the back of Tommy's neck and pulled him closer. "Look, pal. I supposed I'd be a little riled if I inadvertently wrote the funniest script since *Young Frankenstein*, thinking it was *Top Gun*, but that's no reason to take it out on me. I thought I was doing you a favor."

"Favor? Favor? You giving me your highly regarded opinion, thinking it's a favor? This coming from a guy who thinks *Top Gun* is intellectual manna?"

"Manna? What the fuck is that? Some kind of rip?"

Pushing Mike away, Tommy shouted, "Of course, it's a rip. You can't even identify an insult when you hear one? Yeah, it's a putdown. One giant affront. You should feel completely useless now. What do you think of that? How does that register with that sophomoric mind of yours?"

"My percentile scores were unbeatable …"

"On the ACT and SAT. Yeah, I know, and it shows me how useless those tests are because you couldn't identify a work's proper genre if your idiotic football team's very existence depended on it."

"Leave my buddies out of this."

"You know what's weird, Mike? You know what's confusing the hell out of me? You're always talking about all your buddies who follow you around. Well, how come none of them are with you on this little trip? Why? Don't you find that odd? The big academic and sports stud travels alone one week before he's supposed to graduate, and his friends are nowhere to be seen? What, they don't have the same schedule as you? They don't graduate the same day as you? Something's not right, now is it? What's wrong, Mike? Coach got your tongue? Just where are these wondrous masses that supposedly followed you around for four years, throwing themselves at you?"

At first Tommy thought that a cue ball had struck him in the nose, but then he remembered that there was no pool table in the room. Then he thought that he had landed at the bottom of the Grand Canyon, but then he remembered that he was in Wisconsin. And as the sensation of drowning in a pool overcame him, he realized that he was nowhere near one, and that the choking sensation overwhelming him was blood draining down his throat.

"Oh, God, Tom Cat. I'm really sorry. Shit, let me get you a rag. No, better yet, here's the bedspread. It'll cover more space."

The words drifted through the barely conscious adult's confused mind. He had always wondered what people meant when they claimed to have seen stars after a major trauma, and now he knew what they were talking about. Large flashes of crystalline light circled in front of his opened eyes and bounced off the room's furniture, moving mysteriously through inanimate objects.

"Don't move, Tom Cat. Stay on the floor. I'm getting some ice."

Memories of his mother holding him in her arms after he fell out of his tree house filled Tommy's mind as he listened to the Sunday traffic passing by the motel.

"No, ice's bad—I think. Wait. What did Coach say? I before E except after C. Cold compact? Yeah, that's it."

Mike's jumbled thoughts only reinforced the helpless condition in which he found himself. Never one for violence, he knew that in the past two days he had inflicted physical pain on someone who he valued more and more with each passing moment. From the bathroom, the frantic graduate hollered, "Don't worry. I'm gettin' a washcloth super cold for you. That'll bring down the swelling, so you won't walk around with a zucchini instead of a nose. Be great if it were Halloween, but it's not. This'll be way better than ice because, well, we don't have any. Besides, ice that can cause a headrush, which you don't need. Wonder what causes that? You eat a spoonful of ice cream, and suddenly your head implodes. Just a tiny bit of ice cream does that. Do you know why? Stuff like this keeps me up at night. There must have been studies done. Or—wait. Opportunity. Opportunity knocks, my fine writer friend. Maybe you could do a study 'cause it's one of those obvious mysteries that's so obvious that it's been overlooked. Makes sense to me. They came up with solar energy, geothermal energy, fission meets fusion, heated car seats, but never this? I can see how it happened. So, I hand deliver it to you. It's all yours. You can take complete credit. Then you can add scientist to your resume."

Sopping washcloth in hand, Mike rushed to the horizontal man and lifted his head, careful not to raise it too fast. Using his thigh as a pillow, Mike placed Tommy's head on it and held the washcloth under the man's nose. "Here, this'll help. I've seen this done on the field tons of times. The bleeding'll stop once everything clots." Seeing his friend look up with disoriented eyes, Mike continued, but now his voice was shaky, emotional. "Hang in there, Tom Boy. I'm not going to let anything happen to you. Someone comes in here, and he's toast. Someone looks at you the wrong way, and I'm on it; I'm on him. Well, not on him, on him. Just take him out, on him." Tommy's eyes closed. "You know, I know that I haven't been the perfect model of self-control lately, but you hit a nerve with what you said. It's no excuse; I know that, but you don't know how hard this whole thing has been for me, graduation and all. How would you feel if your entire life was filled with praise and congratulations this and congratulations that? After a while you start buying the bullshit, but then it hits you: everything you do from now on is going to be measured against your past. I look around and see my friends, and then I realize that they're not always going to be around, and my teachers aren't going to be with me the rest of my life, telling me how terrific I am. And then I start thinking about having to start over, and you know what? That scares me. It really does. What if I don't measure up? What if my best days were in high school? After being pumped up with their crap about me being so awesome, I'm afraid that I'll fall flat on my face once I'm on my own.

"And you know what? I don't even know what I want to do in life, and I don't care 'cause I don't want to think about it. And do you know what else is painful? Not having any of the people I hung around with in school around me in college; instead of the star football player/Mr. Social/whiz kid, I'll just be another student. I won't stand out. So, I protect myself; I figure the best way to begin is to break away from my friends and pretend that they don't exist. That way I don't have to hurt when they stop calling, which always happens after high school, and I can make believe that they never existed."

Opening his eyes and looking up at Mike, Tommy saw that the seventeen year old was in tears. Long streaks lined his face, a tear falling onto a bloodied face that no longer held a glow. "Get away from me."

The graduate looked down at the man he held in his lap. "What?"

"I said get your stupid, ugly face away from mine, so I don't have to look at it anymore." Sitting up too quickly, Tommy fell back down, his head swimming in pain.

"Don't do that," Mike pleaded.

"Why? So you can keep me here as your punching bag?" Tommy whispered as his eyes shut.

"C'mon, Tom Boy. You're my friend. My first since high school. I wouldn't do anything to hurt you."

"Bashing my head with a beer can, my nose with a fist. You're a real peace loving guy. I can hardly wait to see what's next. And by the way, you're not a graduate yet. For all I know, you're some dropout who can't do simple arithmetic." Pulling himself from the distraught youth, Tommy climbed up to his bed and sat down, still clutching the drenched washcloth. "As soon as the bleeding stops, I'm getting out of here and away from you. You're a fucking lunatic, honor roll or not. I'll find a truck stop or something and call my parents, so they can pick me up. We're not that far from Milwaukee. They should be here in less than two hours."

"What? You're just going to leave me? After all we've been though, you're going to ditch me, walk out of here like none of this meant anything?"

"It doesn't. You got some pathetic notion in your head that you had to explore America, or find America, or whatever the fuck it was, and you ended up taking me. Why? You make me listen to these ridiculous, non-stop football stories that are somehow supposed to represent the Age of Enlightenment, and you end up beating me up. For what? To experiencing violence firsthand?"

"That's not why I did it."

"Look, Junior. You're reasoning doesn't interest me. All I know is that I don't have to sit around and take any more of this, and if you try to stop me this time I'll make sure the cops get here and arrest you for kidnapping, assault, and anything else I can think of, you got that? Is that clear enough for you, or is jail something you want to experience, too?"

Uncharacteristically silent, Mike remained motionless and watched as the unemployed man got up and gathered the articles that the graduate had purchased for him the previous day. Throwing each unused T-shirt, sock, and pair of underwear on the seventeen year old's bed, Tommy said, "I'll leave these with you because I'm not in the mood to walk down the road holding a load of laundry while trying to stop a massive nose bleed. Now, unless there's anything else you want to do to me, maybe pull out my fingernails or torch my hair, I'll be on my way. Have a nice day and thanks for the worst time of my life."

Brushing past the staid youth, Tommy opened the door and left, leaving behind a person who no longer had anyone he could call a friend.

The blinding sun forced Tommy to shield his eyes before walking another step. Smelling the strong scent of diesel fuel and hearing the distant blast of air horns, the man stood and considered the incongruous emotions he was experiencing. Hatred, pain, disgust, confusion, fatigue, understanding.

"Oh, no," he spoke. "That was major weirdness in there. There's no excuse for what he did to me. None."

"Hey, pipe down over there," a distant female voice called out. Looking around, the young man tried to determine from where it originated. For a moment, he believed it was Mike throwing his voice, attempting to intimidate the departing man, but that was too far-fetched, even for Tommy.

Boldness overcame the nineteen year old, and he called out, "Whoever that is, shut up."

"Go soak your head. Can't a woman get a good night's rest without some creep harassing her?"

Then he saw it plain as day: two feet dangled out the Pinto's side window, driver's side. Approaching the car as if it might be radioactive, Tommy peered in and saw an older woman scrunched in the back seat. Their eyes met.

"Mornin'. This your set of wheels?"

Withdrawing his head from the car, Tommy walked back to the motel room and knocked on the door.

"Go away, whoever it is."

"It's me."

Listening to the sounds of scurrying feet, Tommy became apprehensive about the man who would soon appear.

"Tom Boy. You're back," Mike cried with joy, his hand gripping the now opened door, as if to support him.

Deadly serious, Tommy motioned for Mike to move closer. "I don't know how to tell you this, but there's someone camping in your car. Deal with it, 'cause I'm outta here."

Puzzled, Mike replied, "Oh, I get it. This is some kind of plan to get me out of the room, so you can do something to me. Okay. Fine. I deserve it. Give me your best shot."

"I'm not gonna hit you. Just go to your car, and tell me what you see."

Looking over, the Pinto's owner cried out, "Aw, c'mon. Don't tell me someone took a nash and died in my car."

Withdrawing her feet from their position, the woman propped herself up and climbed out. Her long gray hair flew about like a demented woman who was terrorized by neighborhood children who considered her a witch and her house a coven. With arms extended, she ambled towards the two teens and asked, "Hug?"

Chapter 19

"Unreal," Mike shouted upon seeing the woman. Rushing over to her, he offered his hand and said, "Mike Warner. This is my car, and this is my best friend, Tommy Alvin."

Gawking at the nineteen year old, Alma asked, "What happened to your shnoz? You close a car door on it?"

Embarrassed by the torrent of laughs that the pair provided, Tommy looked at the graduate and the slender woman who wore a flowing gauze blouse and replied, "No, I did not. The person you're laughing with attacked me."

Winding up like a major league pitcher, the woman walloped Mike in the arm. "Violence is the root of all evil, you little shit."

"Ow," the teen whined, rubbing his left bicep.

"Name's Alma, global traveler," she directed at Tommy.

Shaking her outstretched hand, the bemused man replied, "Nice to meet you, isn't it, Mike?" Observing the youth's tortured expression, Tommy felt a surge of satisfaction.

"Yeah, great," Mike offered, not in the least bit convincing.

"Just got into town via Denver late last night. Going home, boys. Going home."

"Where's that?" Tommy asked.

"Not as far as it once was," Alma replied with a hint of nostalgia.

"And where might that be?" Mike asked.

"Right here where it counts most," she responded, her hand against her heart.

"Isn't that hard to navigate?" Mike replied, confident that his little jab was both humorous and assertive, thus establishing himself as the alpha dog.

"Not too bright, are you, son? The heart is all that matters."

"Pay no attention to him, Alma. He's a slow learner."

"And getting slower by the second, if you ask me."

"Don't get me started. Barely house broken. Thumb sucker. It's tragic."

"Shut up," Mike protested. "Both of you. I just asked for clarification. Nothing more. And I don't think that's out of line."

"But where is the line, Michael?" Alma inquired. "Is it some self-imposed sense of order that makes people go through life as if it's a series of tasks that needs to be accomplished before the final sendoff? Or is it that which resides in each of us and takes us to the limitless horizons of the soul?"

"Huh?"

Tommy reveled in the treatment that his cohort was receiving and relished every minute. If it were retribution that he was after, then he was positive that Alma would make a fierce ally. Tommy led her away from the Pinto and escorted her to the room. "I can't believe you slept there. The back seat's hard enough to sit in, let alone sleep."

"Tell me about it, but when the cash is gone and sleep calls, it'll do. You should have seen some of the places I ended up in South America. You'd think this car was the Waldorf after spending a couple months in a rubber tree hut."

"Did you say that you were out of money?" Tommy asked.

"Busted flat. Blew my last green back on a bus that took me from Tucumcari, New Mexico to the Mile High City. What's happened to Denver? I could barely breathe. Years ago it was so clear that the mountains looked like they were coming right at ya. Now they look brown. Someone asleep in the White House or what?"

Thrilled with the woman's cavalier disposition and worldly experience, Tommy knew that he had found someone who would appreciate his efforts and plans. Here, he considered, was an anachronism. An artifact. A rare breed of independence, guts, and integrity. The perfect foil to what he viewed as the culture's boring state of affairs.

"Oh, if only the gods would fix this twisted neck," she complained, rolling her head around. "This your room, boys? This ol' bat's gotta rest."

Tommy led the woman into the room, but with one quick glance at the wreckage, she blared, "God Almighty. What went on here?" Surveying the damage, she saw the bloody bedspread and washcloth, clothes strewn about, and crumpled notebook paper that dotted the gray, dappled carpet. Directing her attention to Mike, she asked, "You do this?"

The frightened youth took a step back and covered his groin. "Ah, I guess."

"Guess? Don't you know?" Turning to Tommy, she asked, "Is this his doing?"

Sentencing his friend to a certain dressing-down, the adult replied, "Yep."

Another sharp punch to the arm was leveled against Mike. "Ow. Knock it off, lady. He started it. He looks all innocent, but he's sly. Sly as a fox. Also, somewhat of a tease, if you know what I mean."

"Violence begets violence. Most important lesson I learned from a Peruvian Tribal Chief. And trust me: he knows how to settle a score. Touch this poor guy one more time, and you'll answer to me. Capiche?"

"Capiche? What are you, an extra from *The Godfather*?"

"Could be, rough stuff. Could be. And lose the attitude. If you were my son, I'd hog tie ya and ship you down river. What's the matter with you? You're big as a mountain and act like this? Didn't your folks ever teach you self-restraint?"

As if a dark cloud had been lifted, Mike broke out laughing and threw his arms around the woman, giving her a massive bear hug. "Alma, you're the type of person I've been looking for. You're it. America stands before me."

"What are you talking about?" she asked, throwing him on the bed. "I've been all 'round the world, and you label me? You know what I think of labels? Hate 'em. Spent the last twenty years tryin' to shed them, and you give me a new one within the first five minutes? You need an enema."

"Hey, hang on there, sister. It was a compliment. I've been searching for the real America, and you personify it. You've got more balls than half the guys out there."

"Just half? Let me tell you, kid. Ain't no one who's more on the ball than me. Remember that."

"You hungry, Alma? Mike's a walking Rockefeller. Let's make him feed us."

"That right, Michael? You some rich kid we can exploit?"

"Not rich, but if you wanna get wild you've come to the right place. My bud and I don't know any other way of life. Isn't that right, Tom Cat?"

The woman's rough charm was just what Tommy needed. If it were a champion he sought, he was certain this woman fit the bill. "That's right, Mike. But watch out. One false move, and I'll sic Alma on you."

"That's right, Thomas. Just give me the word, and I'll bean the dolt."

"Unreal," Mike announced. "Unreal."

The motel's restaurant was filled with patrons who frequented the establishment after Sunday Mass. Waitresses bustled about, and the cooks' attention was directed at the endless orders posted on green slips of paper that hung on a metal wheel.

"Wow. Check this place out."

Tommy wondered if the entire restaurant was cued because once they heard Alma's shrill pronouncement, they did what Janesville does best when strangers appear: stop talking. All eyes were on the three; however, the one who secured the most attention was the one who resembled an aging Earth Mother. Yet the short woman paid no attention to the silence and instead tossed her head side to side, absorbing the '80s decor. "These colors bug me. Too cold."

"I do believe we have a live one, Tom Boy."

"No doubt," the man replied, not in the least bothered by Mike's arm wrapped around the nineteen-year-old's waist.

"Hey, darlin'," Alma called out to a passing waitress. "How about a table and cup of java?"

Smiling at the pug woman, the waitress answered, "I'll be with you in a minute. Sunday morning rush. Gotta love it."

"Leave it to me, boys," Alma whispered. "Sleep a week in a Panamanian fish market, and you're ready for anything." Turning to the crowd, the woman added, "Back to your meals. Not a fan of eavesdroppers."

It didn't take long for the three to be seated and served, and as the youths attacked generous portions of chocolate chip pancakes and sausage links, Alma entertained the youths with detailed descriptions of the proper way to prepare Yerba Mate, where to locate the perfect gourd for drinking purposes, how to mix one's own Adobo, and why preparing thatched roofs should be required work for all. The woman was a one-stop resource of knowledge—and quite the food critic. "Get a look at this egg, Michael. Last time I was served one like this a Mexican ran over to me and knocked it off my plate. Said the water was safer. And this orange juice? I think not. More like synthetic fluid made in test tubes. Now, if you want real OJ, you need to head to Ecuador, but I'd push that aside and go for guava juice. Nectar of the gods, boys. Nectar of the gods. It'll recharge even the sorriest of souls."

"Tell us more about the places you've been," Tommy encouraged.

"Yeah, let's find out about the real world out there. Maybe one day I'll want to discover it."

"First America and now the world? What kind of water your folks giving you back home? You remind me of myself twenty years ago, Michael. Long before you were born. Exciting times. Change was in the air, and I had to have it. You can only sit on the sideline for so long before you need to get in the game. Lot of people won't though. And I was one of them for too long." The woman looked down at her napkin and placed it in her hands. Maintaining her stance, she began tearing small pieces. "Don't let anyone ever hold you down, boys. No one. Life's too short to live someone else's dreams. Find your own and make them happen."

Mike looked at Tommy and saw how he observed the woman, his iridescent hazel eyes, his warm smile, kindness emanating from his very being. And he never felt closer to another human being. "Listen to Alma, Tom Boy. She's been there; she knows what she's talking about. We can learn from her."

Recognizing the strained tone in his friend's voice, Tommy knew that in his awkward way Mike was atoning for his prior actions and doubts.

"And don't ever see life through someone else's eyes, boys. Do that, and you'll lose yourself," she added, barely able to continue.

Tommy saw that she was near tears and before he knew it, he had placed his hand over hers. Mike watched and was overcome with a deep sense of pride and love, the type that he had always sought but was positive he would never experience. He now realized how wrong he was.

"The biggest asset any of you has is yourself. I don't care what you plan or who you plan it with. Just make sure that it's someone who believes in you completely and won't abandon you when it looks like your dreams will never come true because they do, boys. They always do. Sometimes it happens early on. Other times it takes what seems like an eternity. But once you stop believing, once you surround yourself with someone who would rather have you settle for second best, then you're nothing more than a shadow of what you once were. And who wants to live like that?"

Reaching over and taking the graduate's napkin, she wiped her eyes and looked out the window, sunlight washing her face in a sea of brightness, revealing her majestic blue eyes surrounded by deep folds, each blended into a face that had weathered decades of expected behavior and the subsequent feeling of betrayal.

"How is everything?" the waitress asked.

"Fine. Can we have the check please?" Mike replied, respectful of the woman's fragile state.

After paying, the trio left the restaurant, Alma holding each teen's hand, walking silently down the cracked concrete that led to their room. Looking over at Mike, Tommy felt that maybe he had been too harsh and reactionary in his response to the youth's earlier words. You do have a habit of being a little thin skinned, he thought. So what if the guy read the screenplay? You pique his curiosity and then get pissed when he takes a look? Classy, Tommy. Classy. And maybe he's right. He couldn't have misread it that much to miss the point. Maybe it's me who's off track. Maybe I've come up with a comedy without even knowing it.

"You say that you're heading somewhere?" Mike asked.

"That's the place," Alma replied.

"Know what, Tom Cat? I think we can be of service. Perhaps Alma fancies a ride to her destination."

"What about your trip?"

"Slight diversion 'cause a journey never ends."

"That's what I'm talkin' about," Alma replied, her hands squeezing each teen's hand tighter. "More people thinkin' this way, and the world'll be just fine."

Jumping in front of the pair, Mike stood before the door and bowed. "Your chamber, my lady. Yours too, Alma."

"Ah, such a funny guy," Tommy replied.

"Sounds like a creep to me," Alma concluded as she brushed past Mike and crawled onto a bed. "Wake me up when there's something that can't be missed."

"Will do. Tom Boy? To the car. A cleaning awaits."

And with that, the two left the woman and proceeded to the yellow Pinto, which now took on a different look. "Good God. Was it always this trashed inside?" Tommy asked.

"Not sure. It does appear to have that lived-in look, though."

"Yeah, for squatters. Should we go to the store and get some cleaning supplies? Windex. Paper towels. Front end loader."

And just as Mike was to respond, he saw it: the driver's side shoulder harness was wrapped around the steering wheel and the directional, the headlight switch pulled outward. "Alma, don't tell me," he sighed. Untangling the harness, he put the seat back in position and turned the ignition key.

"Oh, no."

"Oh, yes, Tom Boy. Dead."

"Alma?"

"Under here," she called out, bed sheets covering her upright body.

"What are you doing?" Mike continued.

"Pyramid power. Draws in energy. You two should try it."

"Maybe later because we have, and I believe this is the technical term, a dead car battery."

"Not to worry. Synchronicity. You two get in the other bed and do what I'm doing. By channeling our energies and thinking positive thoughts, we'll get that sucker juiced if it's the last thing we do."

"Think I'll try a garage first," Mike responded.

"I'll go to the front desk and get a phone book."

"Thanks, Tom Cat. You're my personal savior. Next to Santa."

"See what I mean? The pyramids'll never let you down."

But an aged car battery will.

"Sorry, kid," the tow truck operator said to Mike. "I can jump this all day, but it's not going to do anything. You need a new battery."

"Can you go back to the shop and get a new one?" Tommy asked.

"Sorry, but we're not full service. We only do jumps and tire changes; we're not licensed to do sales. Have to wait 'til tomorrow. Doug's is up the road, and he'll have any battery you need. If you tell him where you are, they'll swing by and replace it. Here's his card."

"Mike, I'm sure this can't be the only operator in Janesville," Tommy assured his companion.

"Think again, kid. This is a religious community. Not much activity on a Sunday and not much outside of town but farmland. Wish I could help, but it's not going to happen. So, which one of you is going to pay me? You're looking at thirty for the service call."

Mike pulled out his sizable wallet and handed the man two twenties.

"Only need thirty."

"Lowest bill I have is a twenty. Would love to add a ten or two fives, though."

"No change. Thanks. You made my day."

"Dick," Tommy said under his breath.

"What did you say?"

"He didn't say anything."

"Yes, I did. You're in the business to help people in need, and you rip them off with your little game?"

"Look, pal."

"I'm not your pal."

"I came out here on a Sunday to help you and don't have tons of cash on me. Got it? I don't steal."

"But you love having someone make your day."

The mechanic glared at Tommy and took one step towards him.

"I don't think so," Mike said as he stepped in front of the man. "Thank you for making time for us. Bye."

The mechanic looked up at the youth who dwarfed him and then around him, Tommy in his sight. "Better watch your mouth, pal."

"He's working on it. And such a trick to pull off. Bye."

And with that, the mechanic got back in his truck and drove away, a *Jesus Saves* bumper sticker on his back fender.

"Jesus might save, but he doesn't make change," Tommy scoffed.

"Man, you are one dangerous mofo. And quite the blasphemer. That lightning strike should come any second, so I'm staying clear of you."

"Guy's a hypocrite. And a thief."

"And so he is. Now, time to strategize."

Alma opened the door and shielded her eyes from the sun. "Any luck, boys?"

"Nope. But some guy just stole ten dollars from Mike."

"Don't worry. Karma's a powerful force. He'll get his."

"And my ten?"

"You, Michael, will get it back in spades. You're a kind soul; the Universe knows it."

"So, what should we do, Alma? You're a woman of the world."

"Work with the now, Thomas, and forget the past. Follow the basic principle of Zen Buddhism: embrace the moment."

"I think that means we'll be spending another night here," Tommy translated.

"If that's where it leads," the woman responded.

"I'd say it does," Mike concluded. "I'll be right back, Alma. Don't take off with ET when I'm gone."

"Who's ET?"

"Oh, that's right. You've been gone awhile. Tom Cat'll explain it while I'm getting you a room for the night."

Staggering forward, she asked, "Whatta ya mean, my room?"

"I figured you'd want your own room. You don't want to stay with us. We're guys. We're gross. We might even have a sumo wrestling match later. We're unpredictable."

"Not a chance, Michael. I want to stay with you two. It's bad enough that you'll be shelling out money for another night because of me. I don't want you wasting any more of it on me. You were nice enough to make your car available last night, and now the battery's dead. Forget it. I'm staying." Casting a hurt expression at the pair, she added, "Unless you don't want me here."

"Are you kidding?" Mike replied. "You're the second best thing that's happened to me since high school."

As Mike directed his attention to Tommy, the unemployed man felt a deep sense of fellowship and belonging. He'd never felt this way prior to meeting Mike, and he wondered how he managed to live nineteen years without it.

"It's no trouble," Tommy said. "Remember, Mike's loaded."

Mike smiled, walked up to Alma, bent down, and gave her a warm embrace, which only made Tommy for confident that he was witnessing a youth well on his way to adulthood.

"I need to shower. Smell like a monkey," Mike said, grabbing some fresh clothes and making for the bathroom.

Alma stretched out her arms and motioned for Tommy. Taking his hand, she sat on the bed and motioned for him to do the same. "Thomas. You and your friend. You're like two peas in a pod. You remind me of my boys. Like oil and water, but you still manage to get together in the end. Kindred spirits. Must have been friends since birth."

"If you only knew. One day I'll put it down on paper, and you can read it. As a matter of fact, I'll probably use it in my first novel."

"A writer. This your paper mess on the floor?"

"I had some help."

"Then tell me everything about your writing. Don't leave anything out because Alma always gets what she wants. Just ask that Uruguayan high priest who tried to hold out on me. He was bragging like the big drunk that he is about levitation, saying that he could float in the air. Imagine that. So this ol' broad wants a demonstration, and do you know what the phony does? Tells me that he can only do it when certain planets line up. So, I stared him down and said, 'You know what, swami? You've got a lot in common with Uranus.' Shut that sucker up in two seconds flat. So, what about your writing? What's the inspiration that drives Thomas Alvin?"

"Life. I like to capture people at their weakest and bring them to their strongest. That's it."

"A man with few words is a blessed man, indeed," Alma told her captive listener. "There're plenty of fools out there who'd like to think of themselves as great artists, great thinkers. But unless you can see within yourself and tap into that special reservoir that holds your inner self, you'll be just like all the others who pretend and never are."

Squeezing her hand, Tommy confided, "I can't live that way. I can't become one of them; otherwise, I'll die."

"Yes, you will, Thomas. Don't ever lower your expectations." Shaking their clenched hands, she added, "Strive, strive to reach the heights that you know you can. Leave the commoners with their country clubs and transistor radios. Have them spend their money to experience you and not you blowing a wad with them to see someone else. The world's full of watchers, and I expect you to be the watched."

Breaking down, Tommy tried to stop his tears, but they were too strong. "Why couldn't you have been my mother? That's all I've ever wanted to hear my whole life."

Stroking his shiny brown hair, she replied, "Because you have a mother who did more for you than I ever could."

"That's not true," he choked.

"It isn't, is it? Do you think you got this way without any help from her or your dad? Think about it. You just met me; you've known them since you were born."

Sitting up and looking at her, Tommy sobbed, "You don't understand."

"Oh, yes, I do. You're the one who doesn't. Let me give you a heavy-duty piece of advice: don't always think that the people you admire most turned out that way because they enjoyed perfect childhoods. Far from it. Most were driven to achieve through rebellion, lashing out against convention, and most of the time their parents provided the impetus for change. Do you understand what I'm saying? Without a parent's mistakes and shortcomings, we'd be a bunch of non-thinking replicas of them. Is that how you'd like to be? Is that the type of life you want to lead?"

Breathing in and fighting back more tears, Tommy replied, "They humor me. Never encourage me."

"And how does that make you feel?"

"Mad, I guess."

"Don't you 'I guess' me," she scolded. "I want a real answer. Now, tell me how you feel."

"Pissed! Fuckin' pissed! I'm their son. I didn't ask to be born. It's their duty to pay attention to me and make me do things. Stay in school. Get a better job. Make more friends. Pay attention to the ones I have."

"And what if they don't?"

"Then they should quit calling themselves parents because they're not."

"And what would that make you?"

Staring at the woman, the man stopped his infuriated discourse and asked, "Alone?"

"All the novels in the world won't change that, now will they?"

Tommy swallowed hard and approached the window. "Why are you doing this, Alma? I never did anything to you."

"No, you didn't. But neither did your folks. Why not give 'em a break, Tom? They're the only ones you've got and ever will."

The bewildered man walked to the door and opened it without saying anything; Alma watched as he exited.

Clad in a towel wrapped around his waist, Mike ran out of the bathroom and asked, "What's going on? Where's Tom Boy? And what's up with the opened door?"

"It's called life, Michael. Someone experiencing growing pains."

"Come on. He's too old for that," Mike dismissed.

"You can be sixty-five and still come face-to-face with 'em. Remember that when you become a parent."

"Me? What are ya, nuts? That's the furthest thing from my mind. I'm not the marrying type."

"You will be," she assured him "You will be."

Grabbing his shoes and jeans, Mike went back into the bathroom and emerged shirtless, his wet hair slicked back. "Be right back, Alma. Gotta catch Tom Boy. See how he's doin'."

Rushing out the door before the woman could responded, Mike sprinted into the parking lot, just missing a gawking couple. "What're you lookin' at? Haven't you ever seen the wet look before?" he asked, leaving them speechless.

Kennedy Parkway was filled with traffic heading towards nearby parks, lakes, relatives, and churches. Looking both ways down the sidewalk, Mike attempted to secure his friend's direction, but he was nowhere to be found. And this worried the graduate.

"C'mon, Tom Boy. Don't play Hide and Seek."

On-lookers stared at the hurried man as he raced down the sidewalk. Where would I go if I were him? he considered. Where's the first place I'd high-tail-it to? A church? Nah, too religious. A store? Maybe, but I've got the money.

And just as he was ready to try another street, Mike saw Tommy sitting on a bus stop bench, his head lowered, shoes rubbing against each other, and sprinted to him.

"Boy, are you going to piss off the driver when you tell him that the ol' cashola's back in your hotel room."

"What do you want, Mike? I don't feel like company right now."

"That's okay," the teen assured his friend. "Neither do I."

"Then why are you here?"

"Just to see what you feel like doing today."

"Nothing."

"Okay. Are you going to be here tonight, too?"

"Shut up."

"I'm serious because if you are I'll be more than happy to run some food down here."

A city bus crawled to a stop, the noxious diesel scent overpowering the pair. "You guys getting on or waiting for another?" the driver asked.

"Neither," Mike replied. "Just working on our tans."

The driver mumbled something that neither could make out and pulled the massive vehicle away.

"Think I pissed him off. That Alma's too much, isn't she?"

"Do you mind? And what you said to the driver was disrespectful. My grandfather drove a city bus. Hard work. Shitty pay. And stop thinking that everything you say has to be a joke. It's doesn't. You just never let up. You go on and on and on. I feel like a parent who's got a whiny little terror who never shuts up."

Getting up, Mike replied calmly, "I don't know what went on back in the room, but as soon as you're ready, come back so we can get on with our day; we'll be waiting for you."

Stopping at a nearby doughnut shop, Mike picked up a half dozen chocolate covered plains and hurried back to Alma, who was engaged in her morning meditation.

"Chow time, Alma. Got you some rare delicacies from the far corners of Janesville." But before he was able to continue, a pillow flew in his direction.

"Quiet," the woman commanded, never once opening her eyes or breaking her cross legged position. "Can't you see what I'm doing?"

"Sitting on a bed?"

Another pillow sailed across the room.

"Interrupt my concentration one more time, and you'll pay."

Alma then resumed her meditative state. Enthralled with this exhibition, Mike sat on his bed, downed one of his breakfast-styled desserts, and wiped his fingers on the bloody bedspread.

"Oh, forget it. Ever since I got back in the states, my rhythm's been off."

"Here, have a doughnut. It'll take your mind off the state of the union," Mike quipped, tossing her the chocolate-smeared white bag. Watching the woman wolf down a doughnut within seconds, Mike sat back and took a long, satisfied look at this woman who intrigued him so. "Alma, are you one of those New Age people?"

"Who're they?"

"Not quite sure, but they have their own music. One word: boring."

"New Age? Sounds like a science class."

"Exactly."

"What kind of music?" she asked, attacking a second doughnut.

"You know, ocean tides, sounds of the forest. Harp shit."

"What's wrong with that?"

"Nothing, but give me Gun 'n' Roses any day."

Swallowing hard, Alma shook a chocolate-covered finger at Mike and warned, "Don't go making fun of them. You folks might have a nice American label for everything, but down in the real America, South America, nature's nothing less than a way of life. You know what, Mike? You remind me of myself a couple decades ago. Always doubting. But what I discovered changed my life."

Spurred by her intensity, he asked, "And what did you find down there that you couldn't find here?"

"Myself."

"Oh. Okay. But what does a pyramid have to do with the real you?"

"I already told you. Energy. My total being. Why waste your time around here when you can go south and discover your place in nature? There are incredible happenings going on down there, Michael. You ever hear of crystals and how they purify your soul?"

Mike shook his head.

"Then let me be the first to inform you: they'll change your life; they did for me. Hang a couple 'round your neck and go about your business. In no time flat, you'll be a new person. They're a miracle."

Mike examined the woman closely, looked about the room, and saw that she didn't have any on display. "So, where're yours?"

"Gave 'em to a darling ticket agent at the Greyhound station in Denver. She was having a dickens of a day, so I took off the crystal necklace I was wearing and gave it to her. Made her day, I'll tell you that."

"But what if you need them?"

"Ach. That poor girl needed them more than I did; besides, I can always get more. That's the beauty of crystals. They're all around you."

"If you say so," the skeptical graduate replied. "Alma, did your family enjoy their travels as much as you?"

"They didn't go with me. I was alone."

"But when they came down to visit, didn't they have some kind of reaction to your surroundings? Peru's a little different than the Midwest."

"Michael, you surprise me. How could my husband afford a family trip like that? He's not made of gold."

"Well, when you visited them then. You probably brought back a lot of artifacts and stuff."

"No, you've got it all wrong, my friend. I left my family and went to the jungles of South America. They didn't know I was going. One day I just up and left."

Stunned, Mike responded, "With no warning?"

"I left them a note," the woman replied with the slightest tinge of defensiveness.

"A note? You left your children and explained everything on a Post-it note?"

"What's that?"

"Never mind. I mean, didn't your husband chase after you or anything? Didn't he hire a private detective or contact the State Department?"

"Why? He knew that what I was doing was in everyone's best interest."

Getting up and pacing, Mike struggled with his conflicting emotions. "Leaving your family was in their best interest? How? Why? Did you knock off a bank or something?"

"Michael, sit down. C'mon. Right next to me."

Staring at the woman, Mike wasn't sure he wanted to know this woman anymore, yet he complied.

"So, you think I'm a nasty old woman who left her family and didn't have the nerve to contact them for twenty years?"

"Twenty years," Mike repeated in amazement.

"Quiet. Let me continue. Yes, it was twenty years. The longest years of my life. You know how strong a mother's protective instinct is? Plenty strong, I assure you, and there's nothing I wouldn't do for those boys, including a long, painful separation that tore me away from them."

"I still don't get it. Why did you have to leave?"

"Because I was dying."

Mike's mouth dropped open. Examining every inch of the woman's face, he asked, "Are you okay now?"

"More than okay. I'm revived and invigorated. There's nothing that I can't conquer now, and I want everyone to know that."

"But I still don't know why you had to run out on your family. Aren't you worried that they'll hate you for what you did to them?"

"I don't believe in hate," Alma schooled the young man. "Hate is nothing more than our inability to deal with our own insecurities. I got over mine, and I know that I can help my family get over theirs. They say leaving a child is the worst thing a mother can do. Not so. Not being the real you is far worse."

"I don't know. I'd sure be sore if my mom did that to me."

"Then you must be a selfish boy. Do you think that a woman who leaves her children is a heartless coward who can't face the responsibilities of motherhood? Is that how you view me? Then let me tell you something, Michael. It takes a lot more courage to leave those you love than it does to stick around and make them as miserable and unfulfilled as you."

Shaking his head, unsure of the woman's philosophy, Mike asked, "So, now you're returning, but what if they don't want you back?"

Alma looked at the graduate and smiled. "Who could ever reject their mother?"

Chapter 20

Another bus driver stopped and barraged Tommy with a litany of less-than-pleasant remarks after the teen insisted that he had no intention of boarding the vehicle, so the nineteen year old left his resting place and continued up the street, pausing at each storefront window. "One two three four, who the hell we cheering for?" he muttered, gazing at his reflection in a vacant store's window. "Not me," he concluded, his voice somber, crestfallen.

"You got the time?" a female voice queried.

Turning, he saw a young woman sporting leopard skin Spandex pants eyeing him up. Her midnight black dyed hair rose to a dramatic peak and had sharp, jagged bangs masking her mascaraed eyes.

"What?"

"You got the time?"

"No, but I think it it's around noon," he replied, innocent as a newborn.

"Not that kind of time," the female teased.

Tommy stared at the slight, young girl and tried to figure out what she meant. And then it came. "Oh. I, ah—no. I don't. I was waiting for my friend who's looking for me," he fumbled.

"Bet you two could make time for the right girl."

"No, no," he blushed. "See, we're stranded at our motel, and …"

"Perfect."

"No, no. Definitely not perfect because we have an old lady with us who …"

"I like your style, boy," she oozed while drawing the frantic youth towards her. "You're a real tiger. The two of you and the two of us? Me likee."

"No, no. No likee. She's over sixty. See, my friend and I are together, trying to find America, and we ended up in Janesville, and we're trying to find our way. You know. Seeing what can be seen."

"Don't worry, honey," she purred. "You can click your ruby slippers after we're done. I've turned on even the gayest of gays."

Alarmed, Tommy responded, "No, no. Got it all wrong, miss. Straight. Very straight. Card carrying straight."

"Miss? I'm not the prom queen. Let's work with Mumsy."

"Incredibly straight. Hooter alert straight. Love the female form."

"Perfect. Early in the day. Plenty of time to play."

"No, no. That won't work because I'm only looking for my friend, and then we'll be on our way, so if you'll excuse me, miss, I need to …"

"Mumsy."

Swallowing hard, he choked, "Mumsy. Right. Nice to meet you and have a pleasant day. I think it'll be sunny and warm, so …"

"Not for long. Rain's coming."

"Oh. Then stay out of the sun unless you've wearing sunblock and invest in an umbrella. Bye."

Bolting from the woman, his heart beat rapidly as he rushed up the street, only to hear the unmistakable sound of Mumsy calling out, "Hey! Hey, Daddy. Come to me, and everything'll be all right. What's the matter? Don't you like me?"

"Do you mind?" Tommy asked as he increased his stride.

"Of course, I don't mind. Why else do you think I'd be in the business?"

Turning, Tommy stopped and held up a hand, ending her determined advance. "I don't know, and I don't care."

"Oh, you do, too, you big liar," she replied, rubbing the besieged man's chest. "Don't give me that."

What did I ever to do deserve this? he thought. "Look," he began. "I'm not sure of anything or anyone right now. Two days ago I was leading a happy life, making lots of plans, and all of a sudden I'm surrounded by a bunch of people who claim that they know what's best for me. And now you."

"And just think: I'm all yours," the girl beamed.

"No, you are not mine. You have the street, and I have a crummy hotel room."

"For the second time, just in case you have a hearing problem, sounds good to me."

"Will you stop saying that? I'm not interested, got it? Nothing you have interests me. Is that clear enough for you, or do I have to call a cop and have you run in?"

Laughing, she pushed him towards the sidewalk's edge and a line of on-coming traffic. "You wouldn't do that. You're too nice."

"That's where you're wrong. I'm not nice. Everyone thinks I am, but I'm not. I'm mean. Mean as snakes. I'm your worst nightmare. I make Hitler look like Mother Theresa. I steal candy from senior citizens. I give Trick-or-Treaters coffee-flavored hard candy."

"Now, that's the lowest of lows," the girl yawned, smoothing out her low cut ocean blue tank top.

"And that's just the beginning, so take off because I'm not interested in what you have. The sooner I'm out of this city the better. I've got lots of projects that need my attention, and you're interfering with my well-laid plans. Now, is that direct enough for you, or should I issue you a memo?"

"Ooh, the way your face lights up when you get angry. Shows power. Lots of energy."

"And now you can watch it in real time as I walk away. Have a nice day."

Tommy stomped his way up the street, trying to place in perspective the day's revelations. "Alma makes it seem like I'm responsible for my lot in life," he muttered. "Wrong. I could be on top right now if I would've only had some encouragement from home. You can't expect a child to make it without parental support. What a joke. My whole life's a joke."

"Who're you talking to?" the girl asked, breathless after chasing the man.

"Look, lady."

"Mumsy."

"Whatever."

"No, not whatever. Mumsy. My name's Mumsy. Now say it. It's not that hard. Mumsy. Like the flower with a Y at the end."

Without moving his mouth, Tommy hissed, "Mumsssyy. There. Better?"

"You've got a snake thing goin' on, but I'll overlook it. So, where're we goin'?"

Beside himself, Tommy announced, "I'm losing my patience."

"Then you better go back to medical school," Mumsy laughed.

"Oh, funny. Very funny. You must write for Richard Pryor."

"No, but I bet I could," she announced, still laughing. "I've got a whole routine that I'm working on. Soon as I get my break, I'll be filling the best comedy shops 'round the country."

"Yeah, the kind that sells leather teddies in the front window."

"Hey, don't get smart with me, kid," the girl commanded. "We all can't be college boys living off mom and dad's charity."

"No, of course, not. Some live off johns and Gummy Bears."

Grabbing his right arm and digging her nails into his forearm, Mumsy warned, "One more comment like that, and my fingers go to China. Got it?"

Breaking free, the alarmed man screamed, "You are out of your mind. Get out of here before I call a cop."

"You want the police? Do you, college boy? Then here." Tearing through her ripped purse, she pulled out a quarter and threw it at Tommy.

"Hey, watch it."

Pulling out additional change, Mumsy continued to pelt the man. "And then you can call the fire department, the mayor, the high school principal, your dorm director."

"All right, enough," he demanded, grabbing her pitching arm.

"Let me go, college boy."

"Not until you promise not to throw anything else at me."

"Let me go."

"Not a chance. I want a promise first."

But what he got instead was a well-driven knee in the groin. Falling to the pavement, Tommy curled in a fetal position and tried to catch his breath.

"Think you can push a woman around?" she asked the incapacitated man. "I know a lot of ways to deal with mashers like you. The streets are full of you creeps, and I know how to fight, so watch it. I'm on to you. Maybe next time you'll think twice about attacking a defenseless girl."

"You're many things, Mumsy," Tommy groaned. "But you're about as defenseless as a nuclear missile."

"Damn straight." Helping the man up, she brushed off his pants and commented, "Wish the city'd spend more time cleaning this place up. Dirt's everywhere."

"Do you mind?" Tommy protested. "People are watching."

"So what? It'll give 'em a lift."

"Yeah, right. Watching a hooker dressed in leopard pants rubbing against a guy is Sunday picnic conversation."

Pushing him towards traffic again, she insisted, "I am not a hooker. Don't ever say that again, or I'll deck you so fast you won't know what hit you. I'm a model. I get paid. Lots. More than you'll ever make, kid."

"Oh, I'm sure you do," Tommy replied in his sarcastic best. "Mumsy in the raw posters must hang in garages all over Janesville."

Enraged, the girl punched Tommy in the right eye. "There. It'll look good with your mangled nose."

Landing flat on his butt, the assaulted adult swam in pain while breathing in the distant aroma of fried chicken.

"Wanna go three rounds?"

"What did you do that for?" the humiliated nineteen year old asked through a stream of tears.

"Oh, quit your crying. I didn't hit you that hard."

"I am not crying, lady," Tommy insisted. "You bashed in my eye ducts. What did you expect would happen?"

"Well, don't blame me. You need to be more considerate of people's feelings."

"I'll keep that in mind next time I'm at a hooker convention." Struggling to get up, Tommy was pushed back down by a determined foot.

"I am not a hooker! I am a model. Practically famous. Big. Huge. And I don't need some weakling telling me I'm not. Try it again, and I'll reposition your mouth with my shoe."

"Little trick you picked up from modeling?"

Unable to dodge the swiftness of a pink pump traveling towards his chin, Tommy's head arched to the heavens on impact and sent his seated body backwards.

The sound of screeching brakes drifted through his mind as a motorist jumped out of his car and screamed, "What're you doing, lady? Trying to kill this guy?"

"Back off, Chester. He's my boyfriend. I'll treat him any way I want."

"You don't have to kill him," the alarmed man replied.

"Get lost," Mumsy responded.

"Hey, buddy. You okay? You look like a truck hit you."

Propping himself up with his elbows, Tommy looked at the concerned driver and asked, "Mom?"

Completely thrown, the man turned to Mumsy and said, "He's all yours. You deserve each other."

"Yes, we do. Now buzz off."

Shaking his head, the driver got back into his car and drove off, leaving Mumsy and Tommy alone on the sidewalk.

"Here, let me help you up," she said while bending over and latching herself to an arm. "God, you're skinny. You should work out."

Shaking his arm loose, Tommy responded, "So, I heard. You and Mike should get together. You could say it in harmony."

"Boyfriend?"

"No, he is not. Now, knock it off."

"Don't get mad."

"Don't get mad, she says. First, she accosts me, practically tears my clothes off …"

"Hey, who're you talking to?"

"Chases after me, punches me, kicks me in the face …"

"Hey, kid. You're talkin' crazy talk. I'm standin' right in front of you, and you're pretending like there's someone else here. Your head all right?"

Looking up at her, Tommy shot back, "Of course, my head is not all right. What did you expect to happen? I probably have a massive concussion and'll die from a cerebral hemorrhage in my sleep tonight. That's how FDR died, you know."

"Who that, your uncle?"

Amazed at the girl's ignorance, Tommy replied, "Yes. My long lost uncle. Father's side."

"See? I'm an intuitive girl. Is your boyfriend like me—I mean, as far as patience goes because from what I've seen you must be a real pain to be with."

Standing, Tommy rubbed his forehead and announced, "I'm going. Goodbye."

"No, don't do that," she protested. "You're the nicest guy I've talked to today."

"Starting a little early, aren't you?"

"If that's another hooker joke, I'll bust your jaw and rearrange your face."

"You've already done that. Have a nice life."

"Oh, c'mon. Just have lunch with me. There's a great restaurant ahead. Wendy's. Ever hear of it?"

Dumbfounded, Tommy answered, "No. Must be a Janesville institution."

"No, it's a franchise. My brother used to work there. We should check it out. They've got the best shakes."

"Goodbye."

"Please?" Mumsy whined. "I promised not to follow you if you have lunch with me."

"Not a chance."

Sensing that she was about to do something, Tommy cringed in horror as she let out a sharp scream, attracting the attention of motorists who slowed down. Panicked, the youth dove and covered her mouth. "All right, all right," he agreed. "Just stop screaming. You're making a scene."

Delighted with her performance, she jumped up and down. "I won, I won. I love winning. Best feeling in the world."

"So is solitude," he mumbled as she took his hand and skipped down the sidewalk, pulling the nineteen year old as if he were a bruised and bleeding rag doll.

After receiving her substantial order and securing a Coke for her captive guest, Mumsy selected a back booth and brushed away a discarded ketchup pack and some spilled salt. "So, how long have you and your boyfriend been together?"

"There has to be some way we can get around this dating crap that you insist on believing."

Chewing a sizable portion of her hamburger, she replied, "Okay, kid. No more questions about your sex life if you quit making those stupid jokes about me. Agreed?"

"Fine."

"So, what's a good looking guy like you doing in a dumpy city like this?"

"Just passing through. And by the way, I don't think this is a dump. Just needs a fresh coat of paint and a little hope."

"Don't we all?"

"Some more than others," he responded, dodging a tossed French fry.

"Where's home?"

"Suburbanland. Milwaukee."

"Ah, rich kid."

"Not at all."

"Yeah, right. My cousin's husband grew up in that area, and he's rolling in money. Boy, did she luck out. Got it made. But you know, once my modeling career takes off, I'll be way richer."

"I'm sure you will," he replied, trying to sound convincing.

"So, what happened to your nose? You and your friend have a spat?"

Not appreciating the inference, Tommy returned, "I thought we had an agreement."

"Okay," Mumsy relented. "How's this: did you and your friend get in a fist fight?"

"That's better and, yes, we did."

"Bet he won."

"Yes, he won hands down. Let me ask you something: are you always this rude to people you just met? Is it that inconceivable that I could have been the victor?"

"More like Victoria."

"That's it." Getting up and heading towards the door, Tommy was followed quickly by Mumsy who ran up and latched on to his T-shirt. "No, don't go. I'm sorry. That was a cheap shot. Sometimes my jokes don't always come out the way I want them to."

"Then you should be more careful with what you say," Tommy replied. Exasperated, he continued. "God, this whole weekend. Nothing, none of this makes sense. Now I'm stuck in some fast food haven talking to a girl who doesn't even know who FDR is."

"Yes, I do. Only president who was elected to four terms, the last of which was cut short by his untimely death. Succeeded by Harry Truman from the great state of Kansas. I was just messin' with you back there."

"Too late. See you on *Wheel of Fortune*."

"It was just a joke. Don't be so touchy. I'm sorry if it didn't come out the right way. Thought we were having some fun, that's all."

"If you can't figure out what's funny and what's not, then maybe you should consider taping your mouth shut."

Mumsy's mouth quivered and she looked away, her hands rubbing the Spandex's slick material. "You don't have to be mean. I've got feelings, you know. Not everyone has the fortunate background that you have."

Torn between guilt and flight, Tommy relented and ambled back to the table, Mumsy right behind. "Sorry. That was mean."

"I win. I win again. I love winning," she cried, clapping her heads and jumping up and down, putting to rest her downcast performance.

"And I keep losing."

"So, what're your plans for today? You and your friend going to show the old lady a wild time?"

"Tell me if this sounds familiar: be a little nicer to people you don't know. She's a terrific human being."

"What're you talking about? I was being nice," she replied, mustard now smeared above her mouth after sniffing the last piece of her hamburger and wincing.

Using his napkin, he leaned over and wiped off the condiment. "So, don't make a sexual joke at her expense."

Mumsy was taken aback by the act and tried to control a voice that she was sure was about to tremble. "I wasn't."

"Good."

"Look, kid …"

"And stop calling me that. You're probably younger than I am."

"Okay, okay. So touchy."

"Actually, not."

"So, college boy—that better? What school do you go to?"

"I'm not in school at the moment."

"You're still in high school?"

"No."

"Then what do you do for a living, college boy?"

"I'm kind of in between jobs right now."

"Ah, got fired."

"Yes, I did, and I don't feel like talking about it."

"Like your anger, college boy. Makes you sexy."

"Insight from your profession?"

"Hey," she blurted out. "If that's some kind of insult, you're going to be sorry after I wallop you."

"Cowgirl that you are."

"Look, college boy. I've had it with your lip."

"Sorry, dad."

"And your lame humor doesn't mean that I'm incorrect, so watch it." Playing with her scuffed red tray, she added, "Take the compliment. They don't come around often enough."

Tommy slid his extra-large Coke back and forth between his hands and considered the truth that she had just shared. Life isn't always filled with compliments, much less encouraging words. "Thanks. You done yet? I need to leave soon."

"Hey, I'm shoveling it down as fast as I can. You don't want me to fall over and die, do you? When you eat too fast, it's a shock to the system. People've keeled over 'cause of that."

"Fine," Tommy relented. "Take your time then. It'll provide more fuel to get through your hectic day."

"Thanks. That's the way I look at it."

I'm sure you do, he thought, amazed at the girl's missed perception.

"Hey, college boy. I bet you'd never think of me as a brain but when I was in high school, I was on the debate team. Concert choir, too. Not too bad, is it?"

"A true accomplishment. Probably had little difficulty hitting the high notes."

"Right on the money. In fact, I was one of the teacher's favorite students before I had to leave."

"Get kicked out after a bad night's performance?"

"No. My dad and I moved. He got a new job, mom got a new friend and didn't want to leave, blah, blah, blah."

"What was your new school like?"

"Never went."

"You had enough credits to graduate?"

"Nope."

"Oh. Go the GED route?"

"Nope."

"So, nothing?"

"Yep."

"Any particular reason?"

"Dad got sick. Lung cancer. My brother was in no position to care for him, so I did."

"Younger brother?"

"Older. Has a learning disability. Had to take care of him, too."

"Wow. Awful. And mom?"

"Like, did she ever come back and beg for forgiveness and get a job at a Fortune 500 company, and we all lived happily ever after? No. She's dead. Well, not dead dead. Just dead to me. She's still with that guy. New family. New arguments. New drama."

"And your dad?"

"Died in January."

"Wow. And your …"

"Stop saying wow. I'm not a magic act."

"Sorry." The two sat silently and listened to the restaurant's activity. Orders placed, dispensers dispensing, metal utensils hitting metal surfaces, nondescript conversations filling the faux red brick interior. "How's your brother doing?"

"In a home. More like a one source place. Live there, work there, learn there. Menial stuff, but there you go."

"Have you thought about going back to school? Everyone needs a high school education."

"Says who?"

"Well, just think how much more money you could make if you got your diploma and found another job. Maybe even go to college."

Laughing at the suggestion, Mumsy replied, "You have no idea how much money I clear when I decide to work. Tax free. Guys take me to great restaurants, tell me about their wives and kids, the dog, and then let me stay in their hotel room when they leave for an early morning flight. Get to stay until checkout time. Entire place to myself. Know how most of 'em fund their little activity? Expense accounts. Not bad, huh? Nice way to milk the company."

Looking down at her tray filled with hamburger wrappings and napkins, each crumped and smeared with mustard and ketchup, she added, "You know, college boy, it's not that bad. All you have to do is pretend that you're somewhere else like a white sandy beach or a movie set with Richard Gere in your bed, and everything is just fine. Exotic. You should try it."

"No, thanks," Tommy responded. "I'll leave Richard for you."

"It's not so bad. Money's great. Dad got all the medicine that disability didn't cover. Sometimes I can pay the rent four months in advance. Dad used to like these really expensive chocolate chunk cookies at the mall, so I'd buy him a ton. Did this all on my own. No help from anyone. You might look down on me for my line of work, but I'd like to see you or anyone else swing this." Gazing at Tommy, she added, "But you won't. None of you will. Always easier to criticize than try and understand why people do what they do."

The two sat in silence for what seemed like an eternity to the pair. Both felt a distinct pain in their hearts, as if an unspoken truth had been uttered, and its painful implication was devastating. Tommy considered all that he had said to Mumsy and was mortified by his callous words; she in return lamented drawing this stranger into her private world.

"So," she began. "Guess you should be on your way. Your friends are probably wondering where you are."

"Yeah, I guess," Tommy responded. "What are you going to do?"

"What do you think? There's a convention at the Civic Center Monday that goes until Thursday. People are comin' in today. Normally, everyone stays at the Marriot when there's a big gathering, so I'll hang out there for the next couple days." Climbing out of the curved plastic booth, she grabbed her tiny purse and added, "Business calls, you know."

"Mumsy," Tommy said, stopping the girl cold. "How old are you?"

Before replying, she caught her reflection in one of the restaurant's smoked glass mirrors that lined the back wall, each adorned with gold painted swirls. "Ah," she stumbled. "I was sixteen 'bout a million years ago."

"I don't follow."

"Nor should you. Be good, college boy."

Before Tommy could stop her, she sprinted out a side door and disappeared into a crowd that had gathered at the scene of a fender bender. Standing on his toes, trying to peer over the crowd through a nearby window, Tommy searched in vain for Mumsy. She was on to something, he thought. When all else fails, maybe all that's left is to dream and believe.

Walking back to the hotel, Tommy considered all that he had encountered during his days with Mike. The Nike parking lot episode brought a smile to his lips that segued into the image of waking up with Mike's arms wrapped around him. Laughing aloud, the nineteen year old saw the two of them drinking beers, wasted, sprawled on twin beds, and remembered the exchanges that followed, allowing each to discover who the other was. "That was nice," he said. "That was really nice."

Laughing at the weekend memories, he made his way back to the motel and struggled with his key before Mike opened the door. Placing an index finger to his mouth to silence the entering man, the graduate said in a hushed tone, "Shh, Alma's asleep."

As if walking on egg shells, the pair tiptoed into the room.

"Mike, she looks dead."

"Kind of, but she's not. By the way, she's a snorer. Worse than you. Where've you been?"

"Nowhere. Just walked around and came back here. What did you two do when I was away?"

"Played Name that Planet."

"Who won?"

"Astro Alma. Wanna a beer? Our guest couldn't believe that beer cans no longer have flip tops that pull off, so I bought a case just so she could see for herself. Should have seen her at the checkout. Never saw a scanner before."

"We've got twenty-four beers?"

"Twenty. We each had two, and then she fell asleep."

"I could stand one. You?"

"Sure," Mike replied, making for the bathroom's ice-filled sink and returning with two Millers. Sitting next to Tommy, the graduate handed one to his comrade and knocked their cans together. "A toast," he whispered.

"To what?"

"To a Sunday in Janesville. To Alma the Magnificent. To a face that looks like a cement truck drove over it."

"Naturally. Was wondering when you were going to comment."

"Shit, I could see it before I opened the door. Face it, Tom Boy—pun intended: disaster follows you. You're a knock 'em, sock 'em kinda guy. That's why you're a superstar, in my book."

Taking a huge gulp of beer, Tommy gurgled, swallowed, burped, laughed at his action, and turned back to Mike. "I suppose you want to hear every last detail of my latest humiliation."

"Nope. Figure you'll tell me when you want to tell me. If not, I'll read about it in one of your books," Mike replied, the calming sounds of a soft, steady rain becoming nothing less than atmospheric.

Smiling at Mike's recognition, Tommy leaned into the youth, knowing full well that he had made a very good friend indeed.

Chapter 21

"Jonathan, there's no way I'm going to stand around a parking lot selling silly T-shirts to a bunch of wacked out hippies. Am I making myself clear, or do I have to knock some sense in your head?"

Grabbing Shanda's arm, Tony warned, "Show some respect to my brother, or I'll pour bong water down your throat."

"Hades," she roared, pulling herself free. "If you're going to stand there and allow your motley brother to rape me, then I'll call the real police, the ones who aren't afraid to uphold the law and protect its citizenry."

"Oh, don't do that," Ben pleaded. "I don't think I have enough food for all of Jon's friends. When I planned this brunch, I was only expecting the four of us." Looking at his youngest son, the Peters' headman asked, "Jonny, do you think applesauce will tide your buddies over until I whip up another quiche?"

"That is enough," Jonathan declared. "You're being ridiculous, Shanda, and so are you, Tony. Now, everyone stop it, or Ben and I'll leave the two of you here and go somewhere else. Damn!"

"Now, you listen here, Mister Potty Mouth. One more outburst, and you can spend the rest of your life selling drug runner shirts with Poncho Villa here until the cows come home because I will not tolerate verbal abuse. I am a contemporary woman, and you darn well better appreciate that right here and now because I'm not changing, but you sure as heck better if you know what's good for you."

All eyes were on the policeman. Opening his mouth, Jonathan looked back at the three and tried to speak, but nothing came. And just as he was about to try again, the telephone rang.

Leaning past his brother, Tony grabbed the phone. "Hello? Yes, she's right here … Interesting … Just a sec. I'll find out." Turning to his adversary, he asked, "Hey, Painful Rectal Itch. Census bureau needs clarification. Male, female, or other?"

Breathing in, her shoulders rose to the point that they nearly burst out her camouflage blouse. The enraged woman then reached over, grabbed a fist full of butter, and threw it at her nemesis, missing him and showering the refrigerator.

"Oh, my. That looks slippery. Wonder if I'll have to wear weightlifting gloves tomorrow."

Hanging up the phone, Tony announced, "Not to worry. They said they'd mark all three and call it a day."

Ben took a few strategic steps back and stood behind Jonathan. "Oh, Tony. I don't think you should play with the telephone. They have laws against that, and Shanda does like her rules. And let's not forget that she also appreciates a good streak knife."

But all the woman did was pull out a kitchen chair and sit. After surveying the array of food, she nonchalantly dished out various portions and poured herself a glass of orange juice. "Big Ben? Could you please get some more butter?"

"From outside the fridge or in?"

"Either one. I don't want to make any trouble for you. Jonathan, why are you standing there looking like dead wood? Come sit next to your bride. This is quality time we're sharing now."

Looking at both his father and brother, the policeman inched his way to the table and lifted a chair, its back protecting his groin. "Is everything all right?"

"Of course, it is. Lost my temper for a second, but I'm better now. Well, come on, everyone. Grab a seat and dig in. Nothing worse than trying to melt a pad of butter on an ice cold waffle."

So, you little hippie varmint. You want us to help you out tomorrow night? Well, that's just fine with me because the sheriff's department is going to be pleased after catching you red-handed with your marijuana cache. Then with you out of the way, Jonathan can be taught a thing or two about the kind of law and order that I demand, Shanda schemed.

"Hey, Tony. Who's going to be selling your shirts once the concert starts?" Ben asked.

"Don't know. Be a drag to lose a sale to those arriving late."

"Well, I could do it when you three kids are at the show. I don't have a ticket anyway, and I promise to be careful when making change. I'll watch you real carefully and take notes about what I should say. It'll just be like I'm in school. Stay up all night, outline my chapters, cram for my test."

Jonathan heard part of his father's plans, but the suspicious bridegroom had something else on his mind. What are you up, to Shanda? he thought. This is not like you to back down from a fight.

"Isn't it exciting? I've always wanted to go into business with one of my sons, and now I'm doing it. *Peters and Father.* Million dollar name. What do you think, Tony? How's that sound?"

"Sounds like a drag, Ben," his son replied, a waffle corner sticking out his mouth. "More of a solo act; besides, Jon and I need you here. You're our anchor. Isn't that right, bro?"

"He's an institution," Shanda cut in. "Aren't you, Big Ben?"

"I try to be. Hey, Jon Jon. What time will you be home tomorrow? Early, I hope."

Drawn out of his near trance, the bridegroom replied, "I don't know. The Warner case has my sole attention right now. Not quite sure when I can leave because everything hinges on whether something breaks."

"Well, don't you worry about a thing," Shanda said, patting her fiancé's hand. "You'll get to the bottom of this horrible crime and see that justice is served. Don't you agree, Tony?"

Eyeing Shanda, the bastion of counterculture opened his mouth and displayed its mashed, multi-colored contents.

Ignoring the man's actions, Shanda looked away and thought, Go ahead, you lily-livered beatnik. Twenty-four hours from now I'll have you exactly where I want: in the pokey.

Jonathan leaned over to Tony and muttered, "By the way. Who called?"

"Not a clue. Took a chance and ran with it."

Chapter 22

As the morning sun shone on Tommy's face, drawing him into consciousness, he noticed that once again Mike's arm was wrapped around him, and the nineteen year old never felt more secure. After all the confusion, trauma, chaotic situations, and off-beat people, the aspiring celebrity felt a strong bond with his newfound friend, one created by strange and intense encounters that became more intriguing by the day. Getting up, yet careful not to awaken his friend, Tommy looked over at the sleeping woman and snickered, amused by the two people with whom he found himself.

"Hey," Mike's groggy voice called out. "You up for the day?"

"Think so. Travels seem to bring out the adventurist in me. Maybe the sentimentalist, too."

"Perhaps next will be nudist. They travel in threes, you know," Mike offered, dragging himself off the bed. "Another day gone, numerous days left, Tom Boy. Options are limitless."

"Why don't you get cleaned up and call a garage? Must be open by now."

"Nah, I'll just walk over to the place up the road that the service guy told us about. Catch a ride back with a mechanic."

"Don't you feel grungy?" Tommy asked.

"Do I look it?'

"A tad."

"Then I'm set."

After dressing and a quick toothbrushing, Mike scurried out the door and up the road. There he walked along motorists inching their way to full-time jobs and unfulfilled careers. "Better you than me," he directed to a Saab that tore through the right shoulder, passing a semi while assaulting the youth with gravel. "One more stunt like that, and you'll be spitting out your teeth, bucket brain," he shouted at the car, waiving a clenched fist as if he were an elderly man screaming, "Get off my lawn."

As Mike continued his trek, Tommy worked quietly around Alma, hoping not to awaken her. Gathering up his belongings and placing them in a chair, he continued with Mike's but just as he was about to reach for his friend's dirty socks, Alma awoke, and she wasn't pleased. "What the hell are you doing, Thomas? Don't you know that you make twice as much noise when you sneak around than you do if you just work normally?"

"Sorry. Was trying to be quiet."

"And that's the problem," she moaned, kicking her bed sheets away. "Do you think the jungle beasts worked quietly around me? If a rhino thought it could get a charge out of a human, it'd ram ya 'til you screamed uncle."

"Since when do they have rhinos in South America?"

"When you're not lookin', smarty. Where's Wonder Boy?"

"Getting help for the car. Someone should be here soon, so we'll be out of here in no time. Why don't you call your family and let them know that you're coming? You can do that, you know."

"Of course, I know. I remember what a telephone does."

"So, be my guest."

"Surprises are more fun."

Sounding as if a one man Fourth of July parade was approaching, Tommy and Alma walked to the window and brushed aside the partially opened nicotine-stained curtains and witnessed a large red panel truck pull into the parking lot, navigating its way to the empty space next to the disabled car. Leaning over, and leaving little room for the driver who was wedged against the door, Mike honked the horn as if to celebrate royalty's arrival. His infectious smile beaming.

"He knows how to make an entrance, doesn't he?" Alma asked.

Tommy smiled at the spectacle and watched the amused mechanic climb out the truck with Mike following—driver side door, of course.

"Hey, monkeys. Check this truck out," Mike yelled to the pair peering out the window. And then it hit: that miraculous moment when life stops, defines itself, and the world is safe for democracy. Mike stopped in mid-step, arms out, and then raced to the driver's door. Jumping in, he reached over and turned up the radio to its near-maximum capacity, pulled back, and danced about the immediate area to Boston's *Smokin'*.

Tommy and Alma watched as the mechanic popped the Pinto's hood and smirked at the dancing queen who moved about. "Ha. Good rockin'," the graduate announced to no one in particular.

"I need to get my groove on. Move it, buster. Chuck wagon's over," Alma decreed as she made for the door and danced her way to Mike.

"Well, if you can't beat 'em," Tommy declared to the empty room. Making his way outside, he walked to the repairman who examined decaying battery cables. "Bet you see a lot of these."

"Batteries or rockers?"

"Take your pick."

The middle-aged mechanic with a rotund mid-section held up a cable and said, "These need to be replaced soon. I can't do it here, and a new battery won't do the trick forever, so you need to schedule an appointment at some point." Glancing over, he added, "Your brother and grandma make quite a pair."

"Yes, they do."

"Mind if I put you to work?"

"Not at all."

"Can you hold this cable? Gettin' in my way. These old cars might as well be from ancient Egypt. Makes servicing them next to impossible."

As the song's bridge began, Mike moved both hands outward, the right miming the classic keyboard lick as Alma danced a jitterbug/go-go/robot hybrid, her hair flying from side to side, her palms out as if channeling Bob Fosse.

"Where are you guys headed?"

"Not sure. Alma wants to meet up with her family, so we'll take her wherever she wants."

The mechanic stopped and stared at the battery. "Thought she was your family?"

"She is. Both of those two are. In an extended sense. Like the family you always wanted but never had."

"Uh-huh. If you say so," the man said as he lifted the old battery and walked to the back of the truck.

"That was Boston, welcoming you back to the work week," the disc jockey interrupted, losing the last third of the song.

"What? Sacrilege. Butchery. Savage butchery," Mike decried.

"As opposed to kindhearted butchery?"

"Well, now you're just being silly, Tom Boy. That's madness."

"You might need to be smokin' as you begin your Monday or, if you're lucky enough, making your way to Alpine Valley for the first of three shows by the Grateful Dead. If you're going, start soon, as 94, 43 and 12 are already showing signs of congestion, which will only get worse as the day goes on. And, of course, stay right here for traffic updates, on your Dead central station, 'ZMF."

"Grateful Dead! Unreal. Alpine's only a few miles this way. Let's do this," Mike insisted, pointing south.

"Wrong way, friend. East, just head east about forty miles or so," the mechanic instructed.

"Half the rain forests wouldn't be here if it weren't for the Dead," Alma educated the three. "They're heroes down in South America."

"Where they have pet rhinos."

"You are such a smart ass, Thomas."

"Yes. Yes, he is, Alma. Indubitably. And it is most unappealing."

"What are you talkin' about, Michael? You're nothin' to write home about."

Tommy and Mike exchanged looks and cracked up over the observant woman whose maternal instincts were in fine form. Here was a woman who possessed more worldly experience than the two of them many times over. Yet unbeknownst to them, here too was a woman who held more emotional wounds than they would ever know.

"Never got into the Dead," Tommy offered. "Too much meandering."

Rushing over and placing his arm around the man, Mike said, "Look, Tom Cat. Face it. We were destined for destiny, you and me. The open road is our friend, and we never let our friends down. We embrace them. We coddle them. We bring them to cobblers. We love clotted cream. We do this so we can experience all that the world offers, so we can transcend the transcendent, remake what others view as immovable, and then share it for all to see. Coach used to pull me aside, much like I'm doing with you now but without his stinky breath—my god, the breath. It was as if a slaughterhouse and a sewage treatment center got busy and bore evil spawn. We're talking s.t.i.n.k.y. Then on a bad day he'd tell me about his lawn. His lawn. Can you believe it? Who talks to a high school kid about his lawn? Even asked if I'd help pull weeds. Kind of creepy, huh? So, he tells me, 'Son, crunch time. Make the impossible possible. Do the unthinkable. Go beyond what you know, and you just might find yourself on the other side with me waiting.' Like I say, creepy. So, let's do this. Let's push ourselves and discover what lagoons can be crossed to capture the mighty dragon and see if he is indeed a fire breather or an imposter posing as a …"

"Aw, shut up," Alma decreed. "God, you're annoying. To the room, Thomas. Bodies need washing, clothing needs packing, and beer needs moving to the back of the yellow chariot with the new bigwig battery."

Chapter 23

Anonymous Rd.
Milwaukee, WI 53201
(414) Anonymous

Captain James Manning
Milwaukee Police Department
The Safety Building
Milwaukee, WI 53201

Dear Captain:

Please do not discard this letter simply because I have chosen to remain anonymous. I'm sure you will agree that if I were pulling a prank, I would not pay the enormous fee that a bonded messenger service charges for one hour delivery and would rely, instead, on the postal system.

Captain, it brings me no joy to inform you of an impending crime that will occur at Alpine Valley this evening where the Grateful Dead are hosting their yearly drug festival, for I know of someone who will be possessing vast amounts of the hallucinogen marijuana: Anthony "Tony" Peters (note the name's Italian overtone), who is the brother of a valued officer of yours, Detective Jonathan Peters.

Please be advised, Captain, that Jonathan has been blinded by his sibling's business practices for years and is no longer able to differentiate between family loyalty and lawlessness. I know this is as painful to you as it is to me, but rest assured that I have arranged for Jonathan to receive the help he needs at one of the area's finest treatment centers and will make sure that he makes a full recovery before ever wearing his badge again.

Captain, by coordinating an effort with the Walworth County Sheriff, this is how you can apprehend this felon. He will be selling, and without a proper permit I might add, colored t-shirts from his 1970

Ford Econoline van. White. (Both criminal and vehicle). The license plate is Dead 1. You should have little difficulty spotting it.

Sir, please be gentle with Jonathan upon the arrest of his misguided brother. Some men's hearts lead them the wrong way. Unfortunately, Jonathan's family loyalty helped provoke this.

Thank you for your vigilance and attention to this matter.

Sincerely,

A Concerned Citizen for a Temperate America

Chapter 24

Alpine Valley is a 1,000 acre expanse that rests within the Kettle Moraine State Forest, one of Wisconsin's largest and most pristine natural wonders. Originally built as a ski resort, the enterprise soon took on mammoth proportions as the lucrative temptations of outdoor concert venues proved attractive to the resort's owners, and work began on an amphitheater that soon hosted the likes of the Rolling Stones, Bruce Springsteen, Madonna, Elton John, and the Who.

Surrounded by endless rolling acres of trees several hundred years old, the facility attracted the attention of entertainment giants who insisted that they be booked there. In fact, Alpine became such a sought after market that neighboring Chicago attempted to recreate the Valley's magic; however, all the Windy City ended up with was an archaic, concrete disaster that produced more smirks that awes from performers; even today, the Wisconsin facility remains unchallenged as one of the premier concert attractions in the United States.

And no one knew this better than the Grateful Dead.

Although 2,500 miles separates the facility from San Francisco, the Dead's home base and financial headquarters, it was not unusual for 8,000 tickets to have been sold to Bay area Deadheads who made the yearly pilgrimage from the California metropolis to East Troy, Wisconsin, population 4,000, home of the music theatre.

Constituting a small village, Deadheads congregated and followed the Grateful Dead to wherever their travels took them in the continental US; it's fair to say that few cities were unaware of the psychedelic caravan that accompanied the legendary rock group with a religious zeal. Whether it was New York, Tulsa, Detroit, or Boulder, Deadheads left their mark and invited town locals to spend the next year reveling in memories until the next inevitable reappearance followed.

By the time that Tommy, Mike, and Alma entered the huge field that served as the Valley's parking lot, the caravan had long since established itself with pitched tents, bold colored vans, and rehabbed school buses that became communal modes of transportation.

"This is too much," Alma exclaimed, examining a midnight blue bus with an immense peace symbol painted on the vehicle's two sides, back, and grill. "Are you two sure that this is not 1969?" the astonished woman asked.

Equally awed, the young men looked about them as if they had entered Oz, for never in their wildest imaginations had they ever constructed a sight quite like the one they were observing. "Unreal, Tom Boy. This is beyond cool. It defines cool."

Staring at what he viewed as a giant anachronism, Tommy replied, "It makes you think that we've been transported to hippie heaven. Look at these people. They're every age."

Indeed, what the trio was witnessing was an assembled lineage represented by two, even three generations of devoted enthusiasts.

"Check this out, Alma," Mike began. "You're not even the oldest one here. There're all sorts of people your age."

"Of course there are, Michael. You don't have to be a kid to appreciate a happening. We all like to rock steady."

Charmed by Alma's latest colloquialism, Tommy turned to the woman and said, "That's right. Don't take any guff from this upstart. He's barely out of high school. What does he know about the history of popular culture?"

"And what do you know?" Alma teased. "When these boys were playing the Fillmore, you were learning how to count."

Bowing to the woman's superior jab, Tommy proceeded to walk with his friends, stopping at the markets that sprang out of opened car trunks and vans, and examined the merchandise for which Marshall Field's would charge a fortune. Hand woven ponchos and Indian designed blankets lined the area as did recently erected makeshift racks that sported tie-dyed shirts, many with various Grateful dead logos and Jimi Hendrix images on them. Next to these, entrepreneurs sold imported beers for $1, guaranteeing the counterculture businessman a modest profit that would enable him to purchase a concert ticket and secure the necessary revenue to continue the Dead trek.

"Hey, I'm starved, Michael. Let's grab some food," Alma commanded, and it wasn't long before the three came across a woman with long brunette hair and a skirt made from an old pair of faded jeans, its seams severed and the pants reshaped into a flowing garment. With a vintage olive green Coleman cooler in front of her convertible VW Bug, she announced, “Yogurt, guava, brown rice, acid.”

As if she had just seen the Almighty, Alma raced to the saleswoman and proclaimed, “I’m back in the bowels of Belize. This was breakfast, lunch, and dinner for me back in my jungle days, boys. Eat this, and you’ll live to be one hundred—minus the acid, that is.”

“Oh, that is so beautiful,” the woman fawned. “You brought your children to the show.”

“These two?” Alma laughed. “Thanks for the compliment, dearie, but these two are young enough to be my grandsons, which they are not. They’re my traveling pals.”

Looking at the two young men, the guava marketer replied, “That is so cool. The three of you in this sea of joy. It’s beautiful. It really is.”

“You have any Dannon?” Mike asked as he helped himself to the woman’s cooler.

“Mike,” Tommy protested.

“Oh, not cool. Not cool,” the woman lamented while observing the youth. “You might injure the mangos.”

Grabbing the scruff of the graduate’s neck, Alma pulled him back and barked, “Knock it off, Michael. Where’re your manners? Try that in the jungle, and a warrior’d be using your head as candle holder in no time flat. If you want something, ask.”

Standing over the opened cooler, the woman shook her head back and forth, long hair shielding a thirtyish face, and mourned, “I had everything in order. Now it’s not. Bummer. We have a major bummer on our hands.”

Not understanding the woman’s grave assessment, Mike joked, “It’s a cooler, not a stock trade.”

Placing her fingertips on her temples, the woman closed her eyes and announced, “I need some time to myself. You’ve upset my balance. Please go; leave me to my thoughts. I shan’t return until my mental flow regains its proper groove.” And with that the woman sat cross legged on the cooler and raised her head to the intense sunlight that bathed the area.

“Now, you did it,” Alma grumbled, slapping Mike’s right shoulder. “I’m half starved, and you go and mess with my sister. You need an enema.” Taking off and marching as if she were a paratrooper on a reconnaissance mission, Alma scoured the parking lot's main aisle for another food outlet, the two teens trying to match her pace, and soon ran across a pair selling seeds and dried fruit. "I am scoring today," she cried out, clasping her hands together and rubbing them in glee while examining the various goods. "Look at this, boys. Flax seed. That'll get you goin' even if you're dead."

A shirtless man with long raven hair looked at Alma through a cloud of marijuana smoke. Leaning against his female companion, the man waved one hand above the table displaying his goods and announced, "I tried everything myself. Natural. Everything you see here is. No machines or chemicals. Just the big yellow gift in the sky."

"Is this guy for real?" Tommy whispered to Mike.

"I don't know," the youth replied. "It seems like he's out to a Woodstock lunch."

"And I've got various sunflower seeds, two varieties, along with some apricots, dates, and peaches." Taking a bong hit, he sucked in until a red hot cherry blossomed in the brass bowl. Holding his breath, he passed the instrument to Alma.

"No, thanks, son. But I'll take a bag of your apricots."

"Sure," he responded, passing the bong to Tommy.

"Go ahead. Take it," Mike urged.

Unsure what to do, Tommy turned away and said, "No, thanks. Trying to cut back."

Bobbing his head up and down, the salesman replied, "That's cool."

Twenty miles west, Tony and Big Ben were packing a white van with merchandise that assured the eldest son a sizable nest egg to tide him over another year. "C'mon, Tony," Ben pleaded. "We've got to get everything moved before Shanda gets here. We don't want to keep your customers waitin'."

Not only did the woman take part of her hectic corporate day off, but Jonathan also told his superior officer that since there had been no sighting of Mike Warner's Pinto or a subsequent break in the case, he was taking the afternoon off to spend time with his family.

"And once we get there, Ben, don't forget: keep Caliban away from my customers. Don't need any bad trips." And with that the remaining goods were packed; within thirty minutes, both Jonathan and Shanda had arrived, and the Peters family was off to East Troy, where Shanda expected to see several SWAT teams, ready to take out her nemesis.

"Let's sing a song," Big Ben urged as the family exited the city limits. "You pick one, Tony. You know so many."

"How 'bout a little Sabbath?"

Leaning over to his brother, careful not to let the others hear, Jonathan said, "I don't think this is much of a Black Sabbath crowd. Why don't we go with something that's a little more conventional?"

"Like what? *Ninety-Nine Bottles of Beer on the Wall*? Gross."

"My father loves that song. It's wholesome," Shanda declared.

"Look, Formaldehyde. Just 'cause they play that song at the morgue doesn't give you the right to force it on us."

"Oh, Shanda. I didn't know you were sharpening up on your embalming skills. Good for you."

"I'm not, Big Ben. It's just another one of your stupid son's insults directed at me. Perhaps you should slap him up a couple times, so he'll be more respectful when in the company of others."

"Look, Flipper. Don't ever talk that way about me again, or I'll put you on the menu at Red Lobster. Throw an orange slice on you and call it Frigid Fluke. Bet you'd be a big hit with the Early Bird Special crowd."

"Well, I never …"

"I know. Jonathan told me. So sad to hear about your gag reflex. So unbecoming when one wants to experience the joys of oral love."

Shaking his head so violently that it looked like he was being hit from both sides, Jonathan struggled with "I, I, ah, ah, I, ah, never—ah …"

Oh, are you going to get it, you sorry excuse for a man, Shanda thought. First your brother will go down, and then you're going to pay for every embarrassment that this creature ever subjected me to.

As the four continued their journey to the Valley, scores of thousands descended on the concert site, bringing the day's attendance to over 40,000, a figure even more impressive when added to the two remaining dates that were guaranteed to match, if not surpass, the Monday draw.

"I can't get over these people," Tommy said in disbelief, surveying the vast parking lot that had taken on carnival-like proportions. Because the amphitheater wasn't scheduled to open until late afternoon, patrons milled about and examined the various sale goods, drank beer, splashed on suntan lotions, listened to bootlegged tapes of past Dead concerts blasting from car stereos, and chatted with other revelers whose anticipation of the evening's show reached a near Nirvanic state.

"You were looking for America, Michael? Then look around you," Alma instructed.

Bowled over by the environment in which he found himself, Mike attempted to formulate a decent reply but was too overwhelmed with what he witnessed. Never before had the graduate taken part in anything quite like this, and he was humbled by the mass of humanity that was congregating peacefully, basking in each other's company while experiencing a shared sense of togetherness and purpose. "I don't know what to say. If this is the real America, what's that sad land outside the Valley called?" Looking around, he added, "Maybe this is the way the whole world should be."

"Not on your life," Alma laughed, taking his hand. "This isn't reality, Michael. This is only a sliver of what could be. Humans are too greedy to make something like this last 365 days, so they try it out once a year, wait for their next opportunity, and attempt to duplicate it. Sometimes it works; other time it doesn't. But it's the belief that it will occur again that keeps people going."

"This your first time with the Dead?" Tommy asked.

"Oh, yeah. Back in the late sixties I used to watch the evening news and follow the reports of all the big rock festivals that seemed to occur monthly. I loved looking at all those idealistic young people who seemed to be looking for answers to questions people have since stopped asking. My heart went out to those innocents, although I was one of them at heart. All that freedom and love. Not that I didn't have much of the latter, mind you, but I sure could have used more of the former." The older woman looked at the magnificent sky and stopped talking for a moment, appearing as if she had become transfixed, mesmerized by her recollections. "You have no idea, boys, how hard it is to watch those who do and then look at the person looking back at you in the mirror, realizing that she's the one who doesn't. Don't ever let that happen to you. Life's too short to live under someone else's expectations. Once you start, it's next to impossible to break free and not hurt those who you love more than your own life."

As Tony's van entered the Valley's parking lot, a sea of shirtless males and tube topped women filled the area and the dirt road that would lead the family to their sales spot. Leaning over the front seat, Shanda jammed her hand on the horn and screamed, "Move it, you freaks."

"Oh, Shanda, stop that," Ben urged. "You might startle someone."

"Good. Maybe then they'll drop their drugs. Right, Jonathan?"

Distracted from his people watching, he replied automatically, "Whatever you say."

Pleased with the perceived affirmation, the woman added, "Good. That's more like it."

Maneuvering his vehicle at a snail's pace through the dense crowd, Tony made his way to a prime parking space, adjacent to the lot's main artery that led patrons to the concert area. "Too much, Jon. We've got the best spot," the thrilled businessman announced.

Undeniably, he could not have asked for a better location, for anyone possessing a ticket, or in need of one, had to stroll past Tony's storefront. "I'm gonna make a killing, bro. A few of their trusted dollars, and I can bankroll one more year in one colossal sweep."

Hearing this, Shanda thought to herself, Go ahead and wish yourself to complacent heaven, you burned out hooligan. Any second now the long arm of the law will have you, and there'll be nothing your little brother can do about it. "Tony, are you going to wish upon a doobie all day long, or are we going to set up shop? No one can buy anything if they see you sitting in a van, looking like a drugstore Indian selling cigars without any merchandise around you. C'mon, get the lead out, and let's get going," the conspiring woman insisted.

"That's right, Tony. You know what they say: a bird in the bush is worth two in the parking lot." Three disbelieving pairs of eyes looked at Ben and stared him down. "Did I say something wrong?"

"Never mind, Ben," Jonathan counseled. "Let's set up shop and see how many shirts we can sell before the concert."

Waving his youngest son closer, Ben whispered, "Do you think it'd be okay to have a little contest to see who sells the most shirts?"

Touched by his father's child-like wonder, Jonathan responded, "I think that's a great idea."

Since the van was parked parallel to the congested corridor, all Tony had to do was slide open his side door and conduct business from inside the van, his three partners becoming sales hawks outside. Ben was the first to exit the van. "Get your red hot Grateful Sabbath T-shirts right here, folks. Step right up before they're gone. They're goin' like hotcakes, so don't leave home without one."

"Ben! Ben!" the alarmed son cried out. "What are you trying to do? Drive my business away?"

"Oh, no. Did I do something wrong?"

"Yeah, for starters it's the Grateful Dead, and secondly we want them to buy our shirts, not bring one from home."

"Oh. Oh. Now I get it." Turning to Jonathan, he implored, "If I say something that doesn't seem quite right, you stop me before I put my foot in my mouth. I don't want Tony to lose faith in my sales ability."

"Sure, dad."

"Shanda? You watch John watch me, okay? Shanda? Shanda, are you listening to me?"

Preoccupied with a pair of college students getting high in front of the van, Shanda scoffed, "Get a hold of these two. Do you believe it? The nerve of some people. They might as well be wee-weeing on the American flag because what they're doing is equally disrespectful." Pushing Jonathan in the pair's direction, Shanda commanded, "Now, you march right over there and slap those cuffs on them so fast that they won't know what hit 'em. Go on, get."

"But Shanda," Jonathan protested.

"Don't you but me, or I'll haul off and kick yours until you do what I tell you to do."

A large cardboard box made its way over Shanda's head; Tony leaned forward and said, "You forget what I warned you about? Leave my brother alone."

Waving her hands over her head, Shanda's muffled voiced called out, "Get this thing off me this instant, or there'll be Hades to pay."

One of the pot smoking students shook his head and told his friend, "Now that is fucked up street theatre."

Stopping by a makeshift clothing rack, Tommy was enamored with a collection of indigo tie-dyes hung on a wire stretched between a van and a light pole. "You won't find anything better than these," an eleven-year-old boy offered. "Everything you see is custom made with the best dyes. Most of the stuff sold around here fades after a wash or two, but not ours. Just soak it in saltwater before its first wash, and the colors'll stay with you forever."

Behind the boy stood a man and woman who Tommy assumed were the youngster's parents. Listening to their child's delivery, the couple looked ahead at nothing in particular; it was at this point that the nineteen year old discerned their vacuous stares and the glazed appearance of their eyes.

"You know anything about acid spots?" the boy asked. "They're basic to the business, but most people mess it up when they make their first shirts. Not us. We do the best. Ask anyone around here."

An empty feeling gnawed at the young adult's gut as he looked at the child, and Tommy wondered if this salesman had ever attended school or if instead spent his life traveling with his parents, scurrying across the country in an endless succession of parking lots and nights stuck in a converted van. "What size do you wear?" the boy asked.

"This guy?" Mike inquired, fresh out of breath after racing from stand to stand. "I don't know. He's pretty big. Massive. Have anything in extra small?"

Given a firm kick to the butt, Mike turned around and saw Alma winding up for another. "Not when I'm turned this way," he pleaded, covering his groin. "Need to protect *Master Harold and the Boys*."

"Then watch your manners. You're not as tough as you think you are, buster. I'm three times your age, and I've got you dancin' around like you haven't hit a bathroom in a week."

Glaring at Mike, Tommy asked, "Why do you have to be such an asshole? You go from zero to sixty and then back again. God, you're a pain. Grow the fuck up."

"Thanks for the advice, dad. I know just where to put it."

Turning to the boy, Tommy said, "I'll take a medium. Unless these have a habit of shrinking. Then I'll take a large."

"It won't," the salesman assured his customer. "Just don't forget about the saltwater, though, because you don't want a runny shirt."

Picking out his selection, Tommy turned to Mike. "Can I have a twenty?"

"Apologize first."

"You want an apology. Do I have that right?"

"Yes. You hurt my feelings."

"Perhaps what you said hurt me."

Mike rolled his eyes like a seventh grade drama queen, fished out his wallet, and handed the salesman a twenty.

"You get two bucks back. Here you go."

But before Mike could say anything, Tommy, absorbed by the youth's stoic parents, leaned over to the youth and asked, "This is something you only do during the summer, right?"

Smiling back at the adult, the boy replied, "Summer's all year round when you're happy."

"Cool shirt," Alma said, grabbing it out of Tommy's hand."

"So much for manners," Mike muttered under his breath. "Please. Allow me. Pick one, Alma. On the house. Well, my house that is."

"Nah, you've done enough, Michael. Once I'm home, I'll figure out how to make these and design one myself."

Thirty yards away, Shanda watched in horror as a young woman took her top off and announced to no one in particular, "Check it out. No tan lines."

"Oh, my God. Oh, my God," the appalled woman stumbled. "She's walking around with her bare bosom exposed. Jonathan, march over there right now and arrest her for indecent exposure."

Detecting a thumping sound, the enraged woman turned and saw Tony holding up a cardboard box, a wry smile spread across his face.

"Oh, forget it. Anytime I try to bring order to this madcap mess I become the victim. Just forget that I'm even here and let these lawless criminals carry on with their depraved and perverse existence." Stepping in front of Jonathan and staring him down, she added, "That's right, Jonathan. Just stand there and watch a nearly naked woman flaunt herself and do nothing. I'm sure all your fellow officers will be overjoyed when you tell them everything that went on here and what you didn't do about it. Figure it out. All that time spent at the academy, and you throw away every corrective principle taught. Admirable, Jonathan. Admirable. I hope you're pleased with yourself."

Detecting another round of cardboard thumps, Shanda stopped, looked at the topless girl, tisked a few times, grabbed one of Tony's sale goods, and waved it in the air. "Neat shirts, neat shirts. Grab 'em now before your drugs wear off."

"Hey, Jon. Tell Ursula that she's not helping."

Ben muscled his way between the not-so-happy couple and asked, "Jonathan, do you think I should offer that young lady sunscreen? If she's not careful, she might get a terrible burn."

Glaring at his fiancée, Jonathan's eyes met hers as he replied, "I don't think so, Ben. I'm sure she's aware of the danger."

"Oh, okay."

"Wow!" Mike exclaimed. "Get a look at those hooters." Although the girl was far enough away not to hear, she was close enough to be seen.

"I don't believe it," the fazed Tommy said. "She's practically naked—which is amazing."

"My goodness," Alma added. "Wonder what her cup size is?"

"You got me, but I intend on finding out," Mike replied, removing his shirt and leaving his partners behind.

"Michael, get back here right now. I don't want you bothering that girl simply because your hormones are doing somersaults."

Turning around to face his advancing friends, Mike replied, "Just wanna say hello. Offer a friendly hug."

Alma stared him down and said, "Don't make me get mean. Leave her be. Last thing she needs is your grubby hands all over her."

"Just trying to be friendly."

"She's a beautiful girl who loves her form. You're no different. You walk around with skin tight T-shirts and tank tops, right? You walk around half-naked with shorts one size too small. The sooner everyone accepts people as people and not objects of exploitation is when this planet starts living more peacefully. How's that for an education in life?" Alma said, nearly out of breath from chasing the youth, Tommy right next to her.

"Thrilling," Mike said, turning away.

"Oh, fuckin' grow up," Tommy said.

"Oh, fuckin' grow a pair. Do you always do everything that she says?"

Tommy tore in front of Mike and walked backwards, their faces nearly touching. "When she's right, yes."

"And when she's wrong?"

"She's not. She just doesn't want you to make an ass out of yourself."

"We're not talking about your daily existence. We're talking about me."

"Knock it off, Michael," Alma demanded.

"Quit telling me what to do. Ever since you dropped into my life you've been punching me and telling me what I can and cannot say. That's garbage, Alma. Complete bullshit. I came here to have a good time, and I feel like I've got a leash around me, and you two are holding it."

"Oh, that's good, Warner. That's really good. You, the master of manipulation is complaining because you think we're holding you back."

"I didn't say that," Mike yelled, walking away, with Tommy right on his tail.

"No, of course you didn't. I could have a transcript of what you said, and you'd still deny it. Why don't you just evolve and stop acting like a total tool? God, you piss me off sometimes. You and your clever little put downs, your attempts to have me try something because you're too scared to."

Grabbing Tommy, Mike seethed, "I've never been scared of anything in my life. I was named MVP on our football team. I'm a Top Ten graduate. Every girl in my class, in my school wanted me."

"Yeah, yeah, yeah. How many times are you going to drag out your yearbook just so you don't have to face the fact that you don't have it together as you'd like everyone to think you do?"

"What?"

"You heard me. All this talk about discovering this, trying that—it's such bullshit, and you're full of it."

Although the crowd noise was considerable, more than a few people were drawn to the ruckus, one that scarred the peaceful coexistence that the Deadheads observed.

Visibly shaken by Tommy's volley of accusations, Mike looked everywhere but in his friend's eyes, refusing to acknowledge the criticisms and their painful implications, for he knew that an element of truth had been spoken. Disgusted, he walked away from his companions and headed towards the distant campgrounds.

"Where are you going?" Tommy called out."

"Nowhere."

"Fine place if can ever find it," Alma added.

"Fuck off."

"Did he say what I thought he did?" Alma asked, a hurt expression erasing her once beaming face.

"He said 'I'm off,'" Tommy lied. An all-consuming anger swelled in the young man's heart. There was no way he was going to allow anyone to demean his paternal friend, the one person who made him take stock of himself. Determined to meet up with Mike for what would become their last confrontation, Tommy took Alma's hands and said, "Look, he's just a kid. The guy's going through a difficult time right now, so I'll catch up with him and bring him back, okay?"

Alma nodded, placed her aged hand on his cheek, and reassured him silently that he was destined for greatness. And he was gone. As she watched Tommy slip into the gathered hoards, an intense feeling of dread and loss overcame her. Watching as her departed friend became smaller with each progressive step, disappearing into the anonymous crowd, an intense pain overcame her, and she struggled to keep her balance. She was alone. Again. And the woman's soul screamed for release, screamed for intercession, screamed for hope.

But none of the three came.

Instead, a renewed sense of isolation and despair took hold of her, but this time it wasn't taking prisoners.

Watching Shanda eye each passing individual, while making condescending and curt comments to those who stopped by the van, saddened Jonathan. He wondered what drove people to such a cold, sterile state where insensitivity becomes the benchmark for social interaction, anger seducing a once innocent child into the clutches of disdain, despair, and loneliness. The simple joys of living forever out of reach because of their limited vision and respect for themselves. Shanda, you are determined, he thought to himself, but you lack the most important part that makes a person whole: a heart. Without that, there's no hope, and without hope I'll just become another you.

And I can't live like that.

Wedging himself through the dense crowd that was leaving campsites and heading to the concert, Tommy looked at the marching masses and thought of a battlefield. Acres of vehicles were parked in a haphazard fashion while colorful tents filled whatever remaining space there was on the thick, muddy hill. A few concert goers still lounged on car hoods and roofs, many getting high, listening to music, and trading some of their more celebrated travel stories. As the youth walked by he heard complaints about the Boston police, the way the Dead's home office was handling the New Year's Eve concert in Oakland, the new crop of fans who were too young and inexperienced, and the changing social attitudes that the country was embracing, beliefs that made the traveling assemblage more noticeable and less amusing.

And there was Mike, sitting bare chested with his head below his knees, resembling a party-puking wasteoid who'd seen better days. But Tommy knew that it wasn't intoxication causing this malady, but rather confusion. Honest, gut wrenching, relentless pain that visits those who wrestle with their thoughts and behaviors. Looking up, Mike asked, "Why'd you have to make me look stupid back there?"

Tommy was struck by the tortured sound in his friend's voice: abandoned and betrayed.

"After three days, you should know what I'm capable of and what I'm not."

"Yeah, right," Mike scoffed. Getting up, he dug his heel into the saturated earth. "Nothing like making me look stupid in front of Alma. I hate when you do that. You made me look like a nothing."

A pang of guilt settled in Tommy's gut but not enough to make him sorry for what he had said earlier. "Look, Mike. If we're supposed to be friends, and that's a very big if, you have to expect me to tell you when I think you're wrong. I expect the same from you."

"Don't be such a fucking diplomat—or is that another occupation you plan on conquering?"

Tommy knew that another argument was imminent, so he walked away saying, "Look, I'm heading back. Either come with me now, or meet us at our car after the concert."

"My car. Not our car. My fucking car. My fucking gas. My fucking money. My fucking hotel room. My fucking clothes."

"You are unbelievable." Tearing off his T-shirt, Tommy threw it at Mike, hitting him in the face. "There, it's yours. I'd give you my underwear, excuse me, your underwear, but I don't feel like getting naked. You are such an asshole, Warner. Just another stupid jock whose best days are behind him because he doesn't know anything else than a bunch of football plays and cheerleaders who don't wear panties on their first date. Oh, wait a minute. I forgot. We really don't have any proof that your hot dates existed, now do we? I guess your word is the only thing we've got. How's that? Did you hear how I phrased it? Your word. Your fucking word, to go along with everything else that's fucking yours."

Four rapid punches pulverized Tommy's face as Mike pummeled a man who had gone too far and gotten too close to the insecurities that the youth struggled with daily. Exorcising his frustrations, he continued to beat the nineteen year old like a whipping boy, smashing the man so many times that blood covered his face and the attacker's right arm. Not satisfied that his demons were expunged, Mike kicked his best friend in the chest, knocking him seven feet behind and under a flower painted VW van, held up by a jack that was bending into the saturated earth.

To Mike it seemed like an eternity, but it was only seconds. Brief, unstoppable moments of time that have no conscience and are incapable of respecting an ear-piercing scream.

As a disoriented man tried to drag himself from under a vehicle, another watched as a knee knocked against an unstable jack that capitulated and gave way, the axle more than willing to crash down upon a mass of flesh, forcing its victim to surrender his last moments of life.

And it was done.

Chapter 25

The early morning's rays made Alma appear older than she was, for her pale, creased face seemed to sag in the morning light, the area under her eyes dark and fleshy. Throughout the endless night, the woman battled with consciousness, trying to stop her body's relentless need for sleep. Barely lifting her eyelids, she tried to focus on her surroundings but was too drained to discern the hospital's anesthetic aroma and the various sounds that circled through her exhausted mind, her body demanding restorative surrender.

In the background, a cable news program retold the evening's headlines. Cholera outbreaks drifted into drive-by shootings. Frozen embryos soon became street people. Anarchy and peace became one. A mother's cry filled her head, as did a father's sobbing questions, each broken into a million fragments, unbearable pain negating any sense of structure.

"Sleep," her mind urged. "Sleep."

Motion beside her caused no unrest.

"Sleep," her mind persisted. "Sleep."

A parent's loss became too familiar.

"Sleep," her mind demanded. "Sleep."

"I didn't mean to," a distant voice cried from behind a closed door.

Screams were unable to stir a woman awake as anguish tore a youth apart.

"God. God, I hurt. I didn't see it. I didn't mean to."

"Doctor, I'm Detective Peters. How's he doing?"

"I gave him a mild sedative to calm him down, but it's not doing much."

"Hold off on another. I need him sensate."

Jonathan? Jonathan, it's me. Come here, son. Don't be afraid. I'm not going to hurt you. Don't you remember me? I'm your mother. I'm the one who took care of you until you were eleven. Yes, that's right. It's me, and now I'm home for good to take care of you, to make sure that no harm will ever come your way. I'm the one who's going to protect you. And do you know what else? I'll always be with you. I'll never leave you again because I know how hard my absence has been on you. Come here, Jonathan. You don't have to be afraid. I remember how frightened you used to be of the dark, but now that I'm here that's all going to change. Everything'll be just like it was before I left.

"He didn't do anything. It was my fault. I'm the one who caused this."

Do you remember that song I used to sing when you were little? "Momma's little boy loves shortening/shortening/Momma's little boy loves shortening bread."

"And I never gave him a chance to fight back. Oh, God. I wish I were dead."

And the thunder'd be going, and you'd be crying so hard that you'd cry yourself hoarse until I got there and held you in my arms. Just you and me. Just the two of us, Jonathan. Us. Together. Just like now.

"But he didn't listen. He kept moving. Why didn't he see it? Why didn't he just lie there and catch his breath? It wouldn't have been that hard to do, but he didn't, and now he's dead."

But I already told you: I'm not going anywhere. I'm going to stay with you from now on. We've got a lot to catch up on, you know. I want to see all your pictures and meet your friends. Have a nice chat with one of the girlfriends I'm sure you have.

"Just fuckin' kill me. I don't want to remember any of this."

What? Yes, I know. You don't have to remind me. I know how much you hurt. I know how much of your life I've missed, but I'm going to make it up to you. You'll see. I'll work twice as hard and see that you get everything you've ever wanted. You just wait and see. What? Don't say that, Jonathan. It's the pain talking and nothing else. I won't listen to this. No, I won't. Not as long as you're talking like that. I've already told you the way things are going to be, and that's that. Yes, that's what I said. Jonathan, where are you going? Son? Don't leave. I just got here. Jonathan? Don't do this to me. I've traveled so far just so we can be together. No, don't say that. No, Jonathan. That's now why I left. It was me, not you. Don't ever think that it was your fault. No, don't do that. Jonathan, no. That'll wreck all the plans I have for us. Son, please don't go. I stayed away for so long, but now that I'm back I need to ... No. Please. You don't mean that. Don't make me do that. I've already left once, and I can't bear the thought of having to leave again. Your happiness is all I've ever thought about. Don't make me leave. Don't. Please don't.

The searing cries behind a closed door awoke Alma. Drawn back to consciousness, she recognized Mike's voice and rushed towards the room, wanting so desperately to comfort him as she once did her own children. But as she raced into the room, she saw that Mike was being consoled by a strong, caring man whose face was pressed against the youth's head, his eyes closed, trying not to cry along with the tortured boy who'd experienced more pain than anyone should.

And then she recognized the man.

Swallowing hard, Alma turned and left the room, not a soul aware that she had been there.

And she was gone, never to return.

Epilogue

Although the Warner case was now closed, Jonathan was troubled by his inability to identify the older woman who Mike said accompanied himself and Tommy for part of the weekend. The only lead he got from Mike was that the woman's name was Alma, and that she was returning home after a lengthy trip down South. No last name was provided, and Jonathan's missing persons request from the Southern states provided no leads.

Toying with his former fiancée's engagement ring, he looked at himself in the mirror and asked, "So, where to now?"

Walking to his bedroom window, he observed the hushed summer night and detected the hint of moisture that hung in the air. Gazing at the same front lawn where he and his brother made countless snowmen and played endless football games, he marveled at its smoothness and the way the nearby streetlight spun dramatic shadows across it.

And then he noticed what appeared to be a human form casting its own shadow. Looking closer, it appeared as if someone was standing across the street, next to a neighbor's massive maple tree. His heart racing, he flew through the house and tore open the front door, not exactly sure what he would find.

But no one was there.

A sadness, a gnawing emptiness filled his soul as he stared at the expanse, feeling more alone than he had since he was a child. Turning, he entered the house, went back to his room, and caught his reflection. Gazing into the mirror, he took a long, discriminating look at himself and saw a man whose direction was anything but certain. Looking over, he saw the framed picture of himself and his ex and knocked it off the nightstand and into a wastebasket. Picking up the phone, he punched in a number and then rubbed his chin, his pulse racing with each passing second. "Hi, Karen. It's me … No, everything's fine … Nah. You know me. Stayed in tonight … Look, sorry to bother you. You're probably getting ready to leave work. But I was wondering if you could go into my office and grab the Warner file that's on my desk … No, nothing's wrong … Case is still closed. Need the female witness' contact number. That's all … Yeah, the young woman from the Nike store. Just wanted to let her know that I cleared up a few loose ends, and that everything's settled. Finally."